100
DAYS
OF
SUN
LIGHT

ABBIE EMMONS

Jacket art: watercolor illustrations by Apple Vert; Eastern Bluebird by The
Birds of America: New York: J.B. Chevalier; Butterfly by American
entomology. v.1. Boston: Estes & Lauriat; Pink Flower by The Floral
magazine v.6 London,L. Reeve & Co.; all public domain illustrations
supplied by Creative Commons through Biodiversity Heritage Library
(www.biodiversitylibrary.org)
Interior illustrations by Pranjal Kumari

This is a work of fiction. Names, characters, places, and incidents either
are the product of the author's imagination or are used fictitiously, and
any resemblance to actual persons, living or dead, business establishments,
events, or locales is entirely coincidental.

www.100daysofsunlight.com
www.abbieemmonsauthor.com

ISBN: 978-1-7339733-1-1

In loving memory of Becca,
who brought sunlight wherever she went.

TESSA

DAY 21

THE BLACK PICKUP TRUCK FLIES THROUGH THE RED light, heading straight for us. My blood freezes in my veins. I want to scream, to warn Grandma, who sits next to me, in the driver's seat—but my voice doesn't work.

He'll hit us. He'll kill us.

Those words repeat in my mind like a chant, getting louder and louder as the black blur gets closer and closer. I cringe, turning my back to the door and covering my face.

I hear the

l o u d e s t   c r a s h

It sounds like a bomb.

My head whiplashes and slams into something hard behind me, and pain explodes through my body.

The world goes dark.

I wake up, gasping for air. I open my eyes, but I see nothing.

Nothing.

Nothing.

Darkness.

I'm cold, but sweating. My ears ring; sounds are muffled and distant, like a swarm of mosquitoes in my brain. I feel sheets underneath

1

me, on top of me, curled inside my damp fists.

I'm in bed.

I'm home.

It's okay.

I'm home.

It's just the dream again. Just my subconscious torturing me again.

Again, again, again.

They call it PTSD, the *again, again, again*. But I can think of a better name. Like *hell*.

I feel around in the blankets, looking for my phone. (*Looking* is a funny word to use when you're blind.) I'm still getting used to the concept of feeling for things. You have to pat gently and carefully, not slide or sweep your hands around. You knock things over when you do that. You accidentally throw your phone off your bed when you do that.

After a few minutes, I find it, a glossy little rectangle with one button. The only thing I can use on this device anymore. I press and hold the button until a familiar tone chimes through the speaker.

"What time is it?" I ask, so soft I'm surprised it picks up my voice at all.

Siri replies a moment later, "It is seven twenty-three a.m. Good morning!"

My breath rushes back out, shaken and ragged. I drop the phone in my blankets.

I still can't decide which is worse: the dream of the crash, where I can see everything in haunting detail... or the waking hours, when all I can see is darkness. Each has its own horrors. At least in my dreams, I know I'm dreaming. The worst part is that I can't change any of it. I can't stop myself from hitting my head.

I can't stop myself from losing my sight.

The doctors said the dizziness would last only two weeks. I can't remember who they were—but they were wrong. As I slowly sit upright, it feels like the world is spinning around me.

I push aside the sweaty bedsheets and swing my legs over the side of the mattress. My toes come in contact with the carpet. My right hand finds the edge of the nightstand.

It's okay. I'm home.

I know what home looks like. I can navigate my bedroom. I can locate all my drawers. I can dress myself. I don't need any help.

What do you do when something bad happens, and you know that you could have done something to stop it? Who do you blame?

It wasn't just the drunk driver's fault. It was my fault, too. Not because of something I did, but because of something I *could have* done.

What if we had arrived at that intersection a moment earlier, or a moment later?

What if it was my fault that we were at that exact spot in the road, at that exact moment?

What if I hadn't taken so long to curl my hair? Or wing my eyeliner? Or choose my earrings?

Grandma was taking me to the mall that day. The closest one is fifty miles away, so it's never a frequent outing. I'm not one for frequent outings to begin with. But Grandma had managed to coax me away from my half-finished blog post with a promise that we could run into the bookstore. (Two things have enough influence to separate me from my laptop: books and waffles.) So I left my draft where it was and headed for the mall with Grandma.

But we never made it there. All because of a drunk driver in a black pickup truck.

It was so loud. That's what I remember most about the accident. It was *so loud.*

My head slammed into something hard.

Darkness came. And it stayed.

What a strange feeling that was, to awaken in the hospital and not see a thing—just hear. Beeps and clicks and footsteps and voices. I thought I was dreaming. But then I heard Grandma; I felt her holding my hand. I realized I wasn't dreaming. And I started to cry.

It could have been worse. The only injury I suffered was something the doctors called a cerebral contusion, which meant there was a bruise on my brain, and it was swollen enough to affect my visual cortex. Swollen enough to cause blindness. *Post-traumatic transient cortical blindness.* They said both sides of my brain were damaged and that, with time, I would most likely regain my sight, but they didn't say for sure. And they didn't say *when.*

The driver of the pickup truck was unharmed. They arrested him, but the damage was done.

Grandma wasn't hurt except for a few minor bruises. She stayed with me in the hospital. Always by my side, always apologizing to me. *I'm so sorry, Tessa. I'm so sorry.* But I felt like I was the one to blame. I was the reason we went out. I could have said, "Another day, Grandma." I could have done something differently, something that could have prevented it all.

After I came home from the hospital, we went to see another neurologist. Her name was Dr. Carle and I imagined she had blond hair and blue eyes and a narrow face. She said the same thing all the other doctors had said. Blunt trauma to the head, cerebral contusion, and cortical blindness. Then she said, "I don't believe this condition is permanent. I expect we'll see improvement within twelve to fourteen weeks."

"Really?" Grandma said, hope shining through her voice.

"I'm realistically optimistic," Dr. Carle replied.

There's no such thing.

Fourteen weeks is ninety-eight days. I asked Siri when I got home that afternoon. That was when I started counting down in my head.

Today is the twenty-first day.

I navigate my bedroom and dress myself. I put on the softest pair of sweatpants I can find—no idea what color they are—and slip a bra underneath my pajama top.

Mornings are the worst for me. I'm dizzy; I'm tired of sleeping; I'm haunted by those three little words over and over again.

All my fault.

All my fault.

All my fault.

What am I now? *Who* am I? A prisoner, or at least that's what it feels like. Stuck in my bedroom, my place of refuge. It feels like a cage now. I used to love looking at my room. It's so white and pretty and organized. My shelf of books, all arranged by color. The sunlight as it pours through the window and sketches patterns on the floor. But now sunlight is a ghost—felt, not seen. Warm and patchy and inconsistent. That's all it is. That's all it ever was.

My laptop sits on my desk. I haven't opened it since the accident. I haven't checked my blog. I haven't answered the comments. I haven't spoken to any of my internet friends. I haven't written one verse, one line, one word of poetry.

I have no desire to.

I have no inspiration, no joy. It's all gone.

Grandma and Grandpa think I should carry on like normal—I heard them talking about it. It was evening, and I had pretended to fall asleep on the couch. They were in the kitchen, speaking in low voices.

"Tessa needs to get back into writing," Grandma said. "She's always the happiest when she's writing."

Grandpa agreed. "There has to be a way."

A way to do what? To write? To blog? To go back to normal?

There is no way to do anything normal.

All the "normal" has been knocked out of my life—just as the life has been knocked out of *me*.

I'm blind.

I'm blind.

I'm blind.

Fine, let them think there's a way to help me. Let them try and fail to find a solution to this mess. Let them come to terms with how bad things really are. I've accepted it—but I seem to be the only one.

That's easy for everyone else to say.

Everyone else can see.

They say, "I'm sorry. I know this must be hard for you." But they don't know. Not even the doctors—what have they done? Read about *cerebral contusions* in their medical books. They don't know what it feels like.

The first two weeks, I cried.

The week after that, I felt nothing.

But now, I'm angry.

It's been twenty-one days since Dr. Carle examined me. And there's still no change.

That's why I make myself get dressed and go downstairs. It's dangerous for me to be alone with my thoughts and my world of darkness.

I slowly make my way down the stairs, feeling for the edge of each step with my toes. Grandpa's voice floats from the kitchen, along with the smell of roasted coffee.

The house is familiar—every wall, every chair, every obstacle in my path. I can see everything in my mind's eye. I used to think it would be easy to do everyday tasks without vision. I even tried it a few times when I was little. I would close my eyes and outstretch my hands and try to get around without falling or knocking things over. It was fun, back then, because I could open my eyes and laugh about it.

Now there is nothing to laugh about.

"Good morning, Tessa," Grandma says when I enter the kitchen. She's smiling; I can tell by the sound of her voice. I want to smile back and say good morning. But I can't. I hover in the doorway, with one hand touching the wall.

Grandpa greets me with a cheery good morning, too. I hear coffee being poured into a cup.

"Do you need help, sweetheart?" Grandma asks.

I shake my head no, which makes a sudden wave of dizziness wash over me. Grandpa comes and offers me his arm and guides me over to the table.

"Chair," he says.

I feel the wood rails under my fingertips and carefully sit down.

"Thanks."

"How are you feeling this morning, Tessa?" Grandma's voice is still smiling, and now I'm beginning to wonder why. It can't merely be this *realistic optimism*, which has suddenly become such a trend.

"I don't know," I reply.

"Are you tired?"

"Yeah."

"Dizzy?"

"Yes."

Grandma sighs. She's sitting in the chair to the left of me. She gives my hand a quick squeeze. Whenever someone touches me—even to help guide me to a chair or through a doorway—it startles me just a little. There's no way for me to predict it. But I know Grandma and Grandpa so well, I can almost sense when they are going to touch me.

"What about your sleep?" Grandma continues the daily inquisition.

I shrug one shoulder. "It's the same."

"Do you still have the dream?"

"Yeah."

What I don't tell her is that I dream about nothing *but* the accident. Everyone tells me to get more rest—but how can I, when sleep is more exhausting than being awake? At least when I'm awake, I can distract myself; I can *force* myself to think about other things. In my dreams, I have no control. In my dreams, I have to live the crash over and over again. So loud.

All my fault.

A cup is set on the table and slid closer to me.

"Coffee," Grandpa says. "If you'd like some."

"Yes, I would. Thanks."

I can hear it in Grandpa's voice, too—the hidden note of optimism. They know something that I don't know. It's a surprise of some sort—a good one.

For a few moments, I say nothing. I sip my coffee and wait for one of them to reveal the news.

"Well?" I finally break the silence, setting my cup on the table. "Is someone going to tell me what's going on?"

Grandma laughs a little, the nervous kind. "Well," she says, a strain of hesitation in her voice, "your grandpa was going to tell you."

"Tell me what? If this is about church, I'm sorry, but I'm not ready—"

"No," Grandpa says. He's sitting across from me, I can tell. "This isn't about church. I know you'll come back when you're ready… although I do miss the most valued member of my congregation."

I smile a little, for his sake. The kind of smile you have to pull from its sickbed.

Grandpa takes a measured breath. "Your grandmother and I were talking about different ways we could help you. We both think it would be good for you to get back into writing poetry."

"Well, I can't—"

Grandma lays her hand on mine, this time as a gentle reminder for me to be quiet. "Just listen for a minute, sweetheart."

My jaw tightens. I sip my coffee. I listen for a minute.

Grandpa continues. "So I had an idea. All you need is someone to transcribe your poetry—to type it up and post it on your blog. Right?"

"Yeah, but…" I shake my head. "You and Grandma are too busy. And not at all tech-savvy."

"You're right about that," Grandpa says, and chuckles.

"So who would do it, then?"

"That's what we were discussing," Grandpa says. "And we decided that the best way to find someone would be to place an ad in the newspaper—asking for particular qualifications, of course. The person would have to be a girl, around your age, and we would interview her first—"

"What?" I can't help but cut him off. "That's… that's ridiculous."

Grandma sighs. "Tessa."

"I'm serious," I counter, unable to see the inevitable disappointment on my grandfather's face. "It won't work. I'm not good with new people, and who says I'll even be able to dictate poetry like that? Look, I appreciate you both caring so much, but... there's no way to help me."

"Tessa," Grandpa says, "I think you should give this a try. If you don't like it, we can—"

"No. I'm not ready. To write or blog or meet new people." I cross my arms over my chest. "Let's just... not talk about it anymore, okay? I'm fine. I'm coping. I don't need to write."

A long silence follows my closing statement. Somehow, I know this isn't the end of the topic. A heaviness hangs in the air.

"Just consider it for a minute, Tessa," Grandma insists. Her warm hand rubs my arm. "To be able to do something that you used to do before all this happened—"

"I already said no," I blurt, without devoting another moment's thought to *consideration*. "It's not like you've already placed the ad, so we can just... Wait. You didn't already place the ad... did you?"

No reply.

Surprise. That's what it is. How did I not see that coming?

"Grandpa?!"

"I'm sorry, Tessa. I thought you'd be pleased at the idea."

My heart drops into my stomach, and the dizziness returns full force. "Oh my god."

Grandma tries to stop me. "Now, listen, sweetheart—"

"How could you?" The words explode out of me before I can think about what I'm saying. "How could you do that to me? Publicly humiliate me in the *newspaper*? How could you go ahead and place an ad without asking me? I can't believe this—"

"Tessa, lower your voice." Grandma's tone is firm. "We're only trying to do what's best for you."

"By going behind my back and inviting strangers to intrude on my life?" My chest is tight; my face is hot. I shake my head, swallowing back the sick feeling rising in my throat. "This is *not* what's best for me."

"Like it or not, young lady, your grandfather and I know you better than anyone else does. We know that the best thing for you would be to get back into writing. But if you *really* feel like you're not ready for this, we'll call the newspaper and pull the ad. I'm sure they haven't printed it yet."

"Yes. Do that." My hands are shaking almost as much as my voice. "I know that you and Grandpa are only trying to help, but it's not… It doesn't help, okay? I wish everyone would just give me some more time. I need more time." I rest my elbows on the table and bury my face in my palms.

"I understand, Tessa." Grandpa speaks for the first time since my outburst. "And I see now that we should have talked to you about it first."

No kidding.

"I'll give the newspaper a call right now."

I hear him push back his chair and stand. Footsteps. He picks up the wall phone.

My heart is still pounding, hot frustration blowing through my veins. Grandma sits beside me, silent and grave. I almost wish she would talk, wish she would say something to justify my anger. But I know, deep down, that it can't be justified—not even by my blindness.

They were only trying to help, in their own way.

But I can't be helped.

I'm blind.

I sit at the table with my face in my hands and listen to Grandpa dial the phone number.

11

WESTON

JUNE 17

THE PHONE ON MY FATHER'S DESK STARTS TO RING.

He picks up the call and says, "*Rockford Chronicle.* This is David speaking."

I pace the office, glancing at the walls. My dad likes motivational quotes—he frames them and hangs them all over his office. I swear there's a new one every time I visit, which is once a week during the summer.

Hanging out at the *Chronicle* is like going back in time. We're one of the smallest newspapers in upstate New York, and Dad says that's something to be proud of—believe it or not. Surviving with a disadvantage is harder than surviving with an advantage, and that makes the disadvantaged stronger. (I know Dad didn't think of that one himself—it's a quote hanging on his wall, with a W. M. Penn credited underneath the words.)

"Yes, Mr. Dickinson," Dad says to the guy on the phone. "I remember the ad you placed yesterday. How can I help?"

He frowns, listening to the answer. "You'd like to retract the ad? Of course. That's absolutely fine."

I glance away from the wall of quotes. Dad is writing something on a sticky note. He's nodding even though this Dickinson guy can't see.

"I understand," Dad says, a hint of sympathy in his voice. "It's a… a difficult situation."

By this point, I'm listening closely—trying to figure out what the deal is here. Why does Dad sound so disappointed over this? It couldn't have been *that* good of an ad. He briefly goes over refunds with the guy on the other end, and then he says, "Well, I wish her a speedy recovery."

So someone is sick. Maybe seriously ill. Maybe dying.

I sit in one of the client chairs and wait for Dad to finish the call.

"Thank you… Have a good day… Bye."

He hangs up the phone and sighs—one of his big, long, something-is-wrong sighs.

"What was that all about?" I ask.

Dad shakes his head, glancing at the sticky note. "Oh, just… this ad needs to be pulled."

"Why? What's it for?"

"Help wanted, for a typist. But *why* is none of our business."

I tilt my head to one side. "Come on, Dad. I won't tell anyone."

He hesitates for a moment, then sighs. "Mr. Dickinson has a granddaughter who was recently involved in a car accident. She suffered a head injury and… lost her sight."

The words hit me harder than I expected them to. I look at the floor and whisper, "Wow. That sucks."

"Yeah," Dad agrees. "Apparently, she's a writer, and her grandparents wanted to hire someone to help her start writing again, someone who could type for her. But Mr. Dickinson said she doesn't like the idea of having an assistant, so he decided to retract the ad altogether."

"So the grandfather placed the ad before he even talked to his granddaughter about it?"

"It seems so."

"Why?"

Dad sighs, taking the sticky note and rising from his desk chair. "Like I said, it's none of our business."

"Okay. Just one more question."

He waits, giving me a warning look.

"What's her name?"

Dad grins. "Tessa." And on that final word, he leaves the office. The frosted-glass door swings shut behind him.

"Tessa," I whisper.

Tessa Dickinson, writer.

Tessa Dickinson, blind.

Help wanted.

Suddenly, an idea hits me. A stupid idea, probably. But right now, it seems like a great idea.

"Hey, Dad?" I jump up and swing open the office door.

I spot Dad halfway down the hallway, handing Rachel the sticky note of doom and explaining the retraction of the ad. Rachel nods understandingly from where she sits behind her computer screen.

I change my mind. I won't ask Dad. He's already too suspicious of my curiosity.

Instead I lie low for a few minutes, studying more motivational quotes in the hallway. Everything smells like printer toner and weak coffee. Finally Dad vanishes through a door at the end of the hallway, and I make my move.

Rachel is a Mesopotamian goddess. She has the biggest eyelashes I've ever seen, and she's from Brooklyn, and she's secretly in love with me.

"Hey, Rachel."

She glances up and gives me a smile, but doesn't stop typing. "Good morning, Weston."

"How are you?" I try to keep the riveting conversation alive.

"Fine. How are you?"

"Never been better."

She laughs. "When you say that, it means you have something up your sleeve..."

"But I *always* say that."

"Precisely."

I offer her my most heart-melting smile and get right to the point. "My dad just talked to you about a help-wanted ad, didn't he?"

Rachel nods, typing, typing.

"Well, I was wondering if I could see it. The copy, I mean. Since you're just gonna throw it away."

Her fingers freeze over the keyboard. She blinks at me with her giant eyelashes. "Why?"

"Because... um..." I rub the back of my neck, trying to think of a reasonable explanation. "Uh—"

"You want to apply for the job?"

I shrug one shoulder. "Maybe."

Rachel grins and reaches for a stack of papers to the side of her desk. "Well, Mr. Ludovico, you may find yourself just a bit... underqualified." She hands me an index card with a short piece of copy written on it.

HELP WANTED: typist/home office assistant. Part-time, approximately ten hours a week. Organized and dependable young woman. Experience preferred, with knowledge of blog management and moderate typing skills. $10.00 an hour to start. Contact Joshua Dickinson, 541-555-4579.

"Just a little," I say with a laugh. "Wrong gender. And not organized. Minimum typing skills, unless texting counts. Other than that, I'm perfect."

Rachel smiles. She appreciates my irony. Or maybe she smiles because she's secretly in love with me. I'm guessing it's a bit of both.

"Thanks for this," I say, holding up the index card. "I won't tell my dad if you won't."

She rolls her eyes and goes back to work.

There's a phone number on the index card, but it's probably the Dickinsons' home phone, which would only lead to another disappointing conversation with the grandfather. And the grandfather isn't the one I want to speak with. So I keep the ad to remember the name.

Tessa Dickinson.

Is there a mom or a dad? Does she live with her grandfather, or is he just super overprotective and controlling? Based on the small amount of information I've learned about Tessa Dickinson, I can speculate quite a bit.

She's a writer and she has a blog, which means she probably spends a lot of time on the internet. I've never heard of her, and I've certainly never met her, which means she doesn't go to my school. Maybe she's homeschooled or something like that. Her grandfather placed the ad before he actually asked Tessa if she wanted an assistant, which means he has her best interests at heart but also knows that she would have a problem with someone assisting her. And she recently lost her sight in a car accident, which means her whole world has been turned upside down.

I know what that feels like.

That's why I want to talk to her. That's why I want to help.

I Google *Joshua Dickinson in Rockford NY* and immediately feel like a stalker. Based on the search results, the dude is a pastor at a local nondenominational church. He lives two neighborhoods over, on West Elm Street. House number fifty-two. I jot down the address on the palm of my hand and, that afternoon, I go for a walk. To 52 West Elm Street. To meet Tessa Dickinson.

Her neighborhood doesn't look much different than mine; more trees, better sidewalks. The house itself is two stories and white, with dark green shutters. I take a deep breath and wonder for the first time if this is actually a stupid idea. But I've come all this way, so why not give it a shot?

I mess my blond hair, straighten my shirt, and knock on the front door.

A minute later, it opens—and there stands a middle-aged woman with auburn hair and gentle eyes. She does the same thing every new person does: first glances at my irresistible face; then she gives me a once-over... and her gaze stops on my legs.

My prosthetic legs.

This is when I usually crack a lame joke, like, *"Yeah, sorry, I left my real legs at home."* But I'm on a mission and I don't want to scare this lady.

She tugs her gaze back up to my irresistible face, offers a wary smile, and says, "Can I help you?"

I give her a bright smile in reply. "Are you Tessa's mom?"

"Oh, good Lord no," she says with a nervous little laugh. "I'm her grandmother."

"You're kidding. I never would have guessed."

"Well, thank you." She smiles modestly. "And you are...?"

"Weston Ludovico," I say, reaching into my pocket and taking out the index card with the ad copy. "My dad owns the newspaper, you know, the *Rockford Chronicle*? I happened to be in the office this morning when Mr. Dickinson called about canceling the ad. And I happened to see the ad, and I happened to... Well, I didn't happen to be here, on your exact street, at your exact house. I just... I heard about your granddaughter. And I know that you pulled the ad and she doesn't want an assistant, and even if she did, I know that I'm not who you're looking for, but... I also understand a little bit about what Tessa is going through. And I think I can help."

Mrs. Dickinson stares at me for a long moment. In fact, she does several double takes throughout my entire speech. Then she gets that look on her face, like *I shouldn't be staring; it's rude.* But everyone stares. I don't mind it anymore.

"Um, why don't you come in?" Mrs. Dickinson says, seeming to refocus. "We can... discuss this."

I can't tell if it's just the sympathy talking, but this time I'm glad of a biased opinion. Mrs. Dickinson might have shut the door in my face if I were an average person. But instead she gestures for me to come inside, and I happily obey.

"Can I get you anything?" she asks, leading the way into a bright kitchen. The walls are yellow and everything is neat as a pin.

"Nah, that's okay."

"Iced tea?"

"Sure."

I'm dying to ask her a million questions, but Mom says it's impolite to be so "unfiltered," and that I should wait at least five seconds before opening my mouth again. There's a clock on the wall, so I count.

One, two, three, four, five.

"So, Mrs. Dickinson. Tell me about Tessa."

Mrs. Dickinson sighs. "Tessa is... not herself. You heard about the accident, you said?"

"Yeah, just through my dad. Mr. Dickinson told him."

She hands me a glass of iced tea.

"Thanks."

"It happened about three weeks ago," Mrs. Dickinson explains. "We were hit by a drunk driver."

"You were in the car, too?"

She nods. "I wasn't hurt. Not like Tessa was."

Another five seconds. Ten, this time, because I don't know what to say. There's something about this house—a feeling hanging in the air. It's familiar, suffocating.

Despair.

Mrs. Dickinson frowns curiously at me. "How old are you, Weston?"

"Sixteen, ma'am."

She smiles. "So is Tessa."

That's a relief. I was worried Tessa might be super young—one of these ten-year-old geniuses who somehow run a blog and social media better than a large corporation.

Mrs. Dickinson gestures toward the kitchen table. "Please, have a seat."

I pull out a chair and sit down. "Does Tessa live with you?"

Mrs. Dickinson nods.

I sip the iced tea. *One, two, three, four, five.*

"Does she have any parents?"

"Her mother lives in Pittsburgh…"

I don't dare ask about the dad.

"So Tessa is a writer, you said?"

Mrs. Dickinson nods. "She's been writing ever since she *could* write. We've always homeschooled her. Sometimes I wish she would get out of the house more, but she'd rather stay in her room and blog all day…" She pauses, then sighs. "But that was before the accident. Now? Well… she's lost her sight."

"Is it forever?"

"No. The doctors have told us that it should return within twelve to fourteen weeks, hopefully." She nods slowly, the way people nod when they're trying to convince themselves to believe what the doctors say. But the doctors are usually wrong.

"Twelve to fourteen weeks isn't too bad," I comment. "But I'm sure that sounds like a long time when you're blind."

Mrs. Dickinson looks down at the table, like she has something uncomfortable to say and she isn't sure how to say it. She wants to give me the bad news that I already know—Tessa doesn't want an assistant, the ad was a mistake, and I shouldn't have bothered coming here. But how do you say all that to a kid who's got nothing left below the knees?

I spare her the struggle.

"Look, ma'am," I begin, "I know you weren't expecting me to show up—especially since you pulled the ad before it even printed. And I have no experience in being blind, but… I do know what it feels like to have something important taken away from you. To… to feel helpless."

Mrs. Dickinson listens, looking at me with sad eyes. For a second, I'm afraid she might start crying—and I hope not, because that would be awkward.

"Is Tessa here?" I ask.

"She's in her room, resting."

I feel like this pause needs to be longer. But seven seconds is all I can stand.

"Could I talk to her?" I ask. "Just for a few minutes?"

The sympathy is still there, gathering like clouds in her eyes. I've seen enough of it to last me a lifetime, but I know it's the only way Mrs. Dickinson might let me try to help her granddaughter.

Finally, she says, "Okay." She rises from the table. "I'll go see if she's awake."

Mission accomplished. Kind of.

"Thank you," I reply, also feeling the need to stand for some reason. "Oh, and Mrs. Dickinson?"

She stops on her way to the stairs. "Yes?"

"Could I ask a favor of you?"

"Of course."

I hesitate, not sure if I *should* ask.

Mrs. Dickinson waits for my request—a puzzled frown creasing her forehead.

"I'd really appreciate it if you don't tell Tessa... about..."

It's funny how, even three years later, I can't figure out how to say it. All I can do is gesture toward my prosthetic legs.

"This."

Mrs. Dickinson smiles a little, the pity returning to her face.

"It's just that... it doesn't affect my ability to use a computer— or do almost anything else, for that matter. And I would be more comfortable if Tessa didn't know."

"I understand," Mrs. Dickinson says. "I won't tell her."

"Thank you."

She turns and vanishes up the stairs, leaving me to wait in the kitchen.

TESSA

DAY 21

AT LEAST THEY PULLED THE AD BEFORE ANYONE HAD A chance to read it. At least I won't be publicly humiliated in the local paper. At least I won't have to tolerate the insolence of strangers trying to understand what it's like.

It was a close call. But I've been spared the torture.

"Tessa?"

I hear Grandma's voice, muffled, on the other side of my bedroom door. I'm lying on my bed and I don't bother to reply, knowing that the door isn't locked and she'll only open it and say my name again.

"Tessa?"

My throat is dry, either from too much crying or too little talking. "What?" I whisper.

Grandma doesn't answer right away. She steps inside and softly shuts the door behind her. That means something is serious. That means I wasn't just hearing things a few minutes ago when I thought I detected a new voice downstairs. That means the mystery person is still in the house, and they have something to do with me.

"Who's here?" I ask, to skip past the explanation of what I already know.

Grandma takes a deep breath and lets it all out again—that means something is *really* serious.

A frown scrunches my eyebrows. "Grandma?"

"It's David Ludovico's son."

"Who?"

"The man who owns the newspaper."

My heart begins to sink all over again. "Don't tell me they printed the ad already..."

"No," Grandma says. "They didn't print the ad."

"Then what's his son doing here?"

Grandma hesitates, but not for as long. "He was at the office when Grandpa called. He saw the ad before they cancelled it. He... thought he might be able to help."

A cynical laugh bursts out of me. "That's kind of presumptuous. I hope you threw him out."

"Tessa." Grandma's voice is firm, with a warning edge that says *You're misbehaving.* "I would like you to just talk to him for a minute. I think he might be able to help you."

I spring to my feet, a time bomb of anger detonating in my chest. "I thought this was over! I told you I don't want help. And I certainly don't want anyone touching my laptop. I don't want to write. I don't want some *stranger* coming into my house and feeling sorry for me! I just want to be left alone. I *need* to be left alone."

"Tessa, I think I know what you need much better than you do."

I whirl around, moving closer to what I think is the window. The afternoon sunlight pours through in warm, patchy shafts. I cross my arms over my chest, bracing them hard against my body.

Blood pulses through my ears. I want to scream; I want to break something; I want to throw a rock through this window, to shatter the view of a world I can no longer see.

No. I'm done with crying. I will not cry.

But my eyes are already stinging with tears. Hot, angry, silent tears.

I will not cry.

"I'm going to send Weston in here," Grandma says. "And you're going to talk to him for five minutes. Understood?"

She doesn't wait for my response. She doesn't let me have any say in the matter. She leaves the room.

Leaves me standing by the window.

Boiling.

WESTON

JUNE 17

"YOU CAN GO UP NOW,"MRS. DICKINSON SAYS WHEN SHE returns to the kitchen. "But I have to warn you—she's not in a very good mood."

I shrug. "That's understandable."

The way Mrs. Dickinson says it makes me think I should be somewhat afraid of this Tessa girl. Or maybe she just thinks that her granddaughter will bite my head off.

Either way, I'm intrigued.

Mrs. Dickinson leads the way up a flight of stairs (which she seems surprised I have no problem with) and stops at the first door on the left. It's open a crack, and white light spills out onto the floor.

"I'll wait out here," Mrs. Dickinson says, nodding for me to go inside.

I don't hesitate or even prepare a speech. I just open the door and step through.

Tessa's bedroom looks like something from a home decorating magazine. Everything is white and organized: no clothes lying around, no evidence that anything about her life is out of the ordinary.

She's standing at a window, with her back to me. Sweatpants, T-shirt, messy golden hair. She just stands there, silent and still.

Never mind.

I don't know what to say.

I don't know what to do.

This was a stupid idea.

"Hi, Tessa," I start off, sounding just as unsure as I feel. "It's… good to meet you. I'm Weston."

She doesn't speak. She doesn't move.

"Your grandmother was just telling me about the accident and what happened to you." I pause, not because I should, but because I sense that feeling in the air again—even denser in this room. *Despair.* "It sucks."

Tessa exhales a sharp, sarcastic laugh. That one little sound tells me a lot about her. And then, after a few seconds, she speaks.

"Listen," she begins, still facing the window. "I don't care what my grandmother told you. I don't want help. I don't *need* help. And I certainly don't need you."

"I know. I know you don't need me. But you need to write."

She shakes her head, rigid and sure of herself.

"Tessa… I know this must be hard for you—"

"You don't know *anything!*" she explodes, spinning around to face me. "You don't know anything about me!"

For a moment, I'm speechless.

It's the first time in three years anyone has ever met me without that look of pity on their face. The first time anyone has ever looked at me and not seen me. The first time anyone has stood before me—with perfectly normal legs—and complained about their own problem.

The feeling is exhilarating.

"Are you blind, Weston?" Tessa screams. Her eyes are filled with tears, and the tears are spilling down her face.

"I said *are you blind*?!"

"No," I reply, my voice not much louder than a whisper.

"So you have *no idea* what this is like, do you?"

She's looking at me. And she can't see me. She can't see This.

"DO YOU?"

I shake my head slowly, feeling like the ability to speak has been knocked out of me by a hurricane called *Tessa*. "No."

"Then don't you *dare* tell me you understand." Tessa finally lowers her voice a little, but the tears keep coming. "You understand *nothing*. Now get out of my house and don't come back. The position is no longer open—it was never even open to begin with. It was impertinent of you to come here."

Impertinent, huh?

So she's stubborn. She's rude. She's a spitfire wallflower who lost her sight and now hates anyone who tries to help her.

Game on.

"With all due respect, miss, this isn't your house. This is your grandparents' house. And as long as they're okay with it, I will come back. Tomorrow."

For a moment she just stands there, gaping and covered in tears. She looks shocked—maybe even horrified.

I wait for another explosion.

And sure enough, it comes.

"How dare you! I refuse to be treated like this. I don't want to see you—" she freezes suddenly, noticing her choice of words "—I don't want to talk to you, I don't want you talking to me. Just leave and don't come back!"

A silence settles between us, much longer than five seconds. We both stand our ground, too stubborn to back down.

After a moment, I decide it's time to leave. We're not getting anywhere.

Not today, at least.

"Goodbye, Tessa."

She doesn't respond. She just stands there, trying to catch her breath.

I leave the room and shut the door behind me.

Mrs. Dickinson is waiting in the upstairs hallway. She, along with the rest of the neighborhood, must have heard our entire conversation. She looks concerned—and maybe a little embarrassed—but doesn't say a word until we are back downstairs in the kitchen.

"I'm so sorry for Tessa's behavior—"

"Don't apologize," I interrupt, shaking my head. "I actually kind of enjoyed it."

Mrs. Dickinson's eyebrows lift. She looks concerned for my psychiatric health.

"She's not angry," I explain, though it sounds crazy. "She's scared. That's why she's so upset. It's not about me or you or anyone else. It's about her." I stop myself and laugh because that probably sounded ridiculous. "I'm not usually this philosophical."

Mrs. Dickinson smiles, that same gentle sadness in her eyes. I wonder if it ever goes away. "In any case, there is no excuse for the way she treated you just now."

"Don't worry about it," I insist. "Would it be okay with you if I come back tomorrow?"

She looks surprised. "If you want to…"

"Of course I want to."

Mrs. Dickinson purses her lips and says, "Tessa never would have been so rude if she knew about—"

"I don't want her to know about it." I try my best not to look desperate. "It'll only make things worse if she knows. Besides, no one has ever seen the light by being told there are darker places out there."

Mrs. Dickinson gives me a puzzled smile.

"It's nice to know there's at least one person in the world who doesn't feel bad for me." I grin and head for the front door. "See you tomorrow, Mrs. Dickinson."

TESSA

DAY 21, DAY 22, AND DAY 23

I'VE NEVER BEEN SO UNCIVIL TO SOMEONE BEFORE—LET alone a perfect stranger. Before the accident, nothing would have triggered me to be so impolite, to scream and cry in front of someone I've never even met.

Grandma insists he was only trying to help, but if he really understood, he would know that I want to be left alone. I don't need help, and I don't want help.

I

don't

want

help.

He's gone now, and so is the sun that I felt when I stood at the window. My room is cold despite the fact that it's the middle of June. I sit on the floor by my bed with my face in my hands. The door is locked, and Grandma has stopped trying to open it.

I feel like every beautiful thing in me has rotted and turned ugly. I've become things that I never wanted to become—things that I hate with every fiber of my being.

I'm selfish.

I'm lazy.

I'm depressed.

I'm bitter.

I'm cynical.

And today, I proved it all by yelling at a boy who only wanted to help me. Crying in front of him, too. A *boy*. I don't think a boy has ever been in my room before today. And if that's the sort of experience it is, I'm not sure I want a boy in my room ever again.

Yes, I treated him with contempt. But he deserved it. He came to my house, uninvited, and presumed to understand my pain without even asking me how I felt about it. He just walked in here as if he knew me, saying, "You need to write."

How does he know what I need? How does *anyone* know what I need?

"It sucks." That was all he said about the accident. Not "I'm so sorry." That's what most people would have said. I'm sick of hearing it, myself. But what kind of a person just says "It sucks"? What kind of person has no sympathy for someone like me? Someone whose world has been turned upside down?

I feel like I've gone through a blender. My emotions have turned into a toxic soup—a cocktail of everything all at once. Anger in one heartbeat, sadness in the next. Frustration, then fear. Rage, then regret.

I am a pendulum.

A tornado.

Chaos.

I'm trying to stop a tidal wave with my bare hands. I'm standing on the beach, screaming into the darkness, and I'm alone.

And I'm drowning.

I'm

d r o w n i n g.

God help me.

Help me help me help me help me help me help me help me help
me help me help me help me help me help me help me help me help
me help me help me help me help me help me help me help me help
me help me help me help me help me help me help me help me help
me help me help me help me help me help me.

Help.

True to his word, the stubborn boy returns the very next day. I hear
his voice downstairs, talking to my grandparents. I hear his laughter,
muffled, through the floor. Our house is old, with little to no insul-
ation. It's cold in the winter and warm in the summer. In the winter,
I huddle under giant knit blankets with hot tea and my laptop, and
I write poetry as snow falls outside.

That is, I used to.

Before.

Now it's summer, and now I'm blind.

I lie on my bed in a broken kind of fetal position, my face half-
buried in the comforter. My head is heavy with exhaustion.

Why is he back? How has he persuaded my grandmother to allow
him the liberty to harass me? A complete stranger. What does he
know? What does Grandma know, letting all of this happen? What
does Grandpa know, *making* all of this happen?

Something inside me is still screaming, still howling back at the
wind of the tornado. But I'm tired today. So tired, I don't think I
possess the ability to argue with Weston even if I wanted to.

I hear footsteps on the stairs, coming up. My bedroom door
opens, and I can somehow sense that it's Grandma. She says nothing.
Then her presence vanishes and someone else steps in.

Weston.

"Hi, Tessa," he says, as if yesterday never happened.

His voice is smooth and gentle.

My voice is wet and gravelly. "I thought I told you to never come back."

"And I thought I told you that you need to start writing again," he counters.

A vise tightens around my stomach. I will *not* cry. But I might explode.

"I think *I* should be the judge of that," I say through gritted teeth. "I can only write when I'm inspired."

"And are you inspired?"

"What do you think."

Weston falls silent.

I close my eyes, trying to breathe slowly and evenly.

"Okay then," Weston says. "I guess I'll come back tomorrow."

My eyes snap open, though the darkness remains. "You will *not*. I don't know how you've coerced my grandparents into thinking this is acceptable, but it is *not acceptable*. I want you to stop coming here, understand? I want you to stop bothering me."

"Tessa—"

"Don't talk to me as if you know me," I snap, curling my hands into fists. "You don't know me, Weston. You don't know what I'm going through, and you can't help me. Just leave me alone."

Silence again.

"Weston?"

He's gone. He must have left the room while I was still speaking, taking advantage of the fact that I can't *see*. What else should I expect from such a thoughtless boy?

"Jerk," I mutter, closing my eyes again and pressing my face against the comforter.

For a long moment, I listen to the noises downstairs. Grandpa's voice, low and deep. Dishes in the kitchen. I wonder what time it is. Today is cloudy, or so Siri told me earlier. I haven't felt the sunlight come through my window since yesterday.

"I'm not a jerk."

I gasp. My heart jumps into my throat.

He didn't leave. *Jerk.*

"I'm only trying to help," he says, calm and matter-of-fact.

"You. Can't. Help. Me."

The door opens. The door closes. I hear his footsteps on the stairs, going down.

I let out a long breath, but it's not a sigh of relief. It's just an exhale that leaves me feeling worse than I felt before Weston came in my room.

Why does he insist on coming here? Haven't I scared him away by now? Anyone in their right mind would just leave me alone. Maybe I'm not as intimidating as I think I am.

Maybe I'm just

p a t h e t i c.

Either way, I need to figure out how to stop him from coming. Clearly, I have no powers of persuasion. But perhaps fighting it is the wrong course of action.

Maybe I should give him what he wants—what my grandparents want.

And prove him wrong.

Prove all of them wrong.

Prove myself right.

* * *

"Grandma?"

"What is it, sweetheart?"

I'm standing in the shower, with a towel wrapped around my body. Since the accident, Grandma stays in the bathroom while I take a shower, to help me if I need anything—but by day twenty-three, I've gotten better at bathing myself without assistance.

"Is Weston coming back tomorrow?" I ask, surprising myself by how small my voice sounds.

"Yes," Grandma replies. "Are you okay with that?"

Funny thing to ask me *now*.

"Don't let him come into my room," I say. "But tell him to come back. On Tuesday. At three o'clock."

I can practically *hear* Grandma's surprise. I can hear her smile through her words—it sounds the same as the morning of the unfortunate newspaper event.

She's happy with my decision.

She thinks I've given in.

Little does she know, I've done just the opposite.

I've outsmarted him.

WESTON

JUNE 21

I GO BACK BECAUSE I KNOW TESSA BETTER THAN SHE thinks I know her. She's not angry with me; she's angry with life. She's angry with the shit that life has thrown in her face so unexpectedly. She doesn't want to take the crutch of Help. Nobody wants to. In fact, it feels like giving up to take the crutch. And Tessa doesn't seem like the type who gives up. She's almost as stubborn as I am. Which means this won't be easy.

"Where are you going?" Mom asks me on Monday as I'm about to make my escape.

"Um..."

She's standing in the living room with her hands on her hips. I'm hovering by the front door, trying to think up a reasonable explanation.

"I'm going for a run," I say. "At the track. With Rudy."

Mom quirks one eyebrow. "You do realize those aren't your running legs."

I glance down at my Nikes. *Right.*

"And you also realize that I can contact Rudy and confirm that you are not, in fact, going for a run at the track."

My shoulders slump. "Yes, Mom, I realize that you and Rudy go behind my back to keep tabs on me twenty-four seven."

Mom smiles and turns away. "Be back before sunset."

That's what makes her so cool. She pretends like she cares, and she does, really—but she's not a helicopter mom. I'm free to go running whenever I want, wherever I want.

Life is good.

When I show up at the Dickinsons' front door, the grandmother tells me to come back on Tuesday instead, at three o'clock. She's smiling, and I feel like we've made this progress together. Mrs. Dickinson could have thrown me out on the first day, but she didn't. She actually thinks I can help Tessa. So does Mr. Dickinson, who I met on Sunday. He was still wearing a suit and tie from church service, and he looked like a rich banker from the nineteen forties; but he doesn't look old enough to be a grandparent, either. He has dark hair and a narrow face and he doesn't stare at me half as much as other people do. I like him. And I sense they both like me.

Tessa is the only Dickinson who doesn't like me.

But maybe she's coming around. That's what I tell myself as I walk to 52 West Elm Street on Tuesday afternoon. But honestly? I have no idea what to expect.

The first day, Tessa was a fireball of anger, standing at the window.

The second day, she was a crumpled heap of sadness, lying on a mess of blankets.

Today, she is serious and alert, sitting upright on her tightly made bed.

"Hello, Weston," she says, clear and brisk, like a news reporter. She stares straight ahead, at nothing.

"Hi," I say, softly closing the door behind me. "How are you doing today?"

Tessa seems annoyed by the question. She shrugs one shoulder. "Fine. You?"

"Never been better."

If she was annoyed by the question, she's even more annoyed by my reply. I detect a little sarcastic grunt, but choose to ignore it.

"So. You have some typing you want me to do?"

Tessa nods. "That *is* why you're here, right?"

"Uh, yeah."

A silence passes. Five seconds, easily. But I don't know what to say next.

"Open the laptop," Tessa instructs, nodding toward the desk.

I sit down at her desk and open up her laptop. It's one of those super-thin, fancy MacBooks, with a white marble case to match her bedroom's perfectionist theme.

"Password?" I ask.

She sighs, as if she wasn't expecting to have to give that out. As if I'll try to break into her laptop or something.

"Open every door," Tessa says. "Three twenty-five."

I type it in.

openeverydoor325

"What does it mean?"

Tessa is quiet for a few seconds. "What makes you think it means anything?"

"Because... I don't know. It's a weird password."

The desktop loads and, once again, I'm not sure what to do from here. I wait for Tessa's instruction, but she only huffs impatiently and says:

"'Not knowing when the dawn will come
I open every door;

Or has it feathers like a bird,
Or billows like a shore?'"

I frown at the wall, wondering if that was something I'm supposed
to type.

"Emily Dickinson," Tessa finishes. "That's what the password is
from. One of her poems."

"Oh."

I suddenly realize the similarity in last name, and I could totally
make a joke about it. But something tells me Tessa isn't in the mood
for a joke about her last name.

"What do I do from here?" I ask, trying to stay focused.

"Open Safari," she says, "and go to blogger.com. It should already
be logged into my account. Click the orange button in the top left
corner that says new post—"

"Um, Tessa?"

"What?"

"I'm not even on the website yet."

She sighs, but says nothing else.

When the page finishes loading, I try to remember her directions.
Orange button, new post.

"Okay."

"You ready?" She says it like she's about to punch me in the face.
Maybe she is.

I position my fingers over the keyboard. "Yeah, I'm ready."

She takes a slow, deep breath, and I can sense another explosion
coming. That's the only predictable thing about Tessa Dickinson:
she's a volcano.

"The night burns and the stars breathe their last

They scream into the black void
Void of life, yet crying to be heard
They're gone now, but we can still see them
Like I'm gone now, but you can still see me
I'm home now, but I'm lost at sea—"

I interrupt her with a short sigh. My fingers stop typing. I have two lines. The part about the stars screaming into the black void.

Tessa hesitates for a moment. "Oh, I'm sorry. Am I going too fast for you?"

I take a measured breath, staring at the wall in front of me. "Not at all."

"Good."

I type the rest of what I can remember.

They're gone now, but you can still see them
I'm gone now, but you can still see me
I'm home now, but I'm lost at sea

"Should I continue?" Tessa asks. Once more, her tone is clear and brisk, like a news reporter.

So this is her plan—to scare me away. We haven't made progress; she's just playing the game to get me to buzz off. She thinks that if she talks too fast for me to type, I'll just walk out and give up.

Little does she know how much I can handle.

Wouldn't it annoy her if I didn't complain at all? Wouldn't it be fun to annoy her?

Totally.

"Go ahead," I say.

"My blood is pounding," Tessa continues. "My mind is breaking.

My heart is cracking. My lips are drowning.

"Life is just a fractured weapon
A lucky hand
Your opponent in the ring
Who happens to be stronger than you
Though he, too, is bleeding
Falling
Drowning
Life gets back up so easily
But I stay down on my knees."

I'm still typing *a lucky hand* when she finishes. But I remember the part about the fighter in the ring.

Tessa falls silent as I finish typing.

"Is that all?" I ask.

"Maybe. Read it back to me."

I guess I should have expected this part. I scroll up to find the first line of the poem and start reading.

"The night burns and the stars breathe their last
They scream into the black void
They're gone now, but you can still see them—"

"You missed a line."

I squint at the words. "What?"

"After *they scream into the black void,* it should say 'Void of life, yet crying to be heard.'"

"Oh." I add the line.

"And it's 'They're gone now, but *we* can still see them.' Not *you.*"

I draw in a sharp, annoyed breath, reaching up to rub my forehead.

"Is something wrong, Weston?" Tessa asks, snappy and hot.

Wouldn't it be fun to annoy her?

She must have thought the same about me.

I turn around in the desk chair, throwing her a hard look over my shoulder. She's still sitting rigid and stoic on her bed, staring at nothing.

She's actually really pretty.

Her eyes are bluer than mine—the enhanced kind of blue you see in contact lens commercials. She has freckles, too. Just a few, thrown across her nose and cheeks. Her hair is braided today, less messy. She looks so serious.

I liked it better when she was screaming and crying.

"No," I say at last, having a good time staring at her without her knowing it. "Nothing's wrong."

"Good."

For two hours, I sit at the volcano's desk and type poetry for her. The lava of words is burning and fluid, spilling and making a mess. I feel like a disruption in Tessa's perfect little world of order. My typing skills are nowhere near moderate—and she knows it.

But I don't give up, and neither does she.

Finally, she says, "I think that's enough for today. I need to rest." She tips her head back and closes her eyes. Apparently, that's my cue to leave.

I close the laptop, walk to the door, and say, "See you tomorrow."

She doesn't reply.

I find Mrs. Dickinson in the kitchen, making tea. She looks up when I enter the room.

"How did it go?"

"All right," I say.

Mrs. Dickinson's face falls, as if I'd replied, "Horrible."

"I think Tessa is trying to scare me away," I explain. "By proving that I'm not up to the task."

Mrs. Dickinson sighs, long and disappointed. "I'm sorry. You don't have to do this, you know."

"I know. But I want to. If you don't mind."

"At least let me pay you."

"No, ma'am. Please. I don't want any money."

But she's just as stubborn as her granddaughter and has somehow already produced a twenty-dollar bill from a drawer. She practically shoves it at me. "I insist."

Begrudgingly, I stick the money into my pocket. I'll have to think up a way to repay her later.

"Stay for tea?" Mrs. Dickinson says.

I shrug. "Okay."

The water boils. She pours it into three matching stoneware mugs and carries the tray out to the sunroom at the back of the house. The walls are lined with windows, and Mr. Dickinson sits in one of the wicker chairs, reading a newspaper.

This house is unlike mine in every possible way. Everything is organized to an obsessive standard, it's quiet enough to hear songbirds outside, and it smells like lavender and laundry detergent.

Mr. Dickinson sets down the newspaper and thanks his wife for the tea, then asks me the same question. "How did it go?"

I give him the same reply.

"I'm sorry I ever called about that ad," Mr. Dickinson says. "I should have known that Tessa wouldn't like the idea."

"But you did know," I say, without thinking. "That's why you didn't tell her, right?"

Mr. Dickinson looks at me for a moment. Then he laughs. "You're right, young man. That's exactly why I didn't tell her."

Mrs. Dickinson hands me a cup of tea.

"Thanks."

"Tessa has always been a bit of a loner," she explains. "But it wasn't until the accident that she's become… so cold. So shut off from everyone else."

I nod slowly. "It'll get better."

Mrs. Dickinson smiles a little, in that sympathetic way of hers. "I'm… not sure it will."

"We understand," Mr. Dickinson adds, "if you don't want to continue coming here."

"But I do."

They both stare at me, puzzled.

"It's not easy—for anyone," I explain. "But that's okay. That's good. The hard thing to do and the right thing to do are usually the same."

That's a quote I stole from my dad's wall. But the words feel like mine.

"There is another reason, too," I say. "Another reason why I like coming here and talking to Tessa."

"Because she treats you so poorly?" Mrs. Dickinson says, guilt written all over her face.

I nod. "Yeah. And I know this sounds weird, but… I like being treated poorly—I like being treated like a normal person, not just the remains of one."

A heavy silence follows that comment.

"So, yeah," I say, trying to lighten the mood. "Please keep Tessa in the dark about it. No pun intended."

The grandparents smile—kind of unsure, but still. They smile.

I sigh, pretending to be relieved. "Phew. I wasn't sure if it was still too soon to joke about that."

Mrs. Dickinson gives me a chiding look over the rim of her teacup.

I can tell they want to ask the Question. Enough time has passed—more than enough, because they're old-fashioned and super polite.

"Go ahead," I murmur, looking at the floor. "I know you're wondering."

"Wondering what?" Mrs. Dickinson says.

I give her a half smile. "How I lost them."

She looks a little surprised. "You weren't born without—?"

I shake my head.

"Well, you don't have to tell us if you don't want to, Weston."

"That's okay," I say, setting my cup on the table. "But I have to warn you—it's kind of a boring story."

WESTON

3 YEARS AND 9 MONTHS BEFORE TESSA

IT ALL STARTED ON THE DAY OF RUDY KAUFMANN'S BAR mitzvah. That sounds like the title of a movie, doesn't it? A movie from the nineteen nineties, with sun-bleached film and good child actors and loud rock music. That's exactly what it was like, actually. Minus the rock music. We were at a synagogue, for crying out loud.

It would have been my bar mitzvah too, if I were Jewish. Technically, I was two hours older than Rudy Kaufmann. I loved to torture him with it, saying things like, "Hey, Rudy, when I was your age…" and then I'd tell him whatever I'd done two hours ago. It was one of the many ways I knew how to get on his nerves.

Rudy was a good four inches taller than me, and his voice had already dropped—literally overnight—which made me jealous as shit. Rudy was a powerhouse, but you'd never guess it. He climbed trees like an acrobat; he was a mess of freckles and ribs and sunburn. He was never looking for a fight, but when I made him box me in the schoolyard after class, he'd blast me into the middle of next week. Then he'd apologize for blasting me. Then I would punch him back, and we'd be even.

Fistfights were against school rules, but the adults were the only ones who cared about rules, and they didn't care enough to *enforce* the rules.

Our school was like a relic from the nineteen forties, and Rudy was like a relic, too. He never cheated, never swore, never tried cigarettes. That's part of the reason why I decided to be his friend to begin with. Because he had enough self-control for two, and I had enough self-control for negative one.

But he fought me. And that was something to watch.

The other kids at school thought so, too. They would pour out of the building and gather around the circle of dirt next to the playground to watch us beat each other up. Some of the kids with money would even take bets. I would hit Rudy and Rudy would hit me back until one of us conceded. Then we would go home bleeding. Or sit in detention together and think up new ways to win the next fight (because we'd always do it again).

That day Rudy was wearing a suit jacket and tie—and I made fun of him, because I'd ripped mine off in the car when Mom wasn't looking. She didn't even notice when we all went into the synagogue—she was holding Noah on one hip and trying not to lose Aidan and Henry in the crowd.

After most of the celebration was over, the adults all kind of swarmed together and talked about grown-up things. I pulled Rudy away from his aunt's riveting conversation about his untold future as a rabbi and dragged him out to the parking lot.

"What are you doing?" he asked, in the same voice he used to say *You're getting me in trouble.*

"My board's in the car. Did you bring yours?"

Rudy sighed. "They'll be looking for me—"

I stopped short, keeping a hold on his skinny arm. "Come on, just a quick ride. To celebrate."

Rudy didn't look convinced. He gave me that look, the one where he was trying to be an adult.

"Where are you going?" Henry's voice piped up from behind us.

I turned around and saw my ten-year-old little brother squinting into the sun.

"Get back to Mom and Dad," I ordered, just because I was the oldest and could say things like that. I pointed in the direction of the synagogue.

But Henry didn't move. "No," he said, "I wanna go skateboarding with you guys."

I groaned. "Fine. But you better do everything I say. Or I'm sendin' you back."

He nodded eagerly. Because I threatened him like that a lot— *sendin' you back.* I somehow developed the ability to make it sound like there was a gloomy dark orphanage from where Henry had originally come, and I could "send him back" whenever I felt like it.

"Go get your board, Kaufmann."

Rudy frowned. "But—"

"Come on, man! Don't be a pansyass."

I ran across the parking lot and opened the back of our car, pulling out my and Henry's skateboards.

A derelict body shop sat behind the synagogue, surrounded by an old metal fence that separated the concrete from the grass. The place was almost like a skate park—metal railings and low barriers stuck up all over the place. We found a way around the fence and brought half a dozen boys with us. The day was way too hot, for September— and way too hot for jackets and ties. A few of the other kids stripped theirs off and tossed them into places where they would never be found again.

Henry watched me to learn how to do tricks on his skateboard, and Rudy watched me to make sure I didn't get myself killed. He could've done all the tricks I did, and probably better—if he wasn't such a pansyass.

"Hey, Rudy, let's climb up on the roof."

"No."

"We could jump off, over the fence."

"No."

"Come on, man—"

"Weston? Henry?" my mother's voice called from the other side of the fence. She was still carrying Noah and frowning in that way moms frown when you run off without permission.

I groaned and rode my skateboard over to the fence while the other boys laughed. "Yeah, Mom?"

"What are you boys doing?"

"Skateboarding."

She sighed. "Well, we're leaving. Noah is tired."

"Aw, come on, Mom," I groaned. "Can't I hang out with Rudy a little while longer?"

Mom drew in a breath, but before she could refuse, Henry materialized by my side.

"Please let us stay, Mom!"

He was always more convincing (because he was Mom's favorite), so I seconded this motion and said, "Yeah, Mom, let us stay. I'll look after Henry."

Henry threw me a brief dirty look—because no ten-year-old boy needs "looking after" in a neglected parking lot full of hazards and skateboards and daredevil middle schoolers.

"Fine," Mom said, because we were only a few blocks from home. "But be back within the hour, okay? And, Weston—" she looked me straight in the eyes "—don't let him out of your sight."

"Yes, ma'am."

Little did she know Henry wasn't the one who would get into

trouble.

If only she hadn't let us stay.

If only she had said, "No, you stupid boys, get your butts in the car."

If only.

"We're free!" I cheered, jumping on my board and doing a double kick flip.

Rudy squinted at me. Everyone was squinting that day. The sun was too bright. "You're not actually gonna climb up on the roof, right?"

"I might. You gonna try and stop me?"

He popped his board up into his hand. "I might."

That was when I made the decision—and I have no idea why I did it. To prove something? Or maybe it was just for fun.

Yeah, it was more likely just for fun.

And what a lot of fun it turned out to be.

I ran to the derelict body shop, where a ladder was mounted to one wall. I picked up my skateboard and started to climb. A few of the boys noticed and stopped what they were doing to watch.

"Weston!" Rudy shouted up to me from the ground. "What the hell are you doing?"

I let out a low whistle. "'Hell'? Is that allowed, Kaufmann?"

"Get your ass down here."

"No."

I climbed all the way up to the roof. It was flat and scorching hot. By this point, all the boys were watching. They had congregated in a small confused knot on the pavement—shielding their eyes to look up at me. I always liked to be the center of attention.

I guess that's why you *should* be careful what you wish for.

Out of all of the kids, Henry seemed the most in awe. Out of all of the kids, Rudy seemed the most annoyed. But he was probably just jealous.

I held my skateboard up like a trophy and yelled down to my audience, "I will now attempt! To ride off the edge of this roof and jump that fence! Over there!"

"You're crazy!" one of the boys in the group sneered. "You'll kill yourself."

"No, I won't."

"Yeah, you will, Wes." Rudy crossed his arms over his chest. "Just get down here."

I shook my head. "Don't you see how it's perfectly aligned with the edge of the roof? This will be easy."

"Do it, then!" a different boy shouted. "If it's so *easy*."

Rudy shook his head. I glanced at the fence again. It was so close to the building—I could easily clear it. And there was only grass on the other side. I wouldn't hurt myself even if I did fall at the end.

"Okay, guys! Watch carefully, 'cause I'm only gonna do this once."

I dropped my skateboard and positioned my foot over the grip tape. I cracked my neck just to be dramatic. I surveyed my runway— a clear path straight off the edge of the roof and over the fence. That rock music started playing in my head again—if this had been a movie, the song probably would have been "Born to Be Wild."

I took a deep breath.

Then I went for it. I pushed off, and a murmur of foolish encouragement rose up from my small audience below.

My little brother shouted, "You can do it, Weston!"

I propelled my board forward—harder, faster, harder, faster, and then... I shot off the edge. In slow motion (or at least I like to imagine it in slow motion) I sailed across the gap between the roof and the fence. And I almost cleared that stupid fence, too.

But not quite.

I came down too fast, and the stupid fence ate me alive.

A sharp pain ripped across the backs of my legs. Then my board crashed to the ground, and *I* crashed too.

I landed on my knees and forearms, but I turned my head in time to avoid a broken nose.

"Ow." I said more than just *ow,* but we won't go into details because I was technically on the property of the synagogue.

As I climbed to my feet, the throng of awestruck boys rushed to the fence—peering out like a bunch of prisoners. They watched, dumbfounded, as I grabbed my board from the grass and held it up like a trophy once more.

"That, my friends, is how it's done!"

They all cheered and clapped. Except for Rudy. He just smiled and shook his head.

I walked over to the fence and leaned against it, trying to channel my inner John Wayne.

"You're still crazy," said the boy who told me I'd kill myself. "But crazy brave."

"Hell yeah!" another kid agreed.

Henry, who was latching onto the fence and staring at me with a look of unspeakable awe, suddenly pointed and said, "Hey, Wes— you're bleeding."

I hadn't even noticed the pain until he said something. I glanced down, and sure enough, there were two trails of blood trickling down the backs of my calves. That stupid fence had caught me good, on both legs.

Without thinking much about it, I turned back to my brother and grinned and said, "Well, what do you know? I'm human."

Everyone laughed—even Rudy. But probably just because it was the most modest thing I'd said all week.

"We should head back home," I told Henry. "Mom will be worried."

Henry nodded as the rest of the boys dispersed.

"Go get your board and I'll meet you on the sidewalk."

He scurried off across the parking lot. Rudy and I were the only ones who remained—him on one side of the fence, me on the other.

"You all right?" he asked.

I reached down and swiped at the blood on my legs. Red smeared all over my hands, but the cuts weren't that deep.

"Yeah, I'm cool," I replied, squinting at Rudy. "You've given me worse."

He grinned. "Pansyass."

Henry wasn't allowed to ride his skateboard on the sidewalk, which meant I wasn't allowed to ride my skateboard on the sidewalk, which meant we had to walk home. It took about fifteen minutes.

Halfway to our street, Henry said, "Hey, Weston?"

"Yeah?"

"You're still bleeding."

"No, I'm not. Look, it's almost stopped."

Henry didn't seem convinced. I halted him in his tracks.

"Hey. Don't go telling Mom about this, okay? Or Dad."

My little brother frowned. "Why not?"

"Because it's no big deal." I shrugged, trying to act cool about it. "And if Mom hears about the fence stunt, she'll never let me take you skateboarding again."

Henry considered the weight of this condition for a few seconds. Then he chose the moral high ground. "I think she should know."

"No, no, no," I said, crouching down to get at his eye level.

"Henry, if you breathe a word about this, I'll take your skateboard and never give it back. Understand?"

Ruling by force was a last resort with Henry—but it always worked. He nodded like a good little brother.

When we got back home, I snuck inside through the back door. If Mom saw the blood, she would freak out—but I didn't have time to wash it off. So I threw on a pair of jeans and ignored the pain. I'd been cut and scraped and punched and kicked and thrown on the ground a million times before. What made this any different? Nothing, really. It didn't even hurt that bad. So I took it like a man.

If only I hadn't.

If only I'd told someone.

If only, if only, if only.

TESSA

DAY 26

"SIRI, WHAT TIME IS IT?"

"It is seven forty-five a.m. Good morning!"

I grit my teeth and press the home button again.

"Why is Weston here so early?"

Apparently, I've reached a point of emotional collapse where I ask artificial intelligence questions that artificial intelligence can't possibly know the answer to.

"Here's what I found on the web for: Why is Weston here so early."

I drop my phone somewhere in my bedsheets, huffing a sigh.

He never shows up this early.

I push back the covers and swing my legs over the side of the mattress. My toes touch the carpet. My right hand finds the edge of my nightstand. I slowly stand up. The dizziness has decreased over the past few days.

Voices murmur below the floor, downstairs. Grandma, Grandpa, and *him*. Weston. The stubborn boy who won't leave me alone.

He's laughing. And maybe if I didn't resent him so much, I would notice that he has a really nice laugh—the kind that makes you want to laugh with him even if you don't get the joke.

I think that means I *did* notice it.

Darn.

I make my way across the room to my dresser. I'm certainly not putting on a bra and going downstairs. Not while Weston is here.

And why is he here? I have no idea.

My hands feel the edge of the dresser, the smooth surface of the wood, then come in contact with the mirror. I let my fingertips trace the glass—up, up, up, until I'm touching the spot where my face would be, if I could see.

If I could see.

There's a vise in my middle, squeezing tighter and tighter, like a corset. Anger and regret and fear, that cocktail of chaotic emotions—it consumes me, burns me, blisters me. I want to cry; I want to see; I want to be *normal again.*

I just want to be normal again.

I just want to be normal again.

I just want to be normal again.

My fingertips press into the mirror—harder and harder and harder until they start to tremble and sting. I drag my fingernails down the glass; I clench my teeth together; I curl my toes. It's the opposite of falling apart; the opposite of exploding. I'm like a star before it goes supernova. Collapsing inward.

If he weren't downstairs, I would scream. I would break my mirror, smash it into a million little pieces.

Then it would look like me.

Because I'm not Tessa Dickinson anymore.

I am a million little pieces of what used to be Tessa Dickinson.

I stumble over to my bedroom door, one hand outstretched and one hand clamped over my mouth to keep the sobs from escaping. I collapse to my knees and lean against the door and listen.

I can hear Grandma talking in the kitchen below, then dishes clattering. Grandpa says something.

Weston laughs.

He's not here to see me. He's here for breakfast. He's literally here to have breakfast with my grandparents.

Did I succeed in scaring him away? Did he decide that I was too much to handle? That it was too hard to type my poetry?

Or does he think I'll get better? Be nicer to him? Just because he has such an optimistic attitude about everything?

"Never been better," he said. Of course. *He* has nothing to complain about.

He can see.

And so can Grandma and Grandpa. I envy them and their perfect health and their laughter, as I sit on the floor and cry into my hands and listen to them downstairs, eating breakfast without me.

In fact, I don't think I've ever been so jealous in my life.

So much has been taken away from me. Yet, at the same time, I can't help but wonder if I've taken it away from *myself.* Am I choosing this? Choosing to sit on the floor and cry?

Am I choosing to be defeated?

A voice inside my head screams the very opposite. *I have no choice. This happened to me. I can't do anything to stop it.*

My head and my heart shout two different anthems, covering their ears, pledging allegiance to rival sides. Part of me wants to wash my face and get dressed and go downstairs and have breakfast with them—if only to freak Weston out.

But the other part of me shuts down such a ridiculous idea.

You're blind. You can't be helped. This is all your fault. You have every right to be miserable.

So I stay on the floor. And cry.

Sunlight is exuberant.
Thunderstorms are passionate.
Two extremes, and so much better
than nothing at all.

Cloudy skies are like nothing at all.
Apathetic.
Numb.
The feeling you feel when you have
no
idea
what
you
feel.

When everything has gone so wrong,
it no longer feels wrong.
There suddenly is no right or wrong.
There's just emptiness.

It would be better for the clouds to cry,
or better for the sun to shine.
But curse this bearing wall
where the sky is
nothing
at
all.

WESTON

JUNE 22

"SO, WHO'S THE GIRL?"

I freeze, turning to look at Henry, who has a smirk on his face and a dishcloth in his hands.

"There is no girl," I lie, shoving a clean, dripping plate at him.

Henry nods slowly. He has grown sarcastic in his pubescent age. He has also grown six inches overnight, which makes me wonder if *I'm* actually the orphan in the family.

My little brother twitches his eyebrows. "So you're saying Tessa Dickinson doesn't exist."

"Hey, keep it down, okay?"

"What?" He takes another plate from my soapy hands. "Everybody knows. You told Mom."

"Mom isn't everybody, last time I checked. Although she might be to you."

"You're avoiding the question."

I sigh, running hot water through a handful of silverware. "Okay, fine. The girl is Tessa Dickinson, she's blind, and she doesn't like me. In any sense of the word. So stop looking at me like that."

Henry laughs and tosses the dishcloth onto the counter. "She's blind. Of course she doesn't like you. She can't check you out."

I smile, shaking my head. "That's right, she can't."

"Wait, she doesn't *know*, does she?"

I shut off the water and dry my hands. "No. She doesn't."

"Holy shit." Henry gapes. "What's *that* like?"

"It's frickin' awesome."

Aidan charges into the kitchen in a streak of blue pajamas and body-slams me. "We're reading in my room tonight, right?" He looks up at me with his giant brown eyes.

"That's right, Spider-Man." I laugh, ruffling his hair. "You call the shots. But I'm still wondering if we should allow Henry to come."

Aidan frowns. "Why not?"

"Because he's kind of old for comics, isn't he?"

Aidan bounces off toward his room, yelling, "Nobody is too old for comics!"

"I've raised you well!" I proclaim dramatically, with a hand over my heart.

Henry rolls his eyes at me. "Mom's raised us well."

"Oh yeah, *mom, mom, momma's boy*." I punch him in the shoulder as I walk by.

He tries to hit me back, but misses. "Shut up! I meant they're her comics."

"I know what you meant." I toss a smirk over my shoulder. "Momma's boy."

It's true—my brothers and I would have no real appreciation for superheroes if it weren't for our mom. Some moms collect vinyls or teacups or jewelry—but our mom collected comics. She stole them from her brothers back in the seventies and eighties. Some of them are even considered vintage now. But she doesn't keep them hidden away somewhere—she's always let us read them, lose them, find them again, cut out pages and tape them to our bedroom walls.

Ever since I learned to read, and ever since I had a younger brother to read to, I've religiously practiced story time—or some theatrical form of it, anyway. First it was just me and three-year-old Henry. He was never allowed to talk while I was reading, only to sit next to me on the bed and look at the pictures. Then Mom had Aidan, and I thought it was important for a newborn to learn about superheroes, so we moved story time into the nursery. By the time Aidan was old enough to move into Henry's room, Mom was pregnant again. Pretty soon, I had three younger brothers to read to, boss around, and throw pillows at every night—which made me feel about as important as a ten-year-old boy *can* feel.

Mom stopped having babies after that. I think the doctor told her it was genetically impossible for her to have a girl. So she gave up.

To this day, my brothers and I still read comics at night, on the floor, in each other's bedrooms. These days I make Aidan read, because I enjoy sleeping more than I used to.

But tonight, I'm wide awake. Tonight, I want to read Tessa's blog.

It's called *YesterSummer,* like yesteryear, but different. Does the name mean something to her? Did she make up the word, or is it from an old poem, like her password? Maybe I'll ask her next time I see her. If I dare.

As soon as my brothers are sent to bed with Mom's usual "That's enough reading for one night," I escape to my room, take off my prostheses, and crash into bed with my phone.

I have about a hundred missed text messages from Rudy.

RUDY: dude what the heck
RUDY: WHERE ARE YOU
RUDY: DID YOU LITERALLY TEXT ME

RUDY: and theN THROW YOUR PHONE
RUDY: ACROSS THE PACIFIC OCEAN
WESTON: bro chilllllllll
WESTON: I got distracted doing the dishes
RUDY: for three hours???
WESTON: can't live without me for three hours man?
WESTON: LOVE YOU TOO

I open a new internet tab and type in Tessa's blog address. The latest post was typed and published by yours truly. She had me include a note at the bottom in small font—something vague about being absent, but nothing mentioning her accident or her blindness. It seems she doesn't like to talk about her problems online. (Unlike ninety-nine percent of Earth's population.)

On the "About" page, there's a picture of Tessa. It's a selfie, but a really good one. She's standing in a garden, surrounded by yellow flowers—and she's smiling.

I've never seen her smile.

It's a good smile. Bright.

In fact, just looking at the picture makes *me* smile.

This can't be a good sign.

Realizing that I'm getting distracted, I go back to the homepage and start scrolling, looking for older poems. Poems she wrote when she still had sight.

At the beginning of May, she posted one titled "Sunlight."

Sunlight is everything
And all at once

Sunlight is gentle
And harsh

Sunlight can be blindingly bright
But then sunlight can also be
delicately soft

Sunlight is a paradox

Sunlight is every color in the world
Red in the arid evenings, like scarlet chivalry
Orange minutes or hours later, like a fading memory
Yellow in the sleepy sugary afternoons, and you can still see
the color through your eyelids
Green through the cracks in the clouds of the summer
thunderstorm, like the dancing trees
Icy blue when it's going to rain and
Deeper blue when it actually does
Purple in the winter sunsets and
Pink in the springtime ones
And red in the arid evenings, like scarlet chivalry

Around and around
Sunlight is everything

Sunlight makes me feel like
I am beautiful
Only because without it
I am invisible
grayscale

nothing

Sunlight is my redemption.

I scroll to the next poem. It's shorter and about the ocean—and maybe about love, too. I can't tell. The next one is similar: bright and fresh and visual. I go back up to the top of the page, to the poem I published for her.

My blood is pounding.
My mind is breaking.
My heart is cracking…

Life gets back up so easily
But I stay down on my knees.

Her poetry was so much brighter before the accident—she wrote about the good in the world, the beauty, the hope. She wrote about new possibilities with every sunrise. She wrote about sunlight and oceans and falling in love, when I'm pretty sure she has no idea what it feels like to fall in love.

But now? Her poetry has fallen down a black hole of misery, and she's fallen down with it. She writes about what she *sees*, and the poems I drafted for her yesterday are no different—they're all just as visual, as if Tessa is bracing herself in the doorway of Sight, unwilling to let go. Letting go feels like giving up. But if you don't let go, you'll drown.

I know the feeling.

And it sucks.

But Life sucks sometimes.

And yeah, it gets back up.

But you don't have to stay on your knees.

You can get back up and punch it in the face, over and over and over again, until Life is screaming and crying and bleeding on the floor, just like you are.

I know *that* feeling, too.

And, hell, it feels awesome.

Tessa needs to learn how to punch Life in the face. She needs to learn how to hear. And taste. And smell. And feel. She needs to realize that there is more than one way to see the world. Sure, a lot has been taken away from Tessa—but not everything. She still has four other senses, four other ways to find the beauty in the world.

I'll teach her.

I'll teach her how to see the world without actually seeing the world.

I'll show her.

Starting tomorrow.

TESSA

DAY 26

EVERY NIGHT, WHEN GRANDPA COMES INTO MY ROOM
to say goodnight, we pray together. He sits on the edge of my bed
and holds my hand and gives me lines from the psalms. Short ones,
to recite to myself when I have a nightmare about the crash.

"'I shall say of the Lord, He is my refuge and my fortress...'"

Grandpa says that the words will console me, but they only seem
to bring me true comfort when he says them—when he sits on my
bed and holds my hand. I feel stable and unshakable, like the dreams
couldn't haunt me even if they tried.

Every night, I look forward to hearing my grandfather pray. Even
if his faith is a little too optimistic for me.

I listen to his words—thanking the Lord for the sight that will
return to me sooner than anyone expects it to. I listen as I used to in
church, and when he finishes praying, I say, "Amen."

"Can I get you anything, Tessa?" Grandpa asks me now, as he
does every night before he leaves.

I shake my head. "No. But you can give me some advice."

He waits for my request.

"It's about..." I take a shivering breath and let it all out again.
"It's about Weston."

"Mmm," Grandpa murmurs. "What about him?"

Will I be able to get through this conversation without crying? My eyes are already beginning to sting, for no reason at all. "I feel like… like I've been unfair or something. The other day, when he came and typed poetry for me… I was trying to make it hard for him. I wanted him to give up."

"I know," Grandpa says.

"You know?"

"He told us."

I let out a sad little laugh. "Should've known. What *doesn't* he say out loud?"

Grandpa falls silent for a few moments.

"None of this is happening the way I wanted it to," I whisper, as one renegade tear slips out of my blind eyes. "I didn't want this to happen *at all*. But now it has, and…"

"And you can't fight it forever," Grandpa finishes.

I nod firmly. "I have to fight it. If I don't fight it, that means I've given up."

"No, honey," Grandpa says, squeezing my hand. "It means you've let go. It means you've *decided* to let go. The only thing you're fighting is *you*. And if you keep fighting, you'll only hurt yourself."

My throat tightens and the tears fall faster down my cheeks. I can't seem to go an hour without crying anymore. Grandpa's words have hit me right in my heart, where it hurts the most.

"You're right, Grandpa," I say at last, my voice thick with tears. "You're right."

He holds my hand, but doesn't say anything else. I inhale, exhale. I dry my wet face with the edge of my bedsheets.

"What should I do about Weston?"

Grandpa thinks for a moment before replying, "I think you

should give him another chance."

I sigh. Somehow, I knew he would say that.

"I wasn't sure about the whole thing at first," Grandpa continues. "Especially since I asked for a girl in the ad, not a boy *your age...*"

"Oh, Grandpa—"

"But I've talked to Weston, and I'm impressed by him."

I frown, puzzled. "Why?"

Grandpa takes an even breath. "He... has a very positive way of looking at life. And he seems to me like a good-hearted boy with an earnest desire to help."

I think about his words for a minute—his first impressions. Everyone seems to like Weston except for me. Maybe I've missed something about him. Maybe I've been too blind to see, both literally and figuratively.

"So you think I should let him come back?" I ask.

Grandpa smiles a little—I can hear it in his voice. "Yes. For his sake as much as yours. Remember, Tessa: love is patient, love is kind. We have to show each other love."

Patient, kind.

Two words I could use to describe Weston.

Granted, I could think of a lot of nastier ones. But still.

Patient.

Kind.

"All right." I relent with a small nod. "He can come back. And I'll try... I'll try to be nicer."

"I know you will," Grandpa says. He leaves a kiss on my forehead. "Goodnight, Tessa."

I close my eyes, though the darkness is the same. "Goodnight, Grandpa."

His footsteps cross the room. I hear the lights switch off.

Smell

WESTON

JUNE 23

THE TRICK ABOUT STEALING FLOWERS FROM YOUR mother's garden is minimizing the appearance of damage. You don't take the flowers she always points out and compliments—you cut the ones she never seems to notice, flowers that are almost like ground cover.

On the morning of June twenty-third, that's what I'm doing: picking flowers—lily of the valley—in my backyard. After I've collected a small bunch of them, I walk to 52 West Elm Street.

Mrs. Dickinson answers the door, like always. She smiles when she sees me.

"Is Tessa awake?" I ask before I even say hello.

"I would hope so." Mrs. Dickinson chuckles. "It's almost eleven o'clock."

"Right."

She steps aside and gestures for me to come in. "Those flowers smell lovely. Are they for Tessa?"

I glance down at the lilies. "Yeah. Well, kind of. I'm going to give them to her, but I'm not going to tell her about them. It's... an experiment."

"An experiment?"

"Yeah."

Mrs. Dickinson frowns, looking bewildered. She's probably wondering, *"What's the next thing he's going to ask me not to tell Tessa about?"*

I suddenly remember that she's still holding the door open for me, so I give her a quick smile and walk inside.

"Would you like a jar of water for the flowers?" Mrs. Dickinson asks.

"That would be great—thanks."

In the kitchen, she takes a small mason jar from one of the super-organized cupboards and fills it with water. I wait five seconds.

"Is Tessa in her room?"

Mrs. Dickinson nods and hands me the jar. I drop the flowers inside.

"I'll let her know you're here."

For a few torturous minutes, I am left alone in the kitchen. It's just me and the jar of flowers and the ticking clock. The walls and ceilings are thin in this house—I can hear Tessa's voice upstairs, muffled and low. Is she telling her grandmother to send me away? That I'm too early, or that she never wants to see me again? I prepare myself for the worst.

But when Mrs. Dickinson comes back downstairs, she has a pleasantly surprised look on her face. "Well," she says, "I wasn't expecting *that.*"

"Expecting what?"

Mrs. Dickinson smiles and shakes her head. "Tessa says she's been looking forward to seeing you. Well, not *seeing* you, but…"

I grin. "She's been looking forward to testing me again, you mean?"

"No, I don't think so," Mrs. Dickinson says. "She actually seems much better this morning. Perhaps she's had a change of heart."

I raise my eyebrows and nod, like, *I hope so.*

"Anyway, you're welcome to go up," Mrs. Dickinson says.

"Thanks."

When I reach the top of the stairs, I find Tessa's bedroom door already open. She is sitting on her bed, cross-legged this time, hugging a fluffy white pillow. Her eyes are shut, but she's listening. When I walk inside, she says, "Good morning, Weston."

I smile even though she can't see. "Good morning, Tessa."

She said good morning. *Good* morning.

It's a start.

As quietly as possible, I set the jar of flowers on her dresser. Then I sit down at her desk.

TESSA

DAY 27

WESTON SMELLS LIKE FLOWERS.

It's weird, but it's true.

My room fills with the perfume of summer blossoms. I know it didn't smell like that until Weston came in.

What on earth?

I frown, puzzled, as he sits down at my desk and opens my laptop.

Yes, it's still difficult to face the reality that someone is touching my laptop—a *boy*, no less. A sixteen-year-old boy, with germs that only belong to the male of the species.

It also bothers me that I can't see him. I want to know what he looks like, but I can't ask him. I can't even ask Grandma, because she'll think I have some other reason for wanting to know. She'll think I *like* him, or something. I don't know what she'll think. But I can't ask. It's too awkward.

"Where do you want me to start?" Weston says.

I snap back into reality. "Um, let's answer some comments."

"Comments?"

"Yeah. Just go to the latest post and read me the comments, and I'll tell you how to reply. Start at the top and work your way down." I keep my voice mellow and gentle in an attempt to be nicer.

Weston types something on my laptop. Click, click. Silence.

"Okay," he says at last. "The first comment is from Liv. She says, 'Wow, this was beautiful, Tessa. You have such a gift. Never stop writing these lovely poems.'"

A little smile finds my face. Liv is always the first commenter— it's part of her brand.

"Who's Liv?" Weston asks.

"She's one of my closest blogger friends," I explain. "We've known each other for years. She lives in Florida."

"How many blogger friends do you have?"

"I don't know. A lot." I trace circles on the pillow in my lap with my fingertip. "But only a few of them are my really close friends. We used to talk all the time, on Instagram."

Weston falls silent for a minute. It's almost startling.

"Anyway, type this for a reply: 'Thank you so much, Liv... Your comments always brighten my day. BTW, I'm sorry I haven't been able to keep up with the squad lately. You know why I've fallen off the face of the earth.' Then put a smiley face. And post."

It feels so strange to dictate comments for him to write. I'm usually way more long-winded and expressive. I use too many all-caps words and too many emojis. But now I feel devoid of the capacity to pour much life and sunshine into my replies. Especially since I have to speak them. I've always been able to write much better than I can talk.

Still, we make it through all twenty-three comments. Weston types my answer to each one. Then he says, "Do you want to write any poetry?"

It seems like an impertinent question, coming out of the blue like that.

God, he smells just like some kind of flowers.

I can't figure it out. I can't think about it. I can't think about poetry, either.

I can't think about anything.

I'm too tired.

Tired, tired, *tired.*

"No," I murmur, slouching into more of a reclined position on my bed. "I want to rest for a while. I don't feel like writing."

Another silence trickles by.

Finally, Weston says, "I don't think you should rest."

My eyes snap open. "Excuse me?"

"I said I don't think you should rest," he reiterates. "I think you should write something."

"And I think you should mind your own business."

It comes out sounding rude. I promised Grandpa I would be nice. But Weston is just as impolite. Does he *ever* think before he speaks?

"Look, Tessa…" He sighs. "I'm only trying to—"

"Help, yes. I know. You've told me."

I can almost sense that he's looking at me, which pours gasoline on the flames of my envy. How can he pretend to understand what it's like? He isn't blind.

For a few moments, neither of us says a word.

It's sunny today. Grandma told me there isn't a cloud in the sky. I want to see that vast blue beauty. I want to go outside and breathe in the summer. It's my favorite season. And I'm missing it all.

"You know," Weston says, slow and gentle. "Visual beauty is only one form of beauty. And you won't be without it forever."

Shockingly philosophical for a sixteen-year-old boy. I might have even been able to appreciate a thought like that Before.

But this is After.

So I reply, "My neurologist told me twelve to fourteen weeks.

Which is almost one hundred days. Did you know that, Weston? That's my sentence. One hundred days of darkness."

Silence hangs in the air between us. Weston has nothing to say.

I hear him shut my laptop and walk to the door. I listen to him leave the room and go downstairs and say something to my grandmother.

A moment later, the front door opens and shuts.

He's gone.

Without saying goodbye.

I blow out an irritated sigh, no longer tired—not even a little.

Why is it so hard to be polite to him? I broke my promise to Grandpa, but I don't care about that anymore. I tried, and Weston didn't. Weston was just as stubborn and rude and thoughtless as he always is. *I don't think you should rest.* Who does he think he is, ordering me around like that?

It's insufferable.

I don't know why I gave him a second chance. Even if I *do* like being able to keep up with my blog schedule and answer comments, it's not worth the price of being undermined in my own house. It's not worth some strange, brash, germy boy touching my laptop.

He may be patient and kind, but that's no recommendation when he is so lacking in sympathy. He treats me as if I'm not even blind— as if I have no right to be miserable.

The voice in my head screams, *You have every right.*

The voice in my heart sobs, *One hundred days of darkness.*

The voice of Weston, still resounding in my bedroom, says, *Visual beauty is only one form of beauty.*

What does he know about any of this?

WESTON

3 YEARS AND 9 MONTHS BEFORE TESSA

THE MORNING AFTER RUDY'S BAR MITZVAH, I HAD HELL to pay for jumping over that stupid fence.

I first noticed it when I got out of bed in the morning—my legs were killing me. The cuts had closed up, but they looked kind of swollen and red. For a second, I wondered if I had an infection. But didn't infections give you a fever or something? I'd been on the receiving end of split lips and scraped knees dozens of times before—the stinging, hot pain of a healing cut felt like nothing new.

So I ignored the pain. If I told Mom, it would only cause more trouble. She would freak out and overreact and send me to the doctor's—maybe even force me to wear bandages or something. My superhero reputation would fall to ruin, Rudy would call me a pansy-ass, and the rest of my friends would laugh at me and say things like "See? Told you not to jump over that stupid fence."

If I was going to save face, I had to keep my mouth shut and suck up the pain. And that was exactly what I did.

I wore jeans—even though it was too hot for jeans—and I shot Henry warning looks whenever I thought he might tell Mom about the fence incident. I scared him into submission. He was afraid of losing his skateboard and the privilege of hanging out with me and

Rudy. So he kept quiet.

Nothing changed. I went to school like normal, I fought with Rudy like normal, I went skateboarding like normal—but resisted the urge to do anything crazy again despite the tempting dares from the other boys. A couple of times, Rudy noticed that I was in pain. He never asked about it; he just gave me that look—the one where he was trying to be an adult. I shook my head and said, "It's nothing. Just pulled a muscle during gym class."

A week later, the cuts were totally healed. There was no sign of infection—my legs looked normal. But they didn't feel normal. In fact, the pain only got worse.

I almost fell on my face when I got out of bed one morning. It felt like iron weights tied to my ankles—no, worse than that. It felt like needles sticking into my skin, my bones, my muscles. Both legs felt the same, and that could only mean one thing.

But could it? After all, if the cuts had healed, how could they be infected? Maybe it was just a pulled muscle, like I told Rudy.

Yeah, it was probably nothing.

And I couldn't worry Mom if it was probably nothing.

So I popped some Advil and went to school. It worked, for a little while. The pain faded almost completely. But it came back around noontime. I obviously needed more than two pills.

The next day, I emptied the whole bottle of Advil into my backpack. Henry caught me red-handed in the bathroom before we left for school.

"What are you doing, Wes?" he said.

"You keep your mouth shut," I answered.

I was sweating that morning. And I felt sick.

The bus ride was longer than usual, because our school had recently moved across town, to a new building with more students. I put my headphones in and tried to focus on something other than the pain and dizziness.

When we arrived, I immediately ran into Clara Hernandez, who was, at the time, my unofficial girlfriend. She had golden-brown skin and a smile like a movie star. We were thirteen years old, which is a stupid age to even think about dating someone, but we weren't really a thing. I'd never even kissed her.

Rudy Kaufmann was the one who really wanted to kiss her—I could tell by the way he stared at her in class, especially after his bar mitzvah. I would have harassed him about it, calling into question his straight-and-narrow morals, but I couldn't judge. That's just how it goes when you turn thirteen. Weird stuff happens in your stomach when you look at girls—and you can't do anything about it.

But Rudy was too shy to talk to Clara, so I talked to her instead. She liked it when I walked to class with her. She fluttered her eyelashes and said my name like it was her favorite word in the English language. But that morning, when I ran into her, I felt like hell.

The ibuprofen hadn't kicked in yet—and the pain was almost crippling. I don't know how I missed the last step at the top of the stairs. I tripped, but caught myself before I fell. My textbooks crashed to the floor. And Clara Hernandez happened to be standing there, at the top of the stairs, when it all happened.

"Weston!" she gasped. "Are you okay?"

A wave of dizziness passed over me, blurring the world for a second. I masked my own surprise and shot her a quick, convincing smile. "Yeah, I'm okay. Just… falling for you, I guess." It was a corny thing to say, but at least it made her blush and smile.

We both stooped down to gather up my fallen textbooks.

"Are you sure, Weston?" Clara asked again, in a lower voice, as we picked up the books. "You seem… not yourself lately."

"Really?" I tried to play it cool. "Well, maybe I'm not myself. Maybe I'm actually an evil twin trying to pry dark secrets out of Weston's closest friends."

Clara giggled. "I find that hard to believe."

"The truth is, I'm naturally super clumsy. I just hide it with my irresistible charm and recklessness."

It actually was the truth—but not the whole truth.

For the next few days, I took Advil and tried to take it easy—skipping out on skateboarding and track practice, using the pulled-muscle story as an excuse. But I knew as much as anyone else, a pulled muscle didn't feel like this. And it didn't last this long, either.

Rudy found out before anyone else did. He caught me popping Advil at my locker during second period. And he had that adult face on, complete with a critical frown.

"What the hell are you doing, Weston?"

I sighed. "Chill out, Kaufmann. I'm not trying to OD, if that's what you think."

"That's not what I think. I think you're hiding something."

"Yeah, my uppercut. Better keep your eyes off the ground if you don't want to get blasted in the face next time we fight."

Rudy ignored my topic change. "How many of those do you take every day?" he asked, nodding toward the bottle of Advil.

"Who says I take them every day?"

He gave me a look. "I've seen you."

"Spy."

"Just answer."

"Two," I said, dropping the bottle into my backpack. "Three times a day."

"Holy shit," Rudy said. "Are you kidding me?"

"No."

"You're gonna kill yourself."

"Okay, thank you for your concern." I shut my locker and swung my backpack over one shoulder. He tried to ask me about my symptoms, if my legs were still bothering me. But I dodged his questions and got away from him as quickly as possible.

It was the wrong move. Rudy will do whatever it takes to save my sorry ass, even if it means going behind my back and talking to my mother.

Which was exactly what he did.

I didn't find out until that night. It was late, and the pain was getting worse.

I couldn't find the bottle of Advil in my backpack. I searched every pocket, dumped all my stuff on the floor. Empty, empty, empty. My hands were shaking, and sweat trickled down my neck.

My first thought was: Henry. He must have told Mom. But I didn't care anymore. I just needed to stop the pain.

Now, now, *now.*

That was all I could think about. The agony.

I rushed into the bathroom and opened the medicine cabinet. I'd seen another bottle of Advil in there the day before. It had to be there, it had to be there, *it had to be there.*

But it was gone.

"Weston?"

My heart jumped into my mouth. I looked up.

Mom stood in the doorway of the bathroom. I'll never forget the look on her face.

"I think we should talk," she said.

She was holding the missing bottle of Advil.

I felt like I'd been caught doing something wrong—and I had. It was wrong of me not to tell Mom in the first place. She made me sit on the couch and didn't allow me to leave until I'd spilled the whole story. I told her all about the skateboarding stunt and how I'd cut myself on the stupid fence. As predicted, she was horrified.

"How could you be so stupid?" she scolded. "You could have gotten yourself killed."

"I knew you'd say that," I muttered, pressing a hand to my forehead. "Which is why I didn't tell you. Because I knew you'd never let me go skateboarding again as long as I live."

Mom clicked her tongue in that chiding way of hers. "I think the pain you're feeling right now is punishment enough."

And it turned out to be one hell of a punishment.

"It sounds like you have an infection," Mom said.

"But it can't be. The wounds healed—there isn't even a scar."

Mom frowned, looking conflicted. "Either way, we're going to the clinic first thing in the morning. I won't rest until I know what's wrong with you. Now go to bed."

The next morning, we went to the clinic. The doctor examined me and asked me a whole shitload of irrelevant questions, like what sports I play and how many hours I spend exercising. He could see the faint evidence of cuts on my legs, but didn't spend much time considering the possibility of infection.

"The day before you started to feel this pain," he said, "were you doing any strenuous physical activity?"

"Yeah, I told you, I was skateboarding."

He nodded. "And do you think you could have torn—or possibly even ruptured—your Achilles tendons?"

"I don't even know what an Achilles tendon is, sir."

The doctor grinned. "It's the largest tendon in your body," he explained, "and it stretches from your ankle to your calf muscles. It's not uncommon to injure your Achilles tendons—lots of people do.

But, if you haven't been resting it, inflammation can set in. I think that's what is happening here."

Most of the medical talk went over my head, but Mom listened closely. "So you don't think it's an infection?" she asked.

"Unlikely," the doctor said. "I've examined his wounds, and they appear to have healed without a problem. I'm glad you mentioned cutting yourself, but I think it's just an unlucky coincidence."

He was wrong.

But we believed every word.

"What can I do for the pain?" I said, feeling very unlike a super-hero.

That was when the doctor told us about cortisone, which came in a needle to the knee joint and promised relief. I practically begged Mom to let me get it. Until this supposed "inflammation" went away, I would be in agony.

Mom looked at me for a long moment, worry still chiseled into her brow. Then she said, "Okay."

The shots didn't hurt half as much as my aching muscles. And the cortisone worked better and faster than the Advil ever did. By the time I got home from the clinic, I was feeling good—almost good enough to jump over another fence on my skateboard.

But the painkiller was just a bandage hiding a bigger wound.

An infection.

"I don't understand why we take showers at school," Rudy said to me one day. "If we're just gonna fight as soon as we finish for the day."

I glanced over at the shower stall next to me, where he stood under the running water. All I could see was his freckled shoulders and his dripping head of dark hair.

"Well, the reason *I* take showers at school is simple," I said. "I can't get through the day without stripping at least *once*."

Rudy laughed, and it echoed. We were the only ones in the locker room.

"And why do *I* take showers at school?" he asked.

"Because you like to smell nice when you sit next to Clara in geography."

He shut off the water and shook his head. "Only you care about stuff like that, pansyass."

I grinned, turning off my own shower and throwing a towel over my shoulders. "Yeah, sure."

I dropped the subject. He was too shy to even talk to *me* about his crush on Clara Hernandez.

We had just gotten out of gym and had five minutes to get to our next class. I tied my towel around my waist and started digging my clothes out of my backpack.

"By the way," Rudy said, "how are you feeling? Your legs, I mean."

I shrugged. "Fine. The cortisone really helped. And my parents are forcing me to lie on the couch more often, which is boring as all hell."

"Still angry I told your mom about the pills?"

"Yeah." I threw him a sharp look. "But don't worry. I'll pay you back. With a nice roundhouse kick to the ribs."

I had the pleasure of paying him back that very same day. Sure, I wasn't supposed to be fighting or running or skateboarding—but I didn't see what difference it made. I felt the same whether I was lying on the couch or punching Rudy in the schoolyard after class. I felt fine.

Until the day I didn't.

The pain came back muted and numb, just kind of sore. It scared me, but I brushed it off as the consequence of not resting enough. But then it got worse—splintering. It felt like my muscles were shriveling away from my bones.

The cortisone was wearing off.

At first, I ignored it. I stayed off Advil and any other painkiller. I pushed through the dizzy spells and waves of sickness and confusion during class. I hoped that I would get better if I just rested.

I was wrong.

But I couldn't let anyone else know that I was sick. So when Rudy pulled me aside after school one day and said, "Want to fight?" I couldn't refuse. When did I ever turn down a chance to brutalize Rudy Kaufmann? It was a bad decision—but in retrospect, I'm glad I did it.

Because that was our last fight.

"I'm feeling lucky today, Ludovico," Rudy said, bouncing on the balls of his feet.

My legs hurt too much to warm up, so I just stood there and swung my arms back and forth. "Didn't think you believed in luck, Kaufmann."

The other kids gathered around to watch. The principal had quit trying to make us stop fighting. They probably figured we would only be in junior high school for this semester before moving on to Rockford High. Then someone else would have to put up with our bullshit.

God, I felt like hell that afternoon. My legs were burning, stinging, screaming with pain. But I swallowed it all back and put my fists up in front of my face.

Rudy did the same. "You ready?"

"Yep."

"Go."

He came at me first—throwing a jab to the face. I blocked it, then took my opening, aiming for his ribs. He blocked, countered—caught me in the stomach with his knee. I stumbled back, coughing. Our spectators made their usual animalistic noises, cheering us on.

I shot Rudy a look over the edge of my knuckles. "Come on, you can do better than that, pansyass!"

He lunged forward with a double punch combination finishing in a roundhouse kick. I grabbed his foot, swung him around, then backed off.

"You gonna stick with defense all day, pansyass?" Rudy shouted between his fists.

Okay, fine. That pissed me off.

I threw a fake at his eyes and took the opportunity to slug him right in the ribs.

"Agh!" He staggered back, gasping for breath, barring an arm over his stomach.

I knew I had some payback coming my way.

Rudy moved in with a jab. I blocked it. He tried again; then I threw a roundhouse kick. He sidestepped and caught my foot, just like I'd done to him moments before. But instead of sending me spinning away, Rudy went in for a takedown.

He pushed me backwards and I hit the ground with a breakfall. Gravel stung my arms as he caught my ankle in the crook of his elbow. He clamped one hand over the top of my shin and pressed his fingers into the nerve, locking out my leg.

It was a perfect technique.

And it hurt like hell.

I wish I knew what I sounded like when I screamed in pain. It would have been embarrassing if it wasn't so painful. Fire tore through my leg and fritzed my whole body. Rudy let go immediately and started freaking out.

"Oh my god, Weston, I'm sorry! Are you okay?"

I couldn't reply. I couldn't breathe. I pressed my head against the ground, clenching my teeth, trying not to scream again.

I'm dying, I'm dying, I'm dying.

What a stupid thought process. I wasn't dying. But everyone thought I was.

Rudy shouted for one of the kids to go get help. Then he turned to me and said, "Is it your legs?"

"No shit, it's my legs!" I yelled back through gritted teeth. My ears were ringing, and I was sweating bullets.

Poor Rudy. He had no idea. His eyes were filled with guilt and terror.

"I'm sorry, man," I whispered. "I should've told you. It's not your fault, it's mine."

Mr. Daniels, our gym coach, skidded to a stop at my side. "What the hell is going on here?" he barked. "Haven't you kids learned to stop beating on each other?"

"It's not that!" Rudy pleaded. "Weston is sick. Somebody call nine-one-one!"

Mr. Daniels looked startled. He frowned at me lying on the ground, in blistering agony, and said, "Weston, should we call an ambulance?"

I couldn't speak.

I nodded.

* * *

It wasn't until they brought me to the emergency room that they figured out what was wrong with me. It wasn't until three different doctors examined me and sucked blood out of my body that they could actually come to an educated decision.

I had something called MRSA, which is short for a bunch of unpronounceable words. It was an infection, sure enough—staph infection, a strain that happened to be resistant to common antibiotics. Maybe antibiotics would have worked if that first doctor had figured out that it was an infection. But we didn't catch it early.

We didn't catch it at all.

Not until I was in the emergency room.

And by then, it was too late.

A guy named Dr. Rosen was the one to break the news. He talked to my parents, not me. Mom and Dad were sitting next to me, sick with worry. Dr. Rosen couldn't look me in the eyes. I should've known that was a bad sign.

"This is a very special case," he said. "Weston is infected with a bacterium called methicillin-resistant *Staphylococcus aureus*, or MRSA, which can cause a condition called necrotizing fasciitis. This is an infection of the tissue that lines the muscles, nerves and blood vessels throughout the body. It began when Weston injured his legs on the fence and the wounds were not properly treated. The cortisone treatment actually made it appear to be clearing up, but it wasn't; the symptoms were simply masked while the infection continued to spread. Unfortunately, now the infection has gone unnoticed for too long, and it has advanced too far for antibiotics to stop it." Dr. Rosen paused and took a measured breath. "Our only option is immediate amputation. I'm sorry to say that we won't be able to save anything below his knees. But we *can* save his life. If we work quickly. Time is of the essence."

It didn't hit me right away. It hit Mom first.

"Amputation?" she blurted. "You have to amputate his legs?"

My stomach twisted. I turned to Dr. Rosen and asked, "Both of them?"

Finally, he looked at me. His eyes were cold and gray, but I could see pain in there somewhere. After all, what the hell do you say to a thirteen-year-old boy who looks you in the face and says, "Both of them?"

He said, "I'm sorry."

That's it.

I'm sorry.

That's what I can't stand about doctors—they never give you direct answers to any questions. Never yes or no. They just say shit like "I'm sorry."

I'm sorry.

The words cut through my insides and flipped my world upside down. It wasn't just the fever that turned my stomach. It was that word: *amputation.* My heart was pounding in my mouth. I asked to use the bathroom. Someone took my arm and walked me to where it was.

I don't remember walking down the hallway. I don't remember locking myself in the bathroom. I don't remember kneeling on the floor and vomiting.

I know that I did, but I don't remember it. All I remember is those words.

I'm sorry.

They scheduled my amputation for that night.

They put me in a hospital bed and shot drugs up my arm. They said the drugs would make me fall asleep, but instead I felt like I was dreaming. My parents were in the room with me, and I could hear them talking.

Mom was crying.

Dad was trying to calm her down.

"God, why did this have to happen to him?" Mom said, her voice ragged with tears. "Anyone else… but not Weston. This will break him."

"Shh," Dad replied, softer. "Weston is strong. Understand? Weston is *strong*." But none of us were strong. Dad sounded like he was crying, too.

Those words stuck with me, both Mom's and Dad's.

This will break him.

Weston is strong.

Those were the two voices warring in my head as they took me into surgery that night. A nurse with pretty green eyes told me to count down from ten.

I got as far as seven.

When I awoke, it was daytime. My eyes hurt from the sudden bright light.

Every part of me felt numb. They could have cut off all my limbs and I wouldn't have even known it until I looked.

Mom was sitting beside my bed, and a heart monitor was beeping steadily somewhere in the room. I had breathing tubes wrapped around my face. My left hand was covered in tape and needles, and my right hand was enveloped in Mom's, though I could barely feel it.

She looked at me. Her face was almost as white as the hospital room. And it was wet with tears.

"Mom," I whispered.

I wanted to say more, but that was all I could manage.

She rubbed her thumb over my hand, something she always did when she couldn't talk without crying.

I forced the rest of my words out. "Are they gone?"

Mom nodded slowly. Her face crumpled, and the tears ran faster. She held my hand tighter. She kissed my knuckles.

I didn't feel anything.

It was as if time slowed to a stop.

And there was nothing.

A little while later, Dad came in and took Mom's place. She went out to the hallway, still crying. Dad sat beside my bed and put a hand on my shoulder and said, "How are you feeling, son?"

"Tired," I whispered.

Dad nodded, leaning his elbows against his knees and staring at the floor. As if it hurt him just to look at me. He didn't say a word, but he didn't have to. A few minutes of silence passed before I finally gathered enough breath to speak again.

"Dad…"

"Yes?" He looked back up at me, and I saw the glint of tears in his eyes. "What is it, Weston?"

I took another breath and whispered, "I heard what you said. Before I went into surgery. You said I was strong… Thank you."

Dad pushed a little sad smile onto his face just as a tear escaped his eye. He tried to swipe it away, but I saw it fall.

"You *are* strong, Weston," he said, hand on my shoulder again. "Remember that."

TESSA

DAY 28

THERE MUST BE FLOWERS IN HERE.

That's my first thought when I wake up on day twenty-eight. The unmistakable aroma didn't vanish when Weston left yesterday—if anything, it grew more odiferous. He must have brought me flowers.

Pushing back my sheets and climbing out of bed, I decide to search my room for them. They have to be somewhere close by.

I feel along the top of the nightstand, moving carefully. If there are flowers, there's also a vase filled with water—and the last thing I want to do is knock over a vase of water.

Nothing on my nightstand. I move across the room to my desk.

My fingers whisper over the familiar shapes—laptop, notebook, jar of pens and pencils, separate jar of whiteboard markers, containers that hold my paperclips, thumb tacks, and rubber bands. I'm surprised to find everything still in its proper place. Not that I expected Weston to disturb anything, but isn't it inevitable for boys to make a mess wherever they go?

Perhaps I'm a little biased. And inexperienced.

I move on to my dresser. This is the last place anyone could leave a vase of flowers. I find a small stack of freshly washed and folded T-shirts, my jewelry box, then—

My fingertips touch something cool and glassy.

A mason jar. With flowers inside.

I feel the blossoms, trying to understand their shape. They are tiny and soft, like little bells, with stems that curve up and then downward. I can't figure out what kind of flowers they are. I pick up the jar and smell them again, though the aroma can be detected easily from across the room.

Nope. I have no idea what kind of flowers they are. But they smell glorious.

Why did Weston bring me flowers, when I can't even see them?

Why did he just leave them here and not tell me about them?

What is he up to?

Part of me wants to believe it's just another strain of his usual mischief—that it's a joke, because nobody would bring flowers to a blind girl.

What's the use of flowers if you can't see them?

I set the jar back down on my dresser and return to bed. But I don't climb under the sheets. I just lie on top of the tangled mess and stare up at nothing.

My nightmares have started to subside. I rarely dream about the accident, and when I do, it doesn't wake me up. I just roll right into another dream. But, last night, Weston's voice played on repeat in my head.

Visual beauty is only one form of beauty.

I stand up and feel my way over to the window. The glass is cool to the touch despite the summer heat. My fingers find the lock and twist it. I push up, opening the window all the way.

My room gets western sunlight, so I won't feel the warmth until this afternoon—but I can already tell, even without asking Siri, that today is going to be clear and bright. The birds are singing outside, and a gentle wind swooshes through the trees in our front yard. I hear faint suburban street noise, and the distant hum of a lawn mower.

"Hey, Siri," I say, without moving away from the window, "what time is it?"

"It is nine forty-two a.m. Good morning!"

I press my forehead against the glass, shutting my eyes to see more darkness. "Yeah," I mutter under my breath. "Good morning to you, too."

Why did he bring me flowers?

It doesn't make sense.

It can't be a gesture of kindness. Despite what my grandparents may think, Weston is not kind. He has no sympathy. He says whatever he thinks, even when it's offensive. He tells me what to do, when I'm supposed to be the one giving *him* orders.

It can't be a gesture of kindness.

He wouldn't bring me flowers after the way I've treated him.

I don't deserve them.

I don't deserve *him.*

My stomach clenches, and that vise returns. Anger, regret. My hands curl into fists, pressing against the windowsill. I squeeze my eyes shut.

No. It can't be a gesture of kindness.

But a little voice in my heart pushes through the murk of my stubbornness.

The voice says, *It is kindness.*

WESTON

JUNE 24

TESSA IS SITTING ON HER BED WHEN I WALK IN. NOT tucked behind a mountain of throw pillows, as she usually is, but perched on the edge of the mattress with her feet on the floor. She must be waiting for me, because the moment I shut the door behind me, she says, "There are flowers in here."

I smile. "How do you know if you can't see them?"

"I can smell them," Tessa says.

Mission accomplished.

"What do you smell?" I ask.

Tessa shakes her head. "I don't know. Flowers."

"What kind?"

"I don't care what kind." She lifts her chin. "I have allergies. Take them away."

I don't give an inch. "What kind of flowers are they?"

Tessa shuts her eyes. Her hair is down today, falling around her face in wispy strands. She wants to close up, give up, brace herself in the doorway.

I want to push her through the doorway.

Who cares if she falls? She's already fallen.

Now she needs to get back up.

I grab the jar of flowers off her dresser and walk right up to her, sticking the blossoms under her chin. My voice comes out sounding so severe, I almost surprise myself.

"What kind of flowers are they?"

Tessa bristles, her body going stiff. Her eyes slowly flutter open. Her fingers grip the blankets underneath her. Those freckles are even prettier up close.

She smells the flowers again, gently. Then she whispers, "I don't know what kind."

"Lily of the valley," I tell her. "Remember that smell. Remember that name." I return the jar of flowers to her dresser. "Tomorrow I'll bring you carnations. Pink ones."

"I told you I have allergies—"

"I'm ready for your dictation, Tessa." I sit down at her desk and open her laptop.

A deathly silence falls. I can practically feel the volcano rumbling underneath me, getting ready to erupt. I log in to her computer with that weird password, *openeverydoor325,* and wait. She's pissed, I can tell—but I don't know how much until I turn around and look at her.

She hasn't moved from her seat on the edge of her bed. Her cheeks are flushed pink, and her fingers curl around the twisted blankets until her knuckles whiten. For a second, I wonder if she's going to throw something at me—probably not, since it would disrupt the perfect feng shui of her bedroom.

She doesn't throw anything—but she does explode.

With poetry.

"I've never met another human as pigheaded as you;
Stubborn and stuck-up and selfish and proud,
The epitome of rude.

I'd tell you to get out, but I've tried that before;
And you just came back to torture me more.
If it weren't my grandparents and God and you,
I'd tell you to go to hell, too."

I just sit there and stare at her for a long moment.

Wow.

No one has ever written a poem about me before.

It takes all my self-control not to burst out laughing.

How funny it is to be judged, cussed at, called *pigheaded* and *the epitome of rude.* How funny it is to be hated by this spitfire of a girl, who sits on her bed and blushes with rage and tells me to go to hell.

I love it.

Tessa Dickinson is the only girl in the world who would think up a hateful poem in response to someone giving her flowers.

I cover my mouth with my fist, unable to stop myself from laughing. Then I ask her, "Would you like me to type that poem for you?"

For a second, I'm afraid it's the wrong thing to say. But Tessa surprises me.

She laughs.

She actually laughs.

It starts out muttered and kind of sarcastic, but then it builds into real, genuine laughter. It's a joyful, freeing sound, like the first scratch of a quill pen on the Declaration of Independence.

She covers her mouth when she laughs, because she clearly has no idea how great her smile is. Her eyes close and crinkle around the edges, and just like that—the volcano turns into a mountain. Another wonder of the world.

Tessa laughs, and I laugh, and finally, finally, *finally*—

I think we might be friends.

TESSA

DAY 29

THE FOLLOWING DAY, WESTON BRINGS CARNATIONS, just as he promised. I'm listening closely, so I hear him set down the jar when he comes in—a barely audible thud of glass on wood. I have him answer comments for me, and he reads me the compliments of my blog readers, in the most literal sense.

He'll say things like: "Jillian writes, in all-caps: 'OH MY GOSH BABE WHAT JUST HAPPENED TO MY HEART' with seven—no, eight—question marks. She also left a crying smiley face with twenty-three apostrophe tears."

Again, he makes me laugh. Just like he made me laugh yesterday. How on earth did he manage it? I thought I hated him. When I sat on my bed and he shoved those flowers in my face and made me try to figure out what kind they were, I wanted nothing more than to throw the jar at his head. But I couldn't see where his head actually was, so I thought up a badly rhymed poem about him instead.

And he laughed.

And I laughed.

For the first time since the accident,

for the first time in twenty-eight days,

I *laughed*.

Now everything seems easier.

Smiling is easier.

Waking up in the morning is easier.

Dealing with Weston is easier.

I'm beginning to put a gag on the voice in my head and listen more closely to the one in my heart. I misjudged Weston before. The flowers weren't a gesture of kindness, but they weren't a joke, either. He wants to give me something to smell.

I have no idea why.

When he finishes answering comments, he tells me I have a few new messages. I tell him that Grandma helps me answer those, because I don't know—it just seems too personal for him to be reading my DMs.

I think of a few lines of a poem that doesn't have a name. He writes them down for me, in a new draft. Then he goes home.

As soon as I hear the front door shut downstairs, I get off my bed and search the room until I find the flowers. He's left the jar on my desk today, not on the dresser. Is that part of the plan? To stay unpredictable, to keep me guessing?

But Weston Ludovico is as predictable as the sun.

I wonder if he's ever unhappy.

Surely, it's not healthy to be so optimistic all the time.

I find the carnations. I feel their petals—soft and silky and smooth under my fingertips. I picture them in my mind's eye, small and baby pink. The color of the dawn in the summertime, when the birds are awake but nobody else is.

I take a single flower out of the mason jar. Droplets of water spring off the stem and onto my skin. I carefully make my way across my bedroom and lie down on my bed, leaning back against the big fluffy throw pillows.

Somehow, the darkness doesn't seem so dark anymore. I wonder if that just means I'm getting used to it. I wonder if that just means blindness is becoming normal to me. I wonder if that's a good or bad thing.

I wonder what Weston looks like.

The blossom in my hand is so delicate, but at the same time it feels strong in its own right. A single pink carnation. It doesn't smell as lovely as the lily of the valley, but it has a scent all its own. Fresh and clean. I twirl the flower under my nose, breathing in the aroma. Then I touch the petals to my lips, closing my eyes.

I can smell it.

I

can

s m e l l

But why does he want me to smell? Why does he bring me these flowers? Why does he keep coming back even after I've been a complete brute to him? Why does he want to help me? Why does he always sound like he's smiling?

Surely, it's not healthy to be so optimistic all the time.

WESTON

3 YEARS AND 8 MONTHS BEFORE TESSA

RUDY WAS THE FIRST ONE TO VISIT ME IN THE HOSPITAL.
He came even before my brothers did. Mom said he had been waiting a long time—waiting in one of those stiff, ugly chairs that I had already grown to hate the sight of. Waiting to be allowed into my room. Waiting to see me.

The drugs were starting to wear off—at least, some of them were. They gave me a button to press for painkillers, but I felt like a pansy-ass using it. Despite the sedatives, I'd regained some feeling in my limbs.

Even the limbs I no longer had.

It was the strangest feeling, the phantom pain they warned me about. Sometimes it was burning, sometimes it was aching, sometimes it felt like my legs were being crushed. Other times, it was just a painless sensation. For a few seconds, I thought that it was all a bad dream. For a few seconds, I thought that every part of me was still intact. But then the sensation would end, and I would realize that it was only that—an apparition.

Usually it happened when I first woke up. I didn't know where I was or why I still had tubes plugged into my arm. I felt like I could just stand up and walk out of there.

But then I remembered.

That was the worst part.

The remembering.

It was like a punch to the gut. And it hurt much more.

Mom was at my side every time I opened my eyes. I wondered if she ever slept or ate or went to the bathroom. She would always just be sitting there, giving me a sad smile or holding my hand. She was the real superhero.

"Rudy would like to see you," she said, pushing my hair off my brow. "Do you feel up to that?"

I had no idea what day it was or what time of day it was. The hospital room wasn't as bright as usual—it must have been cloudy outside.

Truthfully, I was dying to see Rudy.

But no part of me felt "up to it."

That was when Mom told me how long he'd been waiting. Anyone who didn't know better would have thought Rudy was my brother. He didn't want to leave the hospital until he saw me. I wondered if he was missing school because of it.

After a minute, I nodded and said, "Okay, sure."

Mom gave me a weary smile and left the room.

I took a few deep breaths, trying to prepare myself. But I couldn't, not really. I heard my heart monitor pick up, beeping a little faster.

That was when the door opened and Rudy walked in.

I didn't look at him—I looked at the ceiling. But I watched him in my peripheral vision as he moved across the room and sat down in the chair next to my hospital bed. I was trying so hard to hold it together. And the trying only made it worse. The trying made everything hurt.

For a long, long, long moment, neither of us said a word. Then I heard Rudy cuss for the first time in his life. A small, exhausted f-bomb at the end of a long sigh.

That was all we needed to say, really.

That one word pretty much summed up everything.

But I knew that I needed to say something. I stared at the ceiling for a few more seconds, listening to my heart monitor beep.

Finally, I found the courage to speak. My voice felt heavy in my mouth.

"Rudy?"

He looked up from the floor to meet my gaze. "Yeah?"

"Would you do something for me?"

"Course," he said. "Anything."

He looked more like a grown-up that day, and he wasn't even trying. There was a serious frown creasing the space between his eyebrows, and it made him seem two years older than me.

I drew in a shaking breath and pushed the words out before they got stuck in my chest. "Would you just... pretend that none of this is happening?"

Rudy said nothing—he watched me, a steady softness in his eyes.

"I know it's... it's impossible, but..." I paused to swallow, to breathe. "I can almost... deal with it. If you don't look at me like... like I'm... I'm—"

He took my hand. Out of nowhere. He just grabbed it and held on.

I stopped talking. I couldn't talk anymore.

Not with this fricking lump in my throat.

I closed my eyes, feeling the familiar sting of tears. My heart monitor started beeping even faster. But I refused to cry in front of Rudy.

I refused to cry in front of Rudy.

I would not cry.

I was done with crying.

…I was crying.

"Hey," Rudy said, gentle but firm, "it's gonna be all right."

I held his hand, too—as tight as I could, which probably wasn't very tight; I felt like every drop of energy and life had drained out of my body through one of those tubes. But I could feel the warmth of Rudy's hand, strong and desperate. It was like a rescue, someone pulling me out of a black ocean. I would have drowned if he wasn't there. I would have drowned.

My voice came out as a broken whisper. "Thanks, Rudy."

When I opened my eyes, my vision was blurry. But no tears had actually fallen, so I wasn't too much of a wuss.

I glanced down at our hands locked together. My skin looked so deathly pale compared to his. But I wouldn't be weak and drugged and lying here for very long. I would be well enough to brutalize him soon. In fact, I brutalized him right then.

He was asking for it, really. His thumb was in a perfectly convenient position for a lockout. I caught it between two fingers and pressed hard.

"Ow!" He yanked his hand away.

I laughed.

He shot me a look—half stunned, half amused. He shook out his hand. "Jerk."

We were back to normal, just a little. The sun started to come out from behind the clouds.

I closed my eyes and said, "Make yourself useful, pansyass. I'm dying of boredom here."

Rudy briefed me on everything I'd missed at school—how freaked out the kids were that day I was taken to the emergency room.

He told me about the tongue-lashing he got from Mr. Daniels, who had strictly forbidden any and all fistfighting activities for the rest of time. He even wrote an official letter and had Rudy sign it, and he wanted me to sign it when I got out of the hospital. It was a letter that promised we would never beat each other up again.

As if that could stop us.

Rudy didn't know it that day, but I would beat him up again.

And he would beat me up again.

Later.

After I learned how to walk.

The next day, my mom brought my brothers to visit. She didn't even tell me until they were waiting outside.

She came into my room and kissed my forehead and said, "How would you feel about the boys coming in to see you?" She made it sound like they weren't even there.

I was feeling way more alert that day and had at least one fewer needle connected to my body. The nurses still checked on me like they were afraid I was going to run away. But clearly that wasn't an option.

Truthfully, I was dying to see my brothers.

But I didn't want them to see me.

Maybe it was stupid, but I felt like I'd let them down. I was always there for them, always the good (but reckless) example, always the superhero. What was I now?

An amputee.

"I just don't know if I'm ready," I told Mom. "I don't know if I'm ready for them to… see me like this."

"Weston, honey," Mom said, gentle and soft. She placed one

warm hand against my face. "It's not going to be any different tomorrow. Or next week. Or next year."

I don't think she realized how hard those words hit me. Just like she didn't realize I'd heard her on the night of my amputation.

This will break him.

"Besides," she continued, "the boys insisted on coming with me. They were so excited to see you."

"They're here?"

She smiled a little. "They're waiting just outside."

I guess that meant I didn't have much of a choice. I imagined my three little brothers sitting in the ugly chairs, unsure of whether I wanted to see them.

Of course I wanted to see them.

I couldn't turn them away.

"Okay," I relented through a tight sigh. "They can come in."

Mom smiled, and it looked good on her face. I wish it had stayed longer. But her smiles always seemed to fade so quickly those days. Mine wouldn't—not while my brothers were in that hospital room. I could still be the Weston they remembered. But I didn't have much time to psych myself up. In the moments it took Mom to walk to the door and open it, I had to put a smile on my face.

It wasn't so hard once they came into my room. Aidan ran in first, Noah right behind him. They charged across the room, giggling and shouting my name. Mom said, "Take it easy, boys," which made them stop short before jumping on my bed. But I urged them to climb up, and they tackled me with hugs. Henry came in last. Mom had her arm around his shoulders.

"I've missed you guys so much," I said, hugging my two smallest brothers to the best of my ability.

"We miss you!" Noah declared, making himself comfortable on

the bed. He didn't seem to notice that half my legs were missing.

Aidan was a little more aware of the fact. But, for whatever reason, he thought it was cool. He started bombarding me with questions right away. What was the surgery like? Was it scary? Did it hurt? Had they given me new legs yet?

"Honey," Mom said in that chiding voice of hers, ruffling Aidan's hair, "not so many questions."

I gave Mom a crooked smile. "It's okay."

That was when I noticed Henry standing at the foot of my bed.

Poor Henry.

He looked so hesitant. So nervous. So distant. Like he didn't know what to do—like he didn't even want to be here.

Like he didn't even want to see me.

"Hi, Henry."

He looked up from the floor. "Hi, Wes. How are you feeling?" His voice didn't sound like his own.

I couldn't tell him the truth. So I told him, "Never been better."

Then and there, I decided that's how I would reply every time someone asked me how I was feeling—regardless of how I was really feeling.

And, actually, I was feeling pretty good at the time. My brothers were like individual rays of sunshine that had come crashing into my room to drive out the fragments of Despair. For a few minutes, everything was golden. And everything was okay.

"Can we see?" Aidan asked, staring up at me with his giant, curious eyes.

Mom slid her gaze to me with this look of apprehension on her face. I didn't know what she was so nervous about. They would all have to see eventually. It was just like she said: *It's not going to be any different tomorrow. Or next week. Or next year.*

Aidan was sitting where my feet would have been if I had any left. I gave him a smile—feigning secrecy.

"Are you sure?" I asked, in the dramatic voice I used to read him comics. "Once seen, my friend, it cannot be unseen."

Aidan laughed and nodded. Noah was distracted with the bed's remote control. Henry watched me, with his hands in his pockets.

I threw the bedsheets off my legs—or what was left of them.

Aidan gaped. "Whoa! Dude…"

It was still weird for *me* to look at my stumps. I hated to look at them. I hated to face the reality, again and again. I hated to bathe; I hated to sit in wheelchairs; I hated to take medication; I hated to feel my strength fade and my muscles weaken. I hated everything.

But I smiled for my brothers.

I told them jokes—stupid ones, about the routines of the nurses and the horrible movie selections and the awful food. I laughed about it all, like it didn't hurt.

Noah told me that he hadn't had a single nightmare since I'd come to the hospital, which meant he was all grown up now. I gave him a high five and congratulated him on becoming an adult.

Aidan said that he missed story time. He was at the height of his obsession with superheroes and had recently been renamed Spider-Man—for jumping on the furniture and sometimes even running up the walls. I told him that I'd be back home soon, so he'd better start making a huge stack of comics for us to read together.

Henry didn't say anything. He just stood there and looked like he wanted to leave.

Eventually, Mom said, "We should let Weston get some rest now."

"As if I don't get enough rest," I muttered.

But Mom was serious. She shooed the boys off my bed and told them to go wait outside in the hallway. They all said goodbye, in one out-of-sync chorus, and trailed out the door.

It felt like the sun had gone behind a cloud.

Mom was the only one left in the room with me. She was the only one who saw me let go of my act—the only one who saw me let go of my smile.

"God, I miss them so much," I whispered. "Noah doesn't get it. Aidan thinks it's cool, for some reason. But Henry..." I paused, shaking my head. "Henry's scared. Tell him it's okay. Tell him *I'm* okay."

Mom put a hand on my shoulder and smiled a little, tired and uncertain. "Are you, though?"

I just stared at her for a few seconds. My throat tightened. I nodded.

And then I broke down crying.

This time, tears did come out. A lot of tears.

I covered my mouth with my hands so that no one would hear.

And my mother wrapped her arms around me.

And I cried.

TESSA

DAY 33

IT'S BEEN A MONTH SINCE THE ACCIDENT. YET IT FEELS like yesterday.

The dreams have stopped completely, but I'm sure that's only due to my subconscious being so worn down. After all, how many times can my brain project the same memory at me before it gets tired? I'm glad to finally achieve an undisturbed night's sleep, but at the same time, it's difficult. Falling asleep is like catching butterflies—glimpses of sweet unconsciousness fluttering in and out of my bedroom, evading my grasp.

I try to recite the lines of the psalms that my grandfather taught me—but they don't make me fall asleep. I'm tired, but not tired of being awake.

I'm tired of being blind.

Weston brings me a new jar of flowers every day. He doesn't take the other ones away—he just adds to the collection until my whole room smells like a florist's. I lied about having allergies, and Weston must know it by this point.

This morning he brought sunflowers. "Because you write about sunshine so much," he said.

But I haven't written about sunshine since before the accident.

Which makes me think that Weston has read some of the older poems on my blog. Like the one from May, which I can still remember by heart.

Sunlight is everything
And all at once.
Sunlight is gentle
And harsh.

But the sunflowers only make me depressed, because I can't see their bright yellow petals; and they remind me of sunlight, like Weston said. They remind me of the sunlight I can't see.

I can feel it when the sun descends the afternoon sky and its rays pour through the window, soft on my skin and sharp in my eyes. Even though I can't see, direct light still hurts my eyes. It's the strangest feeling.

Ever since I was a little girl, I've hated the darkness. Until I was twelve years old, I couldn't sleep without a nightlight on—soft light was better than no light at all. I wasn't exactly afraid, but the darkness made me feel all alone.

It still does.

I still hate the darkness. I hate not being able to take a shower without Grandma standing by, in case I fall. I hate the fact that my brain hasn't adjusted to the reality—even after thirty-three days. I still turn on the lights when I go to the bathroom. I hate the moment when I first wake up in the morning and I open my eyes, only to find that Grandpa's prayers haven't been answered.

Both my grandparents help me in every way they can. I try not to be angry when I require so much help. I'm just used to doing everything for myself. Now, the only thing I seem capable of doing on my own is falling asleep. And even that I can't do very well.

With the distraction of everything, I almost forgot that I have a period—until one morning when Grandma finds drops of blood in my bedsheets. I cry all over again, and she changes my sheets and washes my pajamas—but it's still difficult and awkward.

Grandpa continues to pray with me every night, and the tenacity of his faith is both puzzling and inspiring. He doesn't ask me about Weston, because he knows things are better between us. He probably hears our laughter through the thin walls. He says that he misses me at church, and he hopes I'll make it out of the house soon.

But the thought of going outside is more terrifying than ever. Even when I could see, I preferred to stay inside, where there is Wi-Fi. Now a weak internet connection is the least of my worries.

In the house, it's safe. I know where everything is: the walls, the furniture, the doors—it's all familiar to me. Outside, it is chaos. The world is a big, scary, disorienting place. Someone gave me a stick, the kind blind people use, to get around. But it has done nothing except sit in the corner of my room, collecting dust. The very thought of using it makes my stomach turn.

On day thirty-three, after Grandpa says goodnight and leaves the room, I lie awake.

I can't sleep.

All I can do is think about the words I don't say out loud.

There are so many words—so many poems—that I would never dictate, especially not to a boy I've just met. There are some words so close to my heart, I would never even publish them on my blog. But I would still write them down, in a journal that no one would ever read. Words like the ones that percolate in my heart right now, as I lie in the darkness and wait to catch the butterflies of sleep.

I wish I could write down the secret poems I don't want anyone to see. I certainly can't dictate them to Weston, because the poem spinning through my head right now is about him—revised from the one about sunlight. I only need to change one word. And it works.

I recite the poem over and over again in my head, like a psalm. It helps me to fall asleep.

Weston is everything
And all at once.
Weston is gentle
And harsh.

Weston can be blindingly bright
But then he can also be
Delicately soft.

Weston is a paradox.

WESTON

JUNE 30

TESSA DOESN'T TALK MUCH. SHE'S ONE OF THOSE people who thinks a lot, but only says about ten percent of what she thinks. Rudy is like that, too—and it drives me nuts.

I know that it must be weird for her to tell me her poetry, when she's so used to writing it all down herself. I also know, without even asking her, that she doesn't tell me *all* her poetry.

The volcano keeps some of her lava hidden underground.

Which is why I don't bring her flowers on the last day of June. Instead, I bring her a notebook—one of those huge ones with a wire spiral binding and plenty of space.

"What kind of flowers are they this time?" Tessa asks, with a tired little smile on her face.

I shut the door behind me. "No flowers today. I brought you something else."

"Oh?"

I cross the room and put one hand on her shoulder—to let her know where I am.

But she gasps and jumps a mile. "God, you scared me. You have to tell me when you're going to touch me, okay? That's the rule."

"Sorry," I murmur, dropping my hand back to my side. "I was

going to give you something. Is that okay?"

Tessa laughs a little, softly. The way you laugh when something harmless just scared the shit out of you, and now you feel stupid for being scared. "Yes," she says.

"Hold out your hands."

She does. I place the notebook on her open palms.

"What is it?" she wonders, feeling the spiral binding. "A notebook?"

I nod. "Yeah. So that you can write down the things you don't want to tell me."

Tessa looks a little taken aback, as if surprised that I'm smart enough to know that there are some things she doesn't want to say out loud. For a moment, she even looks intrigued by the idea. But then she drops the notebook in her lap and says in a disinterested voice, "I can't write."

"Can't write?" I grin, taking a seat on the edge of her bed. "Haven't you learned how? Is this what homeschool is like?"

"No!" she snaps, all fiery and defensive once again.

I say stuff like that just to piss her off.

"Well, then, why not write?"

Tessa sighs. "Weston, I'm blind. There are some things that I just can't do anymore. That's why you're here."

I think about her choice of words for a minute. There was a time when my mother said the very same thing to me.

There are some things you just can't do anymore.

Tessa looks better than she did a week ago, but there's still a shadow of something on her face—defeat. She's still on her knees in the fighting ring, watching Life get back up. The flowers were a start, but they're not enough.

I look at her for a long moment. I look into her blind, unrealistically blue eyes, and it's almost like looking in a mirror. It hurts like hell to believe what other people say about you.

You can't believe it.

There are some things you just can't do anymore.

"Weston?" Tessa says, when I go silent for too long.

"There's nothing you can't do," I reply, standing up and walking over to her desk. There's a fire in my fingertips. Tessa looks confused, sitting on her bed and frowning at nothing. I grip the back of the swivel chair and say it again.

"There's nothing you can't do."

WESTON

3 YEARS AND 7 MONTHS BEFORE TESSA

I HAD A DECISION TO MAKE.

Anyone else would have seen no decision—they would have thought the decisions were over, that everything was done and couldn't be undone.

But that wasn't true.

I had a road to choose.

I lay in that hospital bed with no legs, with needles stuck in my body.

And I had a road to choose.

The first road was flat, easy, and numb. It was simple. It was natural. It was a desert. It would kill me, eventually. Slowly, the same way it kills everyone else. It was a road that would break me, like Mom said. This road was called Despair. It tasted horrible and beautiful all at once.

The second road was rocky, hard, and painful. It was challenging. It was unnatural. It was a mountain range. It was a fighting ring, a boxing match with Life. It was a road that would make me stronger, even if it hurt. This road was called Happiness. It tasted like insanity, like *How can I possibly be happy when I have every right to be miserable?*

I had a road to choose.

And I chose the hard one.

It was even more challenging than it looked. The temptation to take an easy-off exit to the other road would constantly torment me. The mountain range was daunting, and the desert looked like redemption. Happiness felt like hell. And Despair felt like my maker.

The week before I left the hospital, I had nightmares. It was as if Noah and I had traded places—now he was the grown-up and I was the little kid, tortured by sleep. I dreamed about things that hadn't even happened yet—things that would never happen. I saw myself not being able to walk again; I saw myself living the rest of my life in a wheelchair; I saw myself falling and suffering and unable to do anything about it.

During the day, I traveled on the hard road; but when I fell asleep, I wandered into the desert. I couldn't stop the dreams from barraging me. I felt like I was fighting off a multiple-assailant attack. Each thought was an opponent, with bloody knuckles and ragged breath.

When I woke up, there was only one attacker left: Despair. I could feel it and see it as clearly as if it were a person—a dark figure lingering by my bedside, waiting for me with a suffocating embrace. Despair paced my hospital room every night, silent and grim. I closed my eyes and forced myself to ignore it. I forced myself to think about other things: running on the track at school, fighting with Rudy, doing all the things I used to do before this happened. Not because I actually thought I would be able to carry on like normal—but because I couldn't stand the reality of any other option.

Even if I was in denial, who cares? I was punching Life in the face as Life was choking me out. And, even if I didn't win, it felt good to put up a fight.

Finally, they transferred me from the hospital to a rehab center two miles away. My room was smaller there, but at least I was disconnected from machines and they let me wear normal clothes.

Despair didn't come with me to rehab—he stayed in the hospital, patrolling the hallways, the emergency room, the ICU. He had plenty of people on waiting lists. And I wasn't going to be one of them.

Clara Hernandez visited me while I was at the rehab center. I could understand her hesitation—she was a girl, and girls are more shaken and squeamish about stuff like this. But I admired her for coming at all.

Her curly hair was pulled back in a ponytail and she had a serious look on her face. I smiled when I saw her, and she smiled back—but only for a moment. She sat down in the chair next to my bed and looked at the floor.

An awkward silence followed. I didn't know what to say except hello. And we'd already said that.

Finally, Clara murmured in a small voice, "I'm so sorry."

"You should be," I said.

She glanced up at me.

I grinned. "It's all your fault."

Clara smiled shyly. "I didn't mean it like that. I meant—"

"I know," I cut in. "But I've heard it so much already. I'm sick of it. I'm sick of people asking me if I need a hand. Isn't it kind of obvious that I don't need a hand? I need a leg! Two, actually, if that's not too much to ask."

Clara laughed a little, and it was the sound of ice breaking—one of my favorite sounds in the whole world. Especially lately, when the ice always seemed too thick to break with one easy joke.

"So," she said, "how are you doing?"

"Never been better," I replied. "How about you?"

Clara shook her head. "Never mind me. How's rehab?"

"Slow. Stupidly slow. They only give me one physical therapy session every day. Why can't I have two? Or three? Or ten?"

"Because you're still recovering," Clara stated matter-of-factly.

"And I will be forever, at this rate."

She smiled a little. "What else do you do around here?"

I sighed, glancing around the drab room. "Occupational therapy."

"What's that?"

"Awkward. Stuff involving nurses seeing me naked."

Clara giggled.

"But we have free Wi-Fi, so that's a plus." I gestured toward the whiteboard on the wall, which had the nurses' schedules and the Wi-Fi password written on it. There was a moment of silence. Clara had run out of things to say, but I hadn't. I knew what I had to say.

I didn't think about the best way to say it. I just blurted, "Look, Clara… I think we should be clear about something."

She frowned at me, puzzled, waiting for the rest.

I took a measured breath and continued. "I know we were never really a *thing* in the first place, but… I don't think we should be together anymore."

Clara thought about it for a long few seconds. The expression of confusion left her face. In fact, every expression left her face. Her voice sounded flat when she said, "Why not?"

"You know why."

She shook her head, and that same apprehensive look returned. "I don't care about that, Weston."

"Not now," I said, giving her a sad smile in return. "But you will. When everyone is watching."

She thought about it some more. Then she looked down and murmured, "We don't have to talk about it now. Just concentrate on getting better, okay?"

Yeah, yeah, that was what everyone said: concentrate on getting better. If only it was something I could achieve by mere concentration—I would already be the healthiest person alive, with all this time to do nothing but lie in bed and stare at the ceiling and *concentrate on getting better.*

I don't know how long Clara sat there, staring at the floor and not saying anything. I finally pulled myself out of my thoughts and said, "Hey, Clara, did you see those stairs when you came in?"

She nodded. "Yeah. What about them?"

"When I get out of this place," I told her, "I'm gonna run down those stairs."

Well, I didn't actually run down the stairs when I left rehab.

I was still learning how to walk on my new legs.

My prosthetic legs.

At rehab I learned the basics: how to walk using my prostheses, how to put them on and take them off. I wanted to know more. I wanted to train harder, get stronger, get a different pair of legs—the kind runners wear in the Paralympics. But the physical therapists told me that I would continue to regain my strength through personal training. They gave me a piece of paper with safety guidelines on it. I crunched it up and tossed it out the window on the drive home.

For my first week home, I slept downstairs on the pullout sofa bed. Mom had already fixed up a place in the living room for me before I got home. The sight of it disappointed me. I don't know what I was expecting—to sleep in my room upstairs?

"Let's not make things more difficult than they need to be," Mom said. "I'll sleep down here, with you, for the first couple of nights." She gestured towards the other couch, which was too uncomfortable for anyone to sleep on.

"But I can handle the stairs," I insisted. "I can sleep in my own room."

"Honey." Mom put a hand on my shoulder and said those words I would never forget. "There are some things you just can't do anymore. It's all right."

It wasn't all right.

Not even a little bit right.

But at least I could hang out with my brothers again, which was some consolation. Story time resumed, in the living room. Noah and Aidan piled onto my bed and buried me in a mountain of comics. Henry hung out with us, too—but he was always distant, preoccupied, nervous. He never used to talk much, but he talked even less now. I missed him. I knew it must have been difficult for him, but it was even more difficult for me, to see my closest brother so turned off. I just wanted to talk to him—and I wanted him to talk to me.

Mom let us read together for fifteen minutes every night. Then she would say, "Time for bed, boys," and send them upstairs. They would whine and complain but obey. They would say goodnight and then scurry upstairs. I would stay in the living room, listening to their footsteps bouncing around in the ceiling.

I would stay in the living room, like an invalid.

True to her word, Mom slept downstairs for the first few nights, on the other couch. But she didn't get a wink of sleep and I finally convinced her that I'd be all right by myself. She must have said "Are you sure?" eight million times. I promised that I'd holler if I needed her. Finally, she agreed. Finally, she went upstairs with Dad and the boys. Finally, I was alone in the living room.

It was dark, eleven o'clock at night. Everyone else was asleep.

I had to do it.

I had to take the stairs.

Because Mom's voice was still burning in my ears, days later.

There are some things you just can't do anymore.

My own rebellious voice countered, *There's nothing I can't do.*

I pushed aside my blankets and sat upright. My prosthetic legs were leaning against the side of the bed. It was harder to put them on in the dark, but I managed after about ten minutes of trial and error. I eased myself off the mattress and stood up.

Now all I had to do was find my way to the stairs, in the dark, without making any noise or crashing into furniture or falling down.

Easy.

Technically, I had all night. I could take as much time as I needed. And I did.

Slowly and carefully, I moved across the living room and through the hallway to the stairs. I hesitated at the bottom, wondering if this was a stupid idea. Wondering if Mom was right, and there were some things I just couldn't do anymore.

Maybe some things. But walking up the stairs wasn't one of them. There were stairs at school. And I was going to go back to school eventually. Which meant I had to learn how to walk upstairs.

Right now.

I took the stairs, one at a time, in the dark. I have no idea how many minutes passed—maybe ten, maybe twenty, maybe thirty. The whole process was more difficult and more exhausting than I thought it would be, but I made it.

I made it to the top.

I made it to my room.

And when morning came, my mother found me in my own bed.

I didn't open my eyes, but I sensed when she entered the room.

She smelled like cinnamon and home. I felt her touch my shoulder and leave a kiss in my hair.

I heard her whisper, "I was wrong about you, sweetheart. You're stronger than I thought you were."

Taste

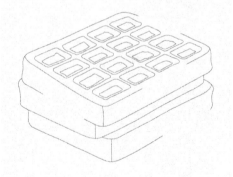

TESSA

DAY 40

I DON'T THINK I'LL EVER GET USED TO IMPROMPTU visits from anyone. Especially Weston, who walks into my room without knocking, at 9:00 a.m., when I'm still in my pajamas.

"Yo," he says, scaring the living daylights out of me.

"Weston!" I gasp, snatching a throw pillow and awkwardly hugging it to my chest. "What are you doing here?"

"What am I always doing here?" The door shuts. I hear him walk across the room and sit down at my desk.

I run my hands through my hair, still a little startled by his sudden entrance. "Working for me?"

"Yeah," Weston replies, peppy as ever. "What do you have for me today?"

"Um… I don't know." I frown, trying to think. It's too early to think. "Where's Grandma?"

"She had an errand, she said. Library or something. Are you hungry? I'm starving."

Without another word, he vanishes. I hear my bedroom door open and his footsteps going down the stairs.

"Weston?" I sigh. "Weston!"

But he's gone. Presumably already in the kitchen.

I groan, tossing the pillow aside and getting to my feet. I go through the tedious motions of feeling my way to the door, then shutting and locking it while I get dressed. Afterward, I make my way downstairs and find Weston in the kitchen. (*Find* is a funny word to use when you can't actually see who you're looking for.)

"What do you want to eat?" Weston asks, regardless of the fact that I never even told him I was hungry.

My fingers find the edge of the island and I perch myself on one of the stools.

"I don't know if Grandma would like you using the kitchen," I say, sounding like quite the prude.

"Why not?" Weston counters. "She told me to make myself at home. And this is what I would do at home. So what do you want? What's your favorite food?"

I open my mouth, then shut it again, then sigh.

"Come on," he groans, and his voice gets closer. He's looking right at me, I can tell. "What's your favorite food?"

I bite my lip. "Waffles."

"Really?"

"Yeah."

"Well, then, Tessa Dickinson—you are in luck. Because I happen to know how to make the most amazing waffles under the sun."

I roll my eyes, but can't help smiling. "You would have said that about any food I picked."

"No way. I'm serious. Let me make you waffles and then you can be the judge. Okay?"

I grin. "Okay."

Weston goes about finding the ingredients. First, I hear him open the refrigerator. He asks me where the eggs are stored. I tell him. Then he asks about bowls. And a whisk. And milk. And flour. And everything else you can possibly think of. I'm surprised by how much I photographically remember where everything can be found in my kitchen.

"So," Weston says after a moment's silence, "have you gone out at all since the accident?"

"Just to doctor appointments."

"Is it weird? To ride in a car?"

I nod slowly. "Yeah, actually… it is. I used to have all these horrible dreams about the crash—but they've pretty much stopped now. Still, it makes me nervous to ride in a car."

"That's understandable." I hear two eggs crack into the bowl. "Um, where's your trash?"

"Under the sink."

Another pause ticks by.

"So," Weston says again, "is it just car rides, or does it make you nervous to be outside in general?"

I shrug one shoulder. "It makes me nervous in general. It's so… disorienting. I don't know where anything is."

"Why don't you use your cane?"

So many questions. Why does he always have to ask so many questions?

I suck in a tight breath. "I don't like it."

"But it would help you."

My jaw clenches. Part of me feels like yelling, *You don't know what it's like!* but I resist the urge to be rude. After all, the boy is making me waffles. And he's been so kind to me. I can't go back there.

So instead I lean forward on my elbows, pressing my fingertips to my brow bone. "I don't want to go outside, Weston." My voice sounds weak. Beaten down.

I'm half-expecting a "Why not?" in response, but instead there's another silence. Instead he asks, "Where do I find the waffle iron?"

"It should be in the cabinet under here." I tap the wood top of the island I'm sitting at.

He crosses the kitchen and opens the cabinet door. He takes out the waffle iron and sets it on the counter. For at least ten seconds, he doesn't say anything.

Then the question comes.

"Did you *never* like going outside, or is it just since the accident?"

I exhale a heavy sigh. At this point, most people would say something polite, like, "You don't have to talk about it if you don't want to." But apparently Weston doesn't believe in formalities. He whisks the waffle batter and waits for my answer.

"A bit of both," I mutter. "I was never much into going outside. Too many people, too many bugs, too many unpredictable things."

I don't mention the lack of Wi-Fi. He would only laugh.

"So you'd rather stay inside all the time?" he asks.

"Basically."

I hear the sweet sizzling of batter being poured into the waffle iron. It's already beginning to smell heavenly in the kitchen. I guess I'm hungrier than I thought.

"So," Weston begins again, for the third time, "does any part of you have any desire to go outside at all for any amount of time?"

Why does he care so much about this?

I pinch my eyes shut. "I said I don't want to go outside."

"Yeah, but—" I hear him cross the kitchen and stop at the island. "Is it because you don't *like* to go out, or is it because you're *afraid* to go out?"

I frown. "Does it matter?"

"I think you know it does."

134

Yes, I do.

I sigh, lacing my fingers together and resting my forehead on my knuckles.

"Listen, Weston," I murmur, "I don't want people to see me... like this. I don't want people to stare at me. I don't want to be *pathetic*. Pitied. I don't want to be blind. I'd rather just stay inside until the whole thing is over. You know?"

He doesn't know. There's no way for him to know.

But he says, "Yeah. I do."

And on some level, I think he does understand. Not as much as I understand. But more than anyone else understands.

Why am I suddenly giving him the benefit of the doubt?

I guess Weston Ludovico is just the kind of person who grows on you.

I can tell he's still standing on the other side of the island, looking at me as I slouch forward against my hands with my eyes shut.

"Is your waffle burning?" I finally say.

"Oh, shit."

He goes back to the counter and then informs me that the waffle is not, in fact, burnt—it is perfect. I hear the silverware drawer, the butter dish, the mason jar of maple syrup Grandma keeps in the fridge.

I don't say anything else about going outside—and neither does Weston. He brings a plate over to the island and sets it in front of me. It smells even more heavenly up close. Heavenlier. Is that a word? It should be.

"Are you ready to judge my culinary genius?" Weston asks.

"Sure."

"Open."

I frown. "What?"

"Your mouth. Open your mouth."

"Oh."

It feels strange, for sure—to be hand-fed breakfast by a boy I scarcely know. But I comply anyway, opening my mouth and shutting my eyes. A moment later, a bite of heaven melts on my tongue.

Wow. Wow. Wow.

"Well?" he asks when I don't open my eyes and silently savor the goodness. "What do you taste?"

I smile despite myself. "The most amazing waffles under the sun."

WESTON

3 YEARS AND 6 MONTHS BEFORE TESSA

MY SOCK DRAWER WAS EMPTY.

I don't know why I opened it—but Mom must have known that I would. So she emptied it.

That was another cool thing about my mom. She might have been a little too pessimistic sometimes, but she always went out of her way to do nice things that nobody else would ever think to do. Things that, oftentimes, went unnoticed.

She let me sleep upstairs in my room, without even discussing it with Dad. For the first time in my life, I felt like I had made a decision without my parents. And for the first time since the amputation, I felt like I was in control of something.

I was in control of my mind.

I could *choose* to be happy, to be stronger, to be me—regardless of everything—and there was nobody standing in my way.

The mountain range was a challenging road, but it was also strangely addictive.

My family still treated me like I was weak—and even though I was, it made me angry. Not because I didn't want to be seen as helpless, but because I could no longer be helpful. Mom would say things like, "Weston, could you—oh, never mind. I'm sorry." And no matter how much I begged her to let me help, she refused to allow it.

Henry had to be the new oldest. The new me, until I could recover enough to be myself again.

He was still distant and nervous and quiet. Every time I saw him, I tried to think of a new way to break the ice. Nothing was working. I couldn't figure him out. Later, I realized that I was trying too hard to figure him out.

One afternoon, the ice broke all on its own. In fact, it melted.

We were the only ones in the house. I was at the top landing of the stairs, beginning my tedious journey down. But I tripped on the first step.

I don't know what happened—anything could have happened, really. I was still getting used to my prosthetic legs. I tripped, and I caught myself on the railing, not unlike the way I'd caught myself at school that day, in front of Clara Hernandez.

But this time it was my brother Henry who saw.

He appeared in the doorway of his room just in time to witness me almost fall down the stairs. He watched me with big worried eyes.

I gave him a lifeless smile and said, "What do you know? I'm human."

Without a word, Henry walked over to me and put an arm around my back. He was still too small to reach my shoulders—but he was stronger than he looked. He helped me down the stairs and we didn't say a word to each other. We didn't have to. There was something about that moment despite how backwards things had become. We were both so weak. We were both so strong. We were boy soldiers, too young for war.

When we reached the bottom of the stairs, Henry's face crumpled. He started to cry. He let go of me and pressed his hands against his eyes and whimpered, "Oh, Wes. I'm so sorry. It's all my fault."

I frowned. "What?"

"I should have stopped you that day," Henry said, taking his hands away from his face and looking up at me through his tears. "Or at least I should have told Mom that you hurt yourself—"

"Henry," I interrupted him, placing a firm hand on his shoulder, "this is *my* fault, okay? Not yours. You were only being loyal to me by not telling Mom. I should have been the one to tell Mom. It was a mistake. And it was wrong of me to make you keep quiet about it."

Henry didn't deny my taking the blame—but he didn't agree with me, either. He rubbed the tears off his face and said, "I didn't think you were, you know."

"Didn't think I was what?"

"Human."

I smiled sadly. "I'm not a superhero, Henry."

He laughed a little—a broken, tired laugh to match my smile. "Maybe not the super part... but you're still a hero. You're still *my* hero."

I couldn't say anything. My eyes were stinging, and my little brother was already crying. If I was going to be a hero, I couldn't fall to pieces, too. Instead, I put my arms around him and I hugged him—with every bit of strength I had left.

And he hugged me back.

And we were okay again.

But Henry wasn't the only one who needed help. Despite Noah's newfound confidence as a "grown-up," he still had nightmares. Only occasionally, but that's all it takes. I had more respect for—or maybe more fear of—bad dreams since my time in the hospital. There's nothing babyish or stupid about a nightmare. You feel like you're drowning, and you can't do anything to stop it. Sleep holds you underwater like a millstone.

Noah was only three and a half, so he couldn't talk coherently about what he dreamed of—but even if he could, I don't think that would have helped. The only thing that seemed to help was me.

Henry and Aidan shared a room, but Noah slept by himself in the nursery, which was right across from my room. Our parents' room was at the other end of the hall, so I was always the first one awake when Noah would start crying.

As the oldest, I'd assumed the responsibility of running to my little brother's rescue. I wouldn't do much—just sit with him and tell him it was okay. Sometimes he'd fall asleep within a few minutes, but other times I would carry him back to my room and let him spend the rest of the night in my bed. It all worked out fine.

Until it didn't.

Noah's nightmare relapse happened two weeks after I came home from rehab. I was startled awake in the middle of the night by the sound of him crying.

It woke me up, but not completely. I was half-conscious, feeling one of those phantom sensations. I thought I still had legs—no, I didn't think. I *felt* it, as real as if it were true.

In a split second, I was out of bed.

And on the floor.

Pain shot through my body like a mortar round. Suddenly, I was wide awake—and cussing like a Marine into the carpet under my mouth.

It never hurt so much to *remember* as it did that night. Even through all those long sterile weeks in the hospital and rehab—I don't think I ever resented my handicap as much as I did at that moment. Because I realized, at that moment, that I could never be the brother I once was.

I remember lying there, listening to Noah whimpering in the next room. My hands were clenched into fists and my forehead was pressed against the floor and I wanted to kill something. But at the same time, I wanted to cry.

Crawling through the dark, I found my prosthetic legs waiting against the side of my bed. I fitted them on, though it took several minutes, and I stood. I went to my brother as quickly as possible, hoping that none of this ruckus would wake Mom or Dad or the other boys.

Noah had quieted down by the time I got to his room. In the soft illumination of his nightlight, I could see tears glistening on his face.

"Shh, it's okay," I said, sitting down on his bed and taking his small shaking body in my arms.

He didn't speak. He only whimpered and clung onto my T-shirt.

I knew that tonight would be one of those nights I needed to take him back to my room. And I had no idea if I could handle it.

But I gave it a shot, anyway.

"You want to sleep with me tonight, bro?" I whispered against the top of his head.

He nodded. Sniffed.

"Okay. Hold onto my neck, and we'll try to do this together."

Noah silently followed my instruction, locking his tiny hands around my neck like a baby monkey. It was a struggle to carry him back to my room—but I made it. I set my shivering little brother on my bed, then took off my prostheses and lay down next to him.

"I'm sorry I took so long," I whispered. "I'll get better at this."

It wasn't just a promise for him. It was a promise for me, too.

I'll get better at this.

I'll get better. I'll get stronger.

I'll do whatever it takes.

Promise.

TESSA

DAY 43

ON SUNDAY, I CONVINCE GRANDMA TO GO TO CHURCH with Grandpa.

He's giving a sermon on forgiveness and it's a good one—I know, because I've heard most of it, bit by bit, every night when he says goodnight to me. I can tell that Grandma misses going to church with him, and since Weston has proven himself to be a responsible person—and had planned on coming over today anyway—there's really no reason for Grandma to stay home again.

After some debating back and forth, I finally win. Both my grandparents leave for church, and Weston shows up just in time so that I won't be alone.

And he brings me chocolate. Dark chocolate, eighty-five percent cocoa.

I don't know why I ever disliked him.

First, we tackle answering comments; then I send him on a paper chase through my pictures folder to find a few specific images I want to include with one of the poems. He follows my somewhat confusing instructions without complaint.

What I don't tell Weston is that I tried writing in the notebook he gave me. It was the strangest feeling, drawing the shapes of letters when I couldn't actually see the words I was spelling. My hand-writing must look like chicken scratches, and I have no idea if I'll be able to make it out when I finally can see again, but it felt good. It felt good to write with a pen in my hand and paper under my finger-tips. It felt like a little bit of normality coming back to me.

His words got stuck in my head, ricocheting back and forth.

There's nothing you can't do.

I stole the line and wrote it down in the notebook, on the first page. One day, if I ever forget where this notebook came from—though I doubt I will—those words will remind me.

"Can I ask you a really personal question?" Weston asks, out of the blue, when I fall silent in thought.

I'm a little taken aback—mostly that he should ask permission to ask a question. That's so un-Weston of him. Then I begin to fear the question itself—because if he is hesitant to ask, it must be *super* personal.

"I guess so," I say, breaking off another square of chocolate and putting it in my mouth.

"Well," Weston begins, "I was just curious about your parents. The first day I came here, your grandmother told me that your mom lives in Pittsburgh—but she didn't mention your dad. And I guess I was wondering why you live here instead of with your mom."

Just a parent question. Good. I breathe a small sigh of relief.

"I never met my dad," I say. "No idea who he is."

"Really?"

I nod.

"That sucks," Weston murmurs.

"Not really. I mean, Grandpa is the best dad I could ever ask for, so…"

"So your mom is their daughter?"

"Yeah," I reply, leaning back against the pillows on my bed. "Mom was kind of a wild child, I guess. Before I was born, she went to college and got all messed up. She slept around with some frat boy who apparently didn't believe in condoms, and... I was the result." I smile a little. "Compelling backstory, huh?"

Weston laughs. He's sitting at my desk, eating the other chocolate bar.

"Anyway," I continue, "Mom dropped out of college when she found out she was pregnant. I don't know what happened to the guy—he just sort of... vanished. Not ready for that kind of responsibility, I guess. So my mom lived with my grandparents until I was born and for a couple of years after. But she had to find work, and I guess Grandma and Grandpa had gotten used to me—they didn't like the idea of three-year-old me being shifted around with babysitters in some other town in some other state while my mom tried to find a job. So they let me live with them. And Mom moved to Pittsburgh to start afresh."

I don't think I've ever said so many words without stopping. I pause, wondering if I'm ranting too much. He *did* ask.

"So, yeah," I conclude, feeling myself blush a little. "I grew up not really knowing my mother. She always comes to visit around Christmastime, but... I don't feel like I know her that well. Grandma and Grandpa are better parents to me than she ever was."

Weston is silent for a few seconds. Then he asks, "Did she come to see you after the accident?"

"No." I manage a dry laugh. "She called me. Asked me if I was all right. Apparently, she was too busy to come up and visit. But... it's fine. I never feel like myself around her, you know?"

He murmurs, "Yeah." But I can tell he doesn't actually know.

"Anyway, enough about me." I shake my head, refocusing. "Tell me *your* story."

"My story?" For the first time ever, Weston sounds a little apprehensive.

I try to clarify. "I mean... what's your family like? Do you have any siblings?"

"Oh, right. Yeah, I have three little brothers."

"Wow."

"Yeah." Weston laughs a little. "Needless to say, your house is... really quiet."

I smile. "What are they like?"

He blows out a long sigh, probably trying to think up the best way to describe them. "Well, Henry is thirteen—and he's my better half. A little too serious sometimes, but that's why he's Mom's favorite."

I put more chocolate in my mouth. "Moms aren't supposed to have favorites."

"Yeah, well, mine does," Weston says. "Aidan—also known as Spider-Man—is nine years old, and he's... my spirit animal."

I raise an eyebrow. "Your spirit animal?"

"The kid is like a bottle of 5-hour Energy. In the form of a human."

"Wow. Impressive."

Weston continues, "And then there's Noah, who just turned six. He'll probably grow up to be an astronaut—like, for real."

A smile warms over my face. "I want to meet your brothers. They sound precious."

"Just don't call them *precious* when you meet them."

I giggle.

"My parents are awesome, too," Weston adds. "Dad owns the newspaper—but you already know that—and Mom wanted to be an engineer, but she decided to be a mom instead. No idea why. Being an engineer sounds like way more fun."

I grin. "To each their own, I guess."

There is a short pause. Then Weston says, just as randomly, "What's homeschool like?"

I think about my reply for a moment. "It's… awesome. I love it."

"Can I ask you a question that you've probably heard a million times and probably hate?"

"You say that as if you haven't asked me such a question already."

He laughs—that infectious kind that makes you want to laugh with him for no reason at all.

"Go ahead," I say, shutting my eyes and waiting for it.

"How do you make friends?"

"Ugh!" I groan, attempting to act enraged. "Not that question *again!*"

He just keeps laughing.

"I make friends through the internet," I explain. "And through church. But mostly through the internet. Remember that Instagram chat I mentioned? There's like seven of us who are super close. We talk all the time."

"Have you met any of them?"

"Not in person," I say. "But we've group called each other before…"

Suddenly, an idea hits me—and I have no idea why I didn't think of it sooner. A group call, of course! All this time I've missed talking to my squad—and I'm sure they've missed me. But maybe I don't have to wait until I'm better to chat with them again. Maybe I can figure out how to use a phone.

The possibility puts a smile on my face. So much has happened since we last talked—even since I had Grandma put up a post on my

Instagram explaining why I wouldn't be responding to any messages. Those six girls are my best friends, even if I haven't met them in person yet.

If I could find a way to talk to them again, my darkness would become a little bit brighter.

WESTON

3 YEARS AND 5 MONTHS BEFORE TESSA

I KNEW THAT I WOULD EVENTUALLY HAVE TO GO BACK to school, but I didn't know which school I would go to. I mean, I'd always assumed I would go back to regular school. But then I heard Mom and Dad discussing it one night.

Mom kept mentioning this place near Albany—a special needs school, for kids with handicaps.

For kids like me.

I understood the point of it. To be in a place where you're not the kid everyone else is staring at—it was a tempting option. But it looked like a desert.

I wanted to go back to Rockford Junior High. I wanted to see my friends and my teachers and those stupid flights of stairs that I liked to trip on so much. I wanted to be normal.

Even though I knew I would never be normal.

I didn't talk to Mom or Dad about school—and they didn't talk to me, either. They must have figured I wasn't ready. This semester was already half over, which meant I would have a shitload of make-up work to do. Sure, it would suck. But I had to do it.

Rudy came over to my house almost every day. He would tell me all about the lousy stuff I was missing at school, and how boring life was without me.

"I miss fighting," he said one afternoon. "I miss sitting in detention with you. I miss taking showers together."

I twitched my eyebrows at him. "You miss taking showers together?"

He smacked my arm. "Shut up."

I laughed—at him, at me, at everything. It was becoming easier to laugh.

"By the way," Rudy said, with a curious frown, "how *do* you take showers now?"

"Not alone," I replied. "It's so frickin' awkward."

If this whole thing had happened just a few years earlier, it would have been better. Of course, no age is a good age to lose your legs— but thirteen is the *worst* age. If I had been nine or ten, I don't think I would have cared much, letting my mother help me take a shower. But now? Hell, now it was just embarrassing.

That was when I decided what my first challenge would be: take a shower by myself. If I could do that, I could do anything.

Of course, I had to do it when Mom was out of the house. One afternoon, she left on an errand with my brothers. And while she was gone, I took a shower.

By myself.

At first, I thought the hardest part was getting in the tub. I'd learned at rehab to do everything in the right order: strip, sit on the edge of the tub, take off my prostheses, then use the grab bars my parents had installed to lower myself in and turn on the water. But I forgot that the hardest part is actually getting *out* of the tub. Because after a shower, everything is wet and slippery and you need about a hundred towels and a mom. The grab bars helped a lot, but I still fell on my ass.

Taking my first solo shower was a thousand times more difficult than walking up the stairs in the dark, but it was worth it.

By the time Mom got home, I was back on the couch—exactly where she'd left me. But my hair was wet. And she noticed right away.

Yeah, I got a lecture. But from that day forward, I took showers without any help.

Still, it was only the beginning. The first step.

I had no idea where to start with everything else.

Then, one day, Aidan burst into my room with a comic book in his hand—it was an older one from Mom's collection, *The Six Million Dollar Man*. Aidan had an excited grin on his face and he was shouting, "Weston! This is you!"

I was confused at first, but my little brother explained himself.

"Steve Austin!" he said. "Remember? He's an astronaut and then he gets into a plane crash and loses his legs. And his right arm. And his left eye. But then they give him bionic implants and he's stronger than anyone. He can run at speeds of sixty miles per hour, and his eye has this crazy zoom lens, and his limbs all have the power of a bulldozer! Wes, he's just like you."

For a few seconds, I didn't know what to say. I was pretty amazed, I guess, that my little brother thought I had some kind of super-human strength, when I could barely even walk.

But he gave me an idea.

I kept the comic book and read it twice. Then I cut it up and taped pages of it to the wall over my bed. Then I printed off motivational quotes, like my dad did, and put them up on the wall, too. Then I found articles about Paralympic runners and added them to the wall. I finished the messy collage with pictures of the various mountains I wanted to climb.

It was like a visual brain dump of my optimism—put on display where anyone could see it. A web of red string would have made the whole thing look way cooler, but I resisted the urge.

When the wall was finished, I took off my prostheses and sat on my bed and called Rudy while I stared at my chaotic masterpiece.

"Hello?" He sounded like he'd just woken up, and it was three o'clock in the afternoon.

"Yo, pansyass. Have you ever heard of the Six Million Dollar Man?"

"The what?"

"You know. Steve Austin. He's the superhero version of me."

Rudy sighed. "What are you talking about…"

"I'm talking about running."

Rudy groaned. "Are you kidding me? You're literally going to try to run?"

"No… I'm not going to *try*."

He told me that I was out of my mind. But this wasn't news to me.

First, I had to get some better prostheses—because the ones I had now would never do the job. I needed running blades, but they were expensive and I'd have to go through all those back-and-forth adjustments with the prosthetist all over again.

But I didn't care. I just wanted to run.

After some discussion, Mom and Dad agreed to the idea. And I got my first pair of running blades. They looked pretty awesome, too—well, as awesome as prosthetic limbs *can* look.

Everyone told me to be careful, to go through so many hours of familiarizing myself with the running blades. They even urged more physical therapy training. But I thought, *To hell with that.* I'd had my fill of being supervised by therapists while walking around a room in a dingy rehab center. If I was going to fall on my face, I'd rather do it when nobody was watching.

At last, the day came when Mom dropped me off at the track. Rudy was already there, waiting for me. He shook his head and smiled, the way he had when I jumped over the fence and didn't die.

"This is for you," I said, tossing him a stopwatch.

He caught it and frowned in confusion. "You're not going to actually time yourself, are you?"

"Nope." I grinned, swinging open the gate to the track. "You are."

Rudy sighed like a tired old man and followed me. It felt good to be on the track again. The morning was cold, but I was wearing a T-shirt and gym shorts. Rudy was dressed to hike Everest. He watched me with a worried, grown-up expression as I sat on the ground and unzipped my backpack.

"What are those?" he asked when I took the new prosthetic legs out.

"Running blades. They make me a blade runner."

He rolled his eyes. "Do you even know how to use them?"

"Not yet, but I'm going to learn."

"Oh, god."

Rudy was a doubter. But I made him a believer. I made him sit there and time me with the stopwatch. It was Shabbat, which meant he wasn't allowed to do anything except frown and be cold.

I learned how to run that day. And yeah, I tripped and fell about eight hundred times. But I would get back up every time, walk back to the starting line, and do it all over again. After a few dozen tries, I was able to run a full lap without even tripping or slowing down.

"Good job," Rudy said, and I could tell he was freezing. "Can we go home now?"

"You kidding? I'm just warming up."

I felt kind of awesome, actually. Sore as hell, but awesome.

For at least fifteen more minutes, I tortured Rudy some more. I ran until I reached my personal best lap time—three minutes and eleven seconds. I let Rudy go home, but I made him promise to meet me at the track again tomorrow.

"And bring the stopwatch."

He shook his head, but not like *no*. More like *you're crazy*.

There was a heavy bag hanging in my garage. And it was fricking cold out there, but I didn't care. I'd gone too long without punching something.

I started with one-minute rounds. I would turn on my dad's old radio to some seventies rock station and blast the heavy bag until I ran out of energy. Then I would stop for about ten seconds and catch my breath. Then I would do it all over again. Until I *really* couldn't breathe.

After that, I would do push-ups—as many as possible without stopping. First that number was five. Then it turned into ten. Then twenty. Then twenty-seven. Then thirty.

Every night, I fell asleep before my head hit the pillow. It felt kind of like being an adult, but better.

I set my alarm for six thirty every morning. I had to get used to waking up early, for when I went back to school. Regular school, with Rudy and all my other friends.

Nobody was standing in my way except for me, right?

Right.

Rudy met up with me at the track every afternoon (except for the afternoons I was stuck at the prosthetist's, getting my running blades adjusted for the millionth time). I ran faster every training session.

Three minutes per lap became two and a half minutes per lap. We must have looked like quite the pair—one boy sitting on a bench with a serious frown and a stopwatch, one boy without legs running laps in the freezing cold and cheering every time he beat his personal best.

I blasted the heavy bag in my garage every chance I got. One-minute rounds turned into two-minute rounds turned into three-minute rounds. Finally, I was able to beat that thing like it was out to kill me. My knuckles bled and I flurried the bag and Led Zeppelin screamed at me from the radio. I felt like I was dying—but at the same time, I finally felt alive again.

I did one hundred push-ups without stopping.

I broke a new record at the track—a two-minute-and-thirteen-second lap.

I woke up at six thirty every morning, and I never hit the snooze button.

I tried harder every day, and it paid off. The muscles that had weakened in the hospital were now strong again—chiseling my arms and shoulders and abdomen and even my upper legs. My bones tasted strength, and it felt incredible.

Finally, I decided that it was time for a real fight. With Rudy.

We were at the track, and the weather was getting a little warmer. I had just broken my record again—a two-minute-and-four-second lap. Even Rudy seemed impressed by this point.

"Wow," he said as I collapsed on the grass, out of breath. "You're fast."

I squinted up at him. "Faster than you."

He rolled his eyes, but couldn't deny it.

"You still think I'm crazy?"

Rudy nodded.

"You still think I'm an invalid?"

He looked taken aback. "What? I never thought that—"

"Then let's fight," I said, getting to my feet. My running blade feet.

He looked even more taken aback. Taken as far aback, in fact, as one can possibly be taken aback. "What? No."

"Come on!" I laughed, putting my fists up in front of my face. "Let's fight."

Rudy shook his head. "Dude, no. Your legs."

"Forget about my frickin' legs! If you *really* don't think I'm an invalid, prove it. Hit me!"

"I don't want to hurt you."

"I'm gonna hurt *you*, pansyass, if you don't hit me. Now!"

Rudy stared at me like I was crazy. "No."

"I'm gonna punch you in the face, then."

He laughed a little, sarcastic. "No, you're not."

But he was wrong. I did punch him in the face. And because he wasn't expecting it, he didn't block it. And, *bam*, I caught him right in the jaw. It must have hurt because my knuckles stung like hell.

"Son of a—" He brought his hand up to his mouth and I caught a glimpse of blood on his fingertips.

For a second, I was shocked—almost as shocked as Rudy was. He looked at me with this freaked-out expression on his face. He was pissed enough to hit me back; I could see it in his eyes.

And it was worth splitting his lip just to witness that look of total rage.

He threw a punch at my nose, but I saw it coming. I blocked it and countered. He barred down on my arm, fritzing a nerve pretty good.

We sparred back and forth, just like we used to. Better than we used to. Because, unlike those times at school, this was a real fight. We were actually angry at each other—Rudy because he got blasted in the face, and me because I wouldn't let my best friend treat me like an invalid. This was the only way to settle the score.

Rudy faked a knee kick to my groin, then hit me in the face— payback. My lip stung and I tasted blood.

Finally.

I threw a kick just to freak him out. He staggered backwards even though I barely tagged him with the tip of my running blade.

"Dude! That's not fair."

I laughed and yelled over my bleeding knuckles, "Nothing about this is fair, Kaufmann!"

Rudy threw a punch and caught me in the ribs, and I pounded him in the collarbone with a hammer fist. Finally, he got up the nerve to reap me. He grabbed my shoulders and knocked my legs out from underneath me. I landed on my back in the grass.

Everything hurt, but in a good way.

"Oh my god—are you okay?" Rudy dropped to his knees beside me, panicking like he did the day he'd brutalized me in the school-yard.

But this time, I was laughing. Despite the fact I couldn't breathe and my lungs were burning and I felt bruised in multiple places.

I was okay. I was more than okay.

I'd never been better.

Rudy started laughing, too. And, again, we must have looked like quite a pair—two boys with blood on their faces and knuckles, sprawled on the grass in the middle of an abandoned high school track, laughing.

"You've... been... practicing," Rudy panted, still trying to catch his breath.

"And you… haven't been… practicing."

That was when my mother pulled into the parking lot to pick us up.

Needless to say, we had a little explaining to do.

By the time we got home, the sun was setting. Dad was in the living room with Henry and Aidan, and Noah was napping. I decided that sleep sounded wonderful and went straight to my room, leaving Rudy to explain his busted face to my dad. I was exhausted and my stumps were sweaty and gross, so I took off my running blades and crashed, face-first, into bed.

I must have fallen asleep immediately. Because not twenty minutes passed before I felt a hand nudging my shoulder and heard Rudy's voice saying, "Hey, Wes. Wake up. Your parents want to talk to you."

I groaned and rubbed my eyes. "But I *just* took my legs off."

"Then put them back on, pansyass. And get downstairs."

Rudy left the room, leaving me no choice but to follow.

I found Mom and Dad in the living room. Aidan and Henry had moved to the kitchen, where they seemed to be trying really hard to be quiet. That could only mean one thing: a serious discussion was going down.

"You want to talk to me about something?" I said, taking a seat next to Rudy on the couch. He had a wet, bloodstained washcloth in his hand, no doubt courtesy of my mom.

And speaking of my mom, she looked less worried than she had in months. In fact, I'd even go as far as to say she had a smile on her face. Dad was definitely smiling.

"Rudy's just been talking to us," Mom said, "about you."

I shot him a questioning look. He ignored me, tending to his split lip.

"What about me?" I asked, glancing between my mom and dad.

"About how hard you've been training," Dad said, picking up where Mom had left off. "Rudy says you've gained a lot of strength—both physically and mentally."

I could sense where this was going. They were going to scold me for not following the stupid safety guidelines—for throwing caution to the wind and working myself to the point of exhaustion. I could practically taste the doom of the you-must-rest sentence that was about to be spoken.

Instead, Dad threw me a curveball: "Would you like to go back to school, Weston?"

"Hell yeah!" I blurted before even considering it. Then I froze. "Wait... Do you mean regular school?"

Mom nodded.

I grinned. "Hell yeah."

She gave me a warning look. "You'll have a lot of catching up to do. And it won't be as easy as it once was. Nor will it be as welcoming as this school I found near Albany—"

"And I'm sure that school is great," I interrupted. "But I just want things to go back to the way they were. I know it won't be easy—that's why I've been training so hard."

Dad looked me in the eyes and said, "We can see that. And we're very proud of you, Weston. If this is what you really want—"

"It is," I cut in, though the look on my face was evidence enough.

"Then we'll do whatever we can to help you," Dad finished.

I smiled.

Mission accomplished.

Well, sort of. The hardest part was still ahead of me.

Rudy's father came to pick him up at our house, and while waiting for him to show, we hung out on the porch.

"Did you talk to my parents about me going back to school?" I asked.

"Yeah," Rudy said. He was still holding the washcloth to his face. I must have popped him pretty good.

"But how did you know that I wanted to go back there? We never even talked about it, I don't think."

Rudy gave me a look, like *come on*. "I know you, Weston." He glanced out to the darkening street in front of our house. "Always trying to prove something. Always trying to show off."

I grinned and leaned against the beam of the porch—channeling my inner John Wayne. For a few moments, I didn't say anything.

"And I also know that you've been working really hard for this," Rudy continued. "But your mom is right—it's not gonna be easy. Sure, you have a lot of friends. But there's lots of jerks, too. People are still gonna stare at you."

"Well, then," I said, shrugging coolly, "I'll just stare right back."

That was when Mr. Kaufmann's car pulled up in front of our house. Rudy tossed me the washcloth and said, "Clean up your face, would you?" before heading down the steps.

I laughed and watched him head across the front lawn to his dad's car.

"Hey, Rudy?"

He stopped with one hand on the passenger's side door. "Yeah?"

I felt a smile pull at the corners of my mouth. "Thanks."

"For beating you up?" He grinned and saluted me. "Anytime, bro."

TESSA

DAY 47

"TELL US MORE ABOUT THE BOY," LIV SAYS THROUGH the phone.

I groan, tipping my head back against the wall. But I can't pretend to be frustrated—not when a smile is taking over my face.

"Ooh, yes," Allison agrees. "What is he like? You haven't given us any details!"

With the help of my long-suffering grandmother, I finally figured out how to group-call my blogging squad—and it's the best thing that's happened in a long time. In the usual chaotic fashion of group calls, we talk over each other and then realize we're talking over each other and then pause and say, "You go ahead," at exactly the same time and then laugh. I ask each one of them to bring me up to speed on everything I've missed since the accident.

Allison is studying music and leading worship at her church, which I've always wanted to attend for many reasons.

Liv is probably working on the next Pulitzer Prize–winning novel, but in secret.

Maria is a literal human sunflower, developing a literary webzine and getting ready to take over the world.

Gracie is choreographing and dancing and starring in too many plays to count (all of which I want to see—in the front row, thank you very much).

Raquel is studying literature at college and simultaneously crafting the next best-selling children's book series.

Kate is buried in writing projects but always has time to give us words of encouragement and make all of us feel like we could be the next president of the United States.

"Tessa?" Maria says. "You still there?"

"What? Oh. Yes. I'm still here."

Allison giggles. "She was lost in thought about *the boy*."

"No, I wasn't," I protest, defending myself, though I'm blushing. Good thing this is just a voice call, and they can't actually see me.

"Tell us about him!" Gracie says. "What does he look like? Oh, wait—sorry. Don't answer that. I totally forgot."

I smile. "It's okay. Even *I* forget sometimes. But hopefully, I'll get my sight back soon, and... everything will go back to normal."

"And you'll be able to see the boy," Kate adds.

I laugh. "Would everyone stop calling him 'the boy'? His name is Weston."

"I love that name," Gracie comments.

"And, yes, I'm kind of dying to see what he looks like."

"I know what you should do," Liv says. "Have him take a selfie and send it to the group chat and we'll tell you whether or not he's cute."

I laugh and bury my face in my hands. "That's... the most ridiculous idea I've ever heard."

"Well, looks aren't everything," Allison states wisely. "What's his personality like?"

I close my eyes, trying to think up an accurate description.

Weston is...

A paradox.

"He's really nice. But stubborn. And obnoxiously optimistic."

Raquel laughs. "Is that a thing?"

"It is now," I say. "At first, I didn't like him. I thought he didn't understand anything about me—even though he acted like he did. And I'm not sure that he understands much, even now. But he's kind. And patient. And he kept coming back to type poetry for me, so I've kind of been forced to make friends with him."

"Aw." Maria is the first one to speak after that monologue. "He sounds really cute."

"He does," Allison agrees. "I ship it."

"Oh my gosh, no." I blush again, squeezing my eyes shut.

"What was his name again?" Raquel asks.

"Don't you dare."

"Weston," Kate offers.

I groan, bracing myself for the most cringe-worthy ship name.

"Westess!" Raquel declares. "Or Tesswes. Or Westa. Or Tesson."

"Okay, enough." I laugh, shaking my head. "I don't like him, okay? Not like that."

Liv grunts. "Well, I bet *he* likes *you*."

"He's only trying to be nice."

"By bringing you flowers every day?" Gracie teases. "And chocolate? I want a Weston…"

"And you said that he made you waffles," Allison adds. "How can you not be in love with a boy who makes you waffles? That's what I want to know."

I sigh, still blushing. Still smiling. "He's only here to type poetry for me and manage my blog. That's all."

"Well," Liv says, and I can hear that she's smiling, too, "we shall see."

WESTON

3 YEARS AND 3 MONTHS BEFORE TESSA

IT WAS THE MIDDLE OF MARCH, AND I WAS FINALLY going back to school. I had to psych myself up to even get in the car that morning. This was the final test—and if I could pass this, everything else would be easy. I couldn't chicken out, not now.

Rudy gave me a T-shirt that said **MY FACE IS UP HERE** and told me that I should wear it on the first day of school—just to freak out the people who stared. I loved the idea.

My dad drove us both to school and I brought my running blades in my backpack, just in case they let me return to gym class. They said they wouldn't expect me to, due to "extenuating circumstances," but people don't always mean what they say. In any case, I would eventually earn my way back into gym class—even if it wasn't today.

My first challenge was just opening the front entrance door and stepping inside.

Man, it was harder than I'd thought it would be to walk down that main hallway of the junior high school—not everyone was watching, like they do in cliché teen movies, but I could definitely feel gazes following me.

I ignored everyone.

Everyone except Clara Hernandez, whom I found digging around in her locker. I snuck up behind the open door and knocked on it twice.

"Anybody home?"

Clara gasped, straightening up. A smile melted over her face when she saw me. "Weston! Oh my god. You're… back!"

There was a long awkward pause right there. I could tell that she was trying really hard to just look at my face—not look down. She was probably the only one who followed the direction on my T-shirt.

I gave her a tired smile and said, "It's okay, Clara. You can look. Everyone else is."

She opened her mouth but didn't say anything and just looked uncomfortable.

One of the guys from the track team walked by and punched my shoulder. "Hey, Wes!"

"Yo, Davis," I said, glancing up and giving him a quick wave.

When I looked back down at Clara, she pushed a polite little smile onto her face. "Want to hang out later? After school?"

"No," I said, without beating around the bush. "No, I don't think we should."

"But—"

"Things can't be like they were before. Let's just be friends, okay? It'll be easier for both of us."

On that final note, I walked away to my own locker, which I half-expected not to be there anymore. I felt like I hadn't been at school in years. Clara didn't chase me down and try to continue the discussion, but I knew that she would stand firm. She was more stubborn than she looked.

My re-entry into school went surprisingly smoothly—at least, socially. (Most academic stuff flew right over my head.) Not many kids were jerks. I think there's this boundary of "catastrophic," and

I'd crossed the line. Beyond that line, people keep their mouths shut. At least, most of them do.

All except for Neil Ferguson. He was the only one rotten enough to say something. I knew him by sight, thanks to a fateful day back in fifth grade when I'd threatened to knock his block off after I caught him picking on Rudy. I remember being dragged away by the principal, shouting in protest, and watching Kaufmann's face turn red.

But this time, I was the one in the line of fire.

"Well, well," Ferguson sneered, coming up behind me in the locker hall with his entourage of dimwitted friends. "Looks like Superman finally got out of his sickbed."

I slammed my locker shut and turned around to face him.

Just like I remembered: frowning, oily, dressed in black like he and his buddies had just returned from a funeral. Maybe it was the last of their compassion they'd buried six feet underground. Rest in peace.

Neil gave me a withering smile. "Shouldn't you be going to 'special school'? You know, for kids who have missing limbs?"

"No," I answered, trying for my best poker face.

"Well, in that case," he said, "shouldn't they at least send you back a grade? You've been gone forever."

I shrugged coolly. "Maybe they will." Then I paused, shooting him a questioning look. "Hey—does that mean we'll be in the same class?"

He didn't get the joke right away. And by the time he did, I was already walking down the hallway. I let him stare.

But he was the minority—and anyone else who agreed with him kept their mouth shut. Still, I didn't get so many rude looks as I did questions.

Everybody wanted to know: "How did it happen?"

And that was where the good part came in—I could answer every one of them differently. Because we had recently moved schools, most of the kids didn't know me. And I took the opportunity to have a little fun.

The first story went something like this:

"Well, I was on this ski trip, right? We vacation to the Swiss Alps every winter and it's awesome. Except for this past time. Clearly, it wasn't awesome. One minute I was flying down the face of this frickin' crazy slope, and the next minute? Blood *everywhere*."

They had no way of knowing that I was lying. Rudy wasn't the type to give out details, and he was the only one who *knew* the details. It was actually kind of funny how many kids bought the story.

I kept getting that question all day.

"How did it happen?"

Sometimes I would just look at them and muster up all the drama I possibly could and say, "Are you *sure* you want to know? It's kind of a gross story."

That was how I spent most of my first day—thinking up new gruesome tales to tell my classmates.

Next, it was a shark attack.

Then a car accident.

Then a zip line that snapped at the wrong moment.

Then I was helping my pretend lumberjack uncle chop down trees in a forest, and this massive oak had crushed my legs. (That one got the most cringes, surprisingly. My personal favorite was the shark attack.)

Rudy caught me red-handed in the library during study hall. I was right in the middle of explaining to a group of girls how I was viciously attacked by a lion while on safari with my grandmother (who has actually been dead for five years, God rest her soul) and had barely made it out alive, when—

"Weston, I have to talk to you," Rudy said, with that grown-up look on his face. He grabbed my arm and pulled me away.

I sighed, retrieved my books, and left the wide-eyed girls in the library, trying to figure out whether or not I was telling them the truth.

Once Rudy had dragged me into the hallway, he said, "What the heck are you doing, man? Telling everyone a different story about how you lost your legs?"

I shrugged. "Why not?"

"Because that's bullshit. You weren't eaten by a lion."

"Yeah, well—this school is full of bullshit." I laughed. "At least mine is interesting bullshit."

Rudy shook his head and sighed. I followed him down the hallway to the boys' bathroom.

"What were you talking to Clara about?" he asked.

I knew he was referencing our conversation in the locker hall; Clara hadn't spoken to me since. I blew out a sigh and leaned against the graffiti-tagged wall.

He of all people deserves to know.

"I dumped her."

Rudy stared at me for a long moment, surprise evident on his face.

A toilet flushed, rudely interrupting our conversation, and a boy exited one of the stalls. He threw a confused glance at me and Rudy, then left the bathroom. We were alone.

That was when Rudy finally replied, with an even more serious look on his face, "Why did you do that?"

"Because I had to."

"No, you didn't."

I leveled my gaze at him. "Yes, I did."

"You're still the same person, Wes."

"Yeah!" I was surprised by the way my voice rose. And the way my throat tightened. "Yeah, I'm the same." I took a step toward him. "And can you even *imagine* how hard that is? To stay the same, when..." The words caught in my throat. I looked down. "When everything is different."

Stupid emotions, always coming at the wrong moment. I clenched my jaw, fighting to control myself. I refused to break down at school. Anywhere else, but not at school.

There was a long silence. I kept my gaze on the floor.

Finally, Rudy said, "No."

I looked up.

"No, I can't imagine what it's like to be you. I couldn't even imagine it before... this." He laughed a little—that sad, grown-up laughter that isn't really laughter at all. "Why do you think I always fought you, Weston?"

The question seemed irrelevant. I shook my head. "I don't know... You have self-harm issues?"

He grinned. "No. Fighting was an education. Every time you won, I thought, 'Someday... I'm gonna win. I'm gonna beat him.'"

"You did," I pointed out. "Several times."

"And when I did, I thought..." Rudy nodded a little, looking me right in the eyes. "'This is what it must feel like. To be Weston.'"

The words hit me hard, one by one.

"I've always admired you, man. I still do. Even more so. Because this..." Rudy shook his head, taking a deep breath. "This takes guts. Guts of fricking steel."

Now my throat hurt more. Even if I could've spoken, I don't know what I would have said to him. But I didn't need to say anything. Because that was when he threw his arms around me and hugged me. And I hugged him back.

And yeah, I was glad we were the only ones in the bathroom.

I remember thinking:

Guts of fricking steel. Ha. I'm crying.

TESSA

DAY 52

"WHAT'S YOUR FAVORITE MOVIE?" WESTON ASKS ON Tuesday.

The question pulls me out of my thoughts, where the chaos of poetry is swimming incoherently. My muse is taking its time today, and Weston can't let much silence pass before he feels the need to talk about something.

And right now, it's movies.

"Um, *The Sound of Music*," I reply. "Definitely."

"Hmm," Weston says. "Never seen it."

"You've never seen *The Sound of Music*?"

"Nope."

I'm appalled. He's a typical uncultured teenage boy.

"Aren't you going to ask me what my favorite movie is?"

I laugh and roll my eyes. "What's your favorite movie."

"*The Princess Bride*," he says. "And I don't care what people think of me because of it."

"Never seen it," I reply, in a terrible imitation of his voice.

He comes right back with an even worse imitation of mine. "You've never seen *The Princess Bride*?"

I throw one of my pillows across the room in the general direction of his voice. I hear him catch it and laugh.

"I thought it was required for all homeschoolers to watch that movie at least once."

"Not this homeschooler. But I'd like to see it sometime."

"We'll watch it," Weston says, "when you get your vision back. It's the kind of movie you have to *see*."

"As opposed to movies you don't have to see."

The pillow hits my legs. I gasp, startled. "You're supposed to tell me when you do stuff like that!"

"Sorry," Weston murmurs. I hear him get up and take the pillow off my bed. "I'm going to throw it at you again. Is that okay?"

I grin, shutting my eyes. "That kind of defeats the purpose, but go ahead."

He throws the pillow at me again. This time it lands in my lap.

"You've probably seen *The Sound of Music* a million times, right?"

I nod hesitantly. "Yes…"

"Okay, cool. Let's watch that."

"Right now?"

He laughs. "Why not?" I hear my laptop shut and the door open.

"Because—"

I stop myself before I can think of a good reason. There's no point in arguing with Weston. Although his reckless spontaneity disturbs me on a number of levels.

I climb off my bed and follow him downstairs. The house is quieter than usual because my grandparents are out, visiting a sick church member in the hospital. We have the living room all to ourselves.

But Weston is in the kitchen, opening the cabinets. He always seems in search of food. Again, typical teenage boy.

"You want popcorn?" he asks me.

I raise an eyebrow, stopping in the doorway of the kitchen. "What time is it?"

"How does that have anything to do with popcorn?"

There's no point in arguing with Weston.

I move into the living room and sit on the couch, and Weston figures out how to turn on the TV and find the library of movies without much help. I feel somewhat guilty, doing nothing to help while he makes the popcorn and starts the movie. But he orders me to just "sit there and not do anything," so I comply.

"Do you know how blind people watch movies?" Weston says, handing me a giant bowl of warm, buttery popcorn.

"Not… really."

"With commentaries. Or narration. Or whatever." He takes a seat next to me on the couch, and I suddenly become hyperaware of his presence, of the warmth of his arm, which is nearly touching mine.

I stuff my face with popcorn and try to ignore the tingly sensations in my hands.

"So," Weston says, "she's running up a hill—it looks like the Swiss Alps—and I think she's going to start singing in a second."

"It's Austria," I correct. "And yes. This is a musical."

"Oh no."

I roll my eyes. "You don't have to narrate the whole thing. I've seen it a million times."

But he narrates it anyway. The whole thing. And it's the best commentary I could ask for, especially since he's never seen it before. I get to hear all the first reactions.

Right from the start he says, "The girl is going to marry Captain, right?"

"Captain isn't his *name.*"

"Whatever."

"And 'the girl' is Maria."

"Whatever. Does she marry him?"

"You'll have to wait and see."

We eat the bowl of popcorn and I listen to the movie and Weston's narration. He keeps trying to predict the first kiss scene.

"They're dancing in the courtyard," he says, even though I already knew what part this is by the music. "Oh, now the blonde chick is watching them. She's gonna be jealous as all hell. They're definitely going to kiss… Wait, nope. Guess not."

Finally, the actual kiss scene happens, and Weston calls it right away.

"The blonde chick is gone, and now they're chilling in the moonlight by the gazebo. Now she's walking into the gazebo… and now he's following her… Okay—EW, THEY'RE KISSING DON'T LOOK!"

Weston covers my eyes. I laugh and throw a handful of popcorn at him.

It feels good to joke about it.

It actually feels *good.*

This stubborn, kind, impertinent, obnoxiously optimistic boy is doing something to me.

And it feels good.

WESTON

3 YEARS AND 2 MONTHS BEFORE TESSA

CLARA HERNANDEZ REFUSED TO BREAK UP WITH ME.
And it was starting to get on my nerves.

I knew that she was only doing it because of the way it would make her look and feel—to dump me after everything I'd been through. But she wasn't even dumping me, and we weren't even dating. We were thirteen years old, for crying out loud. I had to find a way to fix this, and the solution was staring me in the face.

Rudy Kaufmann.

He had been wanting to talk to Clara forever, and now was the perfect opportunity.

Well, almost perfect. It would take a little convincing on my part.

So I cornered Rudy in the locker hall one day and decided to come right out and say it.

"I have a problem."

"Yeah?" Rudy said, glancing up from his algebra notebook, which looked like a more organized version of mine. "What is it?"

The exchange was pretty ironic, now that I think about it.

"I have a problem," says a boy with no legs.

"Yeah?" his friend replies. "What is it?"

"Clara's not going to break up with me unless she has someone

174

else to go out with."

Rudy frowned at his math notes. "What does that have to do with me?"

I gave him a look, like, *Come on.*

All of a sudden, it clicked. His notebook swung shut. "Holy crap. You set this whole thing up, didn't you?"

"Yep. The whole thing, way back to the fence. I hurt myself so that I'd have to lose my legs so that I'd have a legitimate reason to dump Clara so that you guys can be together."

Rudy just rolled his eyes.

"And everything has been going according to plan," I said, crossing my arms over my chest. "So don't mess it all up now."

He wanted to—I could tell. He wanted to resist the whole thing and deny his obvious crush on Clara Hernandez. But he couldn't do anything except laugh and shake his head. He knew I was the best friend he could ever ask for.

"Now ask her out." I gave him a smack on the arm as I walked away. "Besides, I don't have time for girls. I'm too busy trying to get my grades up."

I'd missed a lot of school, and catching up was exhausting, both mentally and physically. I stayed up late every night, studying for the tests they were going to be giving me. In some ways, it was harder than punching the heavy bag or running at the track every day. But I pushed myself just as hard for school. The last thing I wanted to do was take eighth grade all over again.

So I studied, every spare moment I got. Rudy helped me whenever I couldn't wrap my head around something—usually math or geometry. He said that I was ready long before I ever felt ready.

And, apparently, he was right.

Because I passed all the tests.

It was a victorious moment, sure. But there was one test they didn't give me—*wouldn't* give me—because of my "extenuating circumstances."

A physical fitness test.

There was some kind of complication with a note from my doctor and my therapist and probably my mother, too. I needed to get a permit to get a permit to be permitted to join gym class again. It felt like the government—not some small-town junior high school nobody ever heard of.

It was stupid.

All they needed to do was send Mr. Daniels out to the track and let him watch me. I could sprint faster than some of the kids on the track team. I could run the PACER test with zero form breaks. I could do push-ups, sit-ups, anything they wanted me to do. But when I asked the assistant principal, she said, "That's outside of school policy."

What she should have said is, "We've already exempted you and now we're too lazy to push some papers around."

That left me with only one option—talk to my PE teacher myself. Man to man, or something like that. But it didn't help that the first words out of his mouth were, "Weston, hello. Last time I saw you, they were loading you into an ambulance."

I grinned and shut his office door behind me. "Yeah, well… I lived."

"So I see," Mr. Daniels said, gesturing toward the chair on the other side of his desk. As I sat down, he added, "I think I know why you're here."

I raised an eyebrow. "You do? Awesome. So we can skip the bull-shit, then."

He looked a little surprised, but he didn't say anything. So I continued. "I'd like you to give me a physical fitness test."

"Ah." Mr. Daniels glanced down at his desk, that same uncomfortable look on his face that all the other teachers wore. "Well, that might be difficult—"

"How?" I interrupted, already annoyed. "It won't be difficult for me."

Mr. Daniels only sighed and folded his hands like a judge passing sentence. "I'm afraid I can't just... conduct a test."

"Well, what do you need? A note from my doctor? My parents?"

"There would be some form of permission slip involved, yes," he said. "You should speak to the assistant principal—"

"I already did. And she told me that it's outside of school policy."

Mr. Daniels took a large fatigued breath—as if he didn't know what to say to me.

So I kept talking.

"Look, Mr. Daniels. I've been training really hard for this. I'm strong, and I'm a good runner. I know I could pass the test. If you could just work something out with the school board, I promise I won't let you down."

My PE teacher looked at me for a long moment—still uncomfortable. "I don't want to let *you* down, Weston," he said. "But I'm afraid the answer is going to be no."

"So you're telling me you can't do *anything*."

"I'm not... saying that, exactly."

For a moment, I just sat there and stared at him. He acted like his hands were tied, but I knew they weren't. There's always something you can do.

He just didn't want to. And that pissed me off.

So I stood up and said, "You know what? Forget it."

He didn't try to stop me. He just sat there and watched as I left

177

his office.

School was over for the day, and the halls were emptying out. Rudy was probably waiting around for me somewhere—but I took a detour before I tracked him down.

A detour through the gym.

I loved just being in there—the slick floors, the familiar scent of rubber and wood polish, the basketball hoops, the bleachers stacked up at one side of the room, the rock-climbing wall that goes all the way up to the ceiling.

That was where I stopped: at the rock-climbing wall. I looked up at it, thinking about all the stupid, flowery words Mr. Daniels had used back there. Whatever happened to common sense?

To hell with extenuating circumstances.

I dropped my backpack on the floor and leaned against the wall, reaching down to take off my prostheses. I started with the left leg, then grabbed onto one of the holds while removing the right.

Was it crazy to climb up this wall, using arm strength alone, with no harness and no safety net underneath me?

Yeah. But I was used to crazy.

And I had to burn off some energy. Or else I might've accidentally punched someone in the face.

I had already scaled halfway up the wall when I heard the door to the gymnasium swing open. I couldn't turn around and see who it was, but I figured it must have been Rudy. Nobody else obsessively kept tabs on me except for my mom. And nobody else gave me a tongue-lashing for my reckless stunts, like rock climbing without legs. But I spoke up before he could.

"Don't waste your breath, Kaufmann! I'm not trying to kill myself. I'm just so angry at them—these stupid teachers." I latched onto another handhold, pulling myself up higher. "They think they know what's best for me? They think they're doing their job? Following the rules?" I let go of a cynical laugh. "Well, they're not! They suck at their jobs! You see that sign over there on the wall? Sure you see it—we've all seen it. 'You never know how strong you are until being strong is the only choice you have.' I've pretty much lived up to that, don't you think, Rudy? How the heck am I supposed to make them see that I have what it takes? I might look different from everybody else, but I'm just as capable. I know about endurance; I know about hard work; I know about getting up at the crack of dawn and training until I'm exhausted. How can they think I'm not ready for this?" I was close to the top by that point—and I was out of breath. "Actually, never mind," I said, finishing my speech, "I know why. Because they *suck*."

I paused, hanging on tight to the holds on the wall. I had reached the ceiling. My arms were burning and my lungs were thirsty for air, but I felt amazing. I felt alive.

Then the victorious moment ended, as the person on the ground cleared his throat.

And it wasn't Rudy. It was Mr. Daniels.

My eyes widened.

I carefully glanced over my shoulder, down at the place where he stood next to my backpack and my prosthetic legs. His arms were crossed and he was staring up at me with a puzzled (but impressed) look on his face.

"If you're ready to climb back down here," he said, "we can talk about this like civilized people."

I turned back to press my forehead against the wall and catch my breath. I remember thinking: *Haha. Shit. I just told my teacher that he sucks.*

"Uh, sure, Mr. Daniels. I'll be right down."

He figured out a way to let me take the physical fitness test. That whole rock-climbing episode was kind of like the pretest. It convinced Mr. Daniels to take me seriously.

Unlike the academic tests, I didn't have to prepare myself for this one—I'd already spent the past months preparing. And unlike the academic tests, I passed the PFT with flying colors. Mr. Daniels was the examiner, and I was the only student being tested.

He didn't catch one form break—*not one.*

I shook his hand and said, "Thank you, sir," and that was all. We didn't discuss what I'd vented in the gym, or how climbing the rock wall without supervision or safety measures was *"outside of school policy."* We had reached some level of common sense.

And I was back on track—literally.

"How did you do it?" Rudy asked me as we warmed up for sprints one day. He was stretching his shoulders and I was sitting on the bleachers in the sun, changing into my running blades.

"Piece of cake," I said. "Nobody on this school board can say no to my irresistible charm."

Rudy laughed. "Yeah, sure."

"Like those girls over there." I nodded toward a cluster of eighth graders who were waiting for direction from their coach. Most of them were blonde and most of them were staring at me.

"Yeah, they're totally checking you out," Rudy said with a knowing smile.

"Should I show them my awesome six-pack?"

"No."

"You're probably right." I stood, walked over to the track, and began to pace the starting line. "Wouldn't want them all hitting on me."

Rudy just shook his head.

TESSA

DAY 53

I NEED TO KNOW WHAT HE LOOKS LIKE. IT'S TORTURE, not being able to see him. I've been wondering ever since the first day he came to my house.

But on day fifty-three, for whatever reason, the desire to see him hits me full force.

I am sitting at the kitchen table, listening to Grandma cook supper, and playing with the zipper on my hoodie. I zip it up, then zip it down. It's chilly tonight. That's all I know. It feels like the sun has gone down, but I have no idea.

"Something on your mind?" Grandma asks. She's making pasta, and I can hear the water beginning to boil.

I shake my head and immediately feel guilty—because *no* is a bold-faced lie. I do have something on my mind. I have a lot on my mind.

But mostly one thing.

Weston.

I want to know what his face looks like. What his smile looks like. I want to know what color his eyes are. I want to know if he has freckles like I do. I want to know everything about him.

And I want to know so badly, I don't care what Grandma thinks anymore.

My zipper goes up. My zipper goes down. At last, I spill. "Can I ask you a question, Grandma?"

"Of course," she says.

I'm already blushing and I haven't even said the worst part yet. "I just... I'm really curious."

"Mm-hmm..."

"What does Weston look like?"

For the first time in fifty-three days, I'm glad that I can't see her face—because I'm fairly certain her expression is equal parts amused and teasing. I can imagine she has that glint in her eyes, the look she gives me when she thinks I'm interested in a boy.

But I'm not. Not like that.

I just want to know what he looks like.

"Well," Grandma begins, "he's quite a good-looking boy."

My stomach flutters for no reason at all. "Really?"

I don't know why this piece of information changes anything. Lots of boys are good-looking. I've even talked to some of them before. But never has a "good-looking boy" spent so much time with me, transcribed poetry for me, made waffles for me, watched *The Sound of Music* with me.

Maybe I'm getting butterflies because I feel like I'm not all that pretty. Weston has seen me at my worst—without makeup, without dignity, tears streaming down my face. Yet I haven't had the liberty of seeing him at all.

"Describe him," I say as Grandma pours the pasta into the boiling water. I keep playing with my zipper.

"He has blond hair," Grandma says. "And blue eyes. But not like yours—more of a grayish blue. He's tall—but not very tall—and sun-tanned, and he's always smiling."

I begin to construct an image in my mind's eye.

Blond hair.

Gray-blue eyes.

Tall, but not very tall.

Suntanned.

Always smiling.

The description seems to match his personality. I feel the corners of my lips bend toward a grin when I think about him. I can almost see him in my mind. I can almost see his unfaltering smile.

But I refocus before Grandma catches me thinking about it.

"If he's so good-looking," I say, "why doesn't he have a girlfriend?"

Grandma hesitates for a minute before replying. "Perhaps he does."

I feel a twinge of envy—small and prickling—in my gut when I consider the possibility. Weston can't have a girlfriend. She wouldn't spare him to come over here all the time, and she would dump him if she knew he was seeing another girl—regardless of how platonic our relationship is.

But is it?

I didn't think I liked Weston, and my brain still insists that I don't. But my body suggests otherwise. My heart flutters in my chest like a firefly trapped in a mason jar. My cheeks warm with a blood rush when I talk about him. And my hands still do that tingling thing, like they did when he was sitting next to me on the couch.

I didn't think I liked Weston, but now I'm not so sure.

I go to bed thinking about him. I paint the mental picture all over again, with Grandma's descriptions. I breathe in the aroma of the flowers in my room—fresh flowers that he still brings me every week. I lie in the dark and try to catch the butterflies of sleep—simultaneously trying to calm the ones in my stomach.

I want to see him.

I just want to see him.

Weston is everything
And all at once.
Weston is gentle
And harsh.

Weston can be blindingly bright
But then he can also be
Delicately soft.

Weston is a paradox.

Around and around
Weston is everything

Weston makes me feel like
I am beautiful
Only because without him
I am invisible
grayscale
nothing

Weston is my redemption.

Hearing

WESTON

3 YEARS BEFORE TESSA

WHEN I CAME HOME FROM SCHOOL ONE DAY, I FOUND it sitting on my bed. I froze in the doorway, my backpack hanging from my arm, and I stared at it, as if it were a person—an intruder hanging out in my room.

It was a small yellow ukulele.

But I didn't know that at the time. I had no idea what it was— some kind of miniature guitar? I'd never played an instrument in my life until I picked up the ukulele that day. I dropped my backpack on the floor and sat on my bed and took the tiny instrument in my hands.

It had four strings and I had no clue what notes they were. High, lower, even lower, and then another high one. I ran one finger across the strings, listening to the sound they made. It didn't sound like music, but it didn't sound awful, either.

That was when Mom appeared in the doorway to my bedroom. She had a smile on her face, almost as bright as the sunlight pouring through the window.

"What is this?" I asked, indicating the instrument in my hands.

"It's a ukulele," Mom said.

"Did you leave it here?"

She nodded.

"For me?"

She kept nodding.

"Why?"

"Because," Mom began, stepping inside the room and coming over to rest a hand on my shoulder, "it reminds me of you."

I glanced down at the ukulele and said, "Small, yellow, and hopelessly soprano? Mm, yeah. I can see the similarities."

Mom laughed and ruffled my hair. "No, because it makes me happy every time I look at it."

Just when I thought my life couldn't possibly get any more backward, it did.

I learned how to play the ukulele.

Well, I didn't really *learn*. I just messed around with it until it sounded pretty good. Music isn't rocket science (luckily for me), and it just takes some experimenting to get off the ground. I started writing songs—short, nothing-special ones. Some of them had lyrics, but I never sang for anyone (not even my own mother, much to her disappointment).

The ukulele never left my room. I tried to make sure no one found out that I played it in my free time—although Rudy discovered my dark secret eventually.

I was glad that Mom had given it to me.

Because I knew that someday it would leave my room.

Someday I would take it somewhere and play it for someone else.

And I had no idea who or when or how or why that would be.

But the unknown is something to look forward to.

TESSA

DAY 58

I FIGURE OUT HOW TO CALL WESTON ON THE PHONE.
Grandma enters his number into my contacts list and Siri quickly
learns the command "Call Weston." He always picks up my calls, no
matter what time of day it is.

I get into a habit of calling him at night, when I'm lying awake in
bed and inspiration for a poem strikes me out of nowhere. I can't
write it down, so I call Weston and ask him to write it down for me.
But our conversations don't end with the dictation. We start talking
and then we don't stop talking until late into the night. It's an interesting thing, not being able to glance at the clock every few minutes—it's freeing. You sleep when you're tired. You wake up when
you're rested. You watch movies and eat popcorn in the middle of
the day.

On the night of day fifty-eight, Weston says to me, "Can I come
over tomorrow morning?"

"Sure," I reply, without even pausing to consider it.

"Good. Because I have a surprise for you."

I feel myself smile. "Oh? What is it?"

"A surprise."

"So was the ad my grandparents almost published in your father's

191

newspaper. And I didn't take very kindly to that surprise."

Weston laughs—softly, because his family is probably asleep. I have no idea how late it is, but I can smell the fragrance of midnight in the air.

"Well, that newspaper ad made a lot of good stuff happen, didn't it?" Weston says.

I shut my eyes, relenting. "I suppose so."

"She *supposes* so."

"Fine," I groan, hoping he can't hear that I'm actually grinning from ear to ear. "It made a lot of good stuff happen."

"And more good stuff is to come, Tessa Dickinson," he whispers. "Tomorrow."

TESSA

DAY 59

ON THE MORNING OF DAY FIFTY-NINE, I PREPARE MYSELF for a good surprise.

I'm still not sure if you're supposed to prepare yourself for a surprise, but it was Weston who gave away the hint, and I'm glad he did. Because I have something to look forward to.

I am wearing a sundress, and Grandma tells me it's yellow.

While waiting for him to show up, I attempt to tidy my room. I make my bed, arrange the pillows as best I can, straighten anything on the desk that may have fallen out of perfect alignment, and, finally, I line up the mason jars of flowers on my dresser.

There are seven of them at the moment—all containing different flowers. And I know them each by smell. Daisies, roses, lilies, chamomile, hydrangeas, violets, and zinnias.

"Which one's your favorite?"

I gasp as my heart jumps into my throat. "Weston! I didn't even hear you come in the house."

"Really? I was talking to your grandmother downstairs."

I let out a sigh, feeling my cheeks flush. "Well, I didn't... hear you."

"So you said."

My jaw accidentally clenches. I put my hands on my hips. "Where's my surprise? Please don't say it was just you scaring me for no reason."

He laughs and walks past me, moving across the room. He smells good; like fresh air. I hear the chair slide out from its place under my desk. "No, that wasn't the surprise. Come sit down."

With a puzzled frown on my face, I return to my neatly made bed and take a seat, cross-legged.

"You ready?" Weston asks.

I hold out my hands. "Mm-hmm."

But he doesn't actually give me a tangible thing. Instead, he gives me a sound—music. A chord from a melodious stringed instrument. Not a guitar, but similar.

I feel a smile light across my face. My hands drop into my lap. "What *is* that?"

"Ukulele," Weston says. He continues playing, going through four different chords and then repeating them. I wish I knew how to describe how beautiful it sounds—like audible sunlight, bright and happy and intricately simple.

He stops, and I hear the soft thud of his hand against wood, muting the strings.

I'm still smiling. "You never told me you're a musician."

"I'm not," Weston says. "Not really. It's easy. Here, try it."

"Oh, no, I couldn't—"

He sits next to me on the bed. I feel the mattress shift slightly and my heart rate speeds up for no reason at all.

"I'm gonna take your hands," Weston says softly. "Is that okay?"

I swallow. I nod.

He takes my right hand first, guiding it over the smooth, painted surface of the ukulele now in my lap. Then he lifts my left hand to rest it on the neck of the instrument.

"Now I'm going to position your fingers over the strings..."

I nod again. My voice has deserted me.

"This one is the easiest. C chord."

His hands are gentle and warm, bringing my thumb to the back and my index finger to the front, resting against the bottom string.

"Now press on this string," he instructs, voice barely above a whisper, "and with your right hand, strum down."

He guides me through it the first time, running my fingertips down the strings, then up the strings, then down, up, down, up, down. I catch the rhythm of it, and I'm able to do it by myself. It doesn't sound half as lovely as when Weston was playing it, but it doesn't sound terrible, either.

"Good job," Weston says. "Now G chord. This one is a little more complicated."

He repositions my fingers over the strings, pressing down on three and staggering them a little. He tells me to strum again, and I do. Down... up-down, up-down... up-down, up-down...

I catch myself smiling. What a wondrous thing it is to play a ukulele when I've never even *seen* a ukulele in real life before. What a wondrous thing it is to create something beautiful without sight.

They say that sound is the most powerful sense to those who are blind. I have discovered that to be true, over the past fifty-nine days. But what I haven't discovered is all the beautiful sounds. The sounds that I've ignored because I was too busy thinking about what they *looked* like instead of simply *listening*.

I'm listening now.

And I want to hear more.

As if reading my thoughts, Weston says, "My ukulele is just the tip of the iceberg, Tessa. There's a whole world of sound out there."

"Out there?" I ask, finally pulling my voice out of hiding.

"Outside."

The word trembles inside my chest, nervous—like a fledgling bird unsure of how to fly.

I am the fledgling bird, unsure of how to reply.

But the wind tastes wild and sweet, up here in the trees.

I want to know what will happen if I

  just

   let

    go.

I want to know what will happen if I fly.

"Show me," I whisper.

Weston is speechless, for once in his life. And so he should be, after I made a point of saying that I didn't want to go outside, that I resented the very idea of going outside.

And now I actually *want* to go outside.

"But I have one condition," I add quickly before he can reply. "I don't want to use my cane."

"What do you want to use, then?"

I reach out and find his hand. It is warm and strong and much bigger than mine, and I can't believe *I'm holding his hand.*

"This," I say.

I don't even need to see him.

I can tell.

He's smiling.

After Grandma agrees to me going out, she gives Weston a little crash course in how to properly guide me—by lightly tapping the back of his hand against mine to let me know where he is, then walking one step ahead of me while I hold onto his elbow. She warns us to be careful when taking stairs and crossing streets. Weston listens attentively to all the instruction and says, "Yes, ma'am," again and again until, at last, we break free from the safety of the house.

Somehow, free-falling out of the sky isn't as terrifying as I thought.

I don't need to think; I don't need to worry.

All I need to do is listen.

Weston takes me on a whirlwind tour of the place I thought I knew so well.

First, he takes me to the riverbank, a short distance from my neighborhood. It's mostly forest, and I remember being here once or twice before, when I was small. Weston guides me through the scattering of trees and asks me, "What do you hear?"

"Birds singing," I answer, my senses somehow electrified by the fresh air in my lungs. "And water... The river. I hear wind in the trees. Leaves dancing."

"Yes!" He laughs. "Leaves dancing."

At this point, I break the rules a little—I let my hand slide down Weston's arm and interlace my fingers with his. He's taller than me, so it's more convenient to hold his hand rather than his elbow (and even better, because I really enjoy holding his hand).

Before I know it, there's sidewalk under my feet, scattered with soft interruptions of grass. Weston pauses and tells me whenever I have to step up or down at a curb.

He says, "What do you hear?"

"Kids laughing somewhere. A lawn mower. Cicadas."

"Anything else?" he asks.

I listen again. "Songbirds."

Before long, we reach the center of town. I always thought it was a sleepy sort of place, where not much happens. But today, it seems alive like never before. A cacophony of noise surrounds me, buzzing and bright.

"What do you hear?" Weston asks me again.

"Cars. Voices. A radio playing rock music somewhere. More cicadas."

He never lets go of my hand. He guides me ever onward, and I think we must have walked a mile or two by this point—but I don't care about the prickles in my feet or the knot in my lungs. I'm breathing hard, and I'm laughing, and I'm listening.

I'm *hearing*.

Finally, Weston helps me up a short flight of stairs and through a door.

"Where are we?" I wonder out loud, but he doesn't reply. He just keeps walking, and I follow.

Distantly, I hear music. Orchestral music. But it's not distant at all—it's just muted. It's nearby, behind a door.

And Weston opens the door, guiding me through.

Music floods over me like a tidal wave—showering chills across my skin. Violins and flutes and cellos and bells and one steadily pounding drum, like the heart of a great whale. I feel myself smile in awe and astonishment. We're in the concert hall during orchestra practice—and the whole room swells with music. It is dizzying and overwhelming, like spinning through space, surrounded by stars.

Weston takes both my hands in his and laughs over the music. "What do you hear?"

This time, I don't know how to describe it.

I hear my heart exploding.

Weston holds on tight to my hands and spins me around. The beautiful chaos is all around me, raining down. It is disorienting, yes—but in the best possible way.

I know nothing. I feel everything.

My dress swirls around my knees and I laugh and I hear Weston laughing, too.

I am drowning again.

But this time I don't need help.

I don't need a rescue.

Because I am drowning in perfect beauty.

I am drowning in reckless joy.

I've fallen out of the tree.

And now,

I fly.

WESTON

JULY 28

ON FRIDAY, I BREAK MY STREAK OF NEVER LETTING
anyone hear me sing.

But first, I make a habit of bringing my ukulele to Tessa's house.
And I wonder what I must look like, walking to 52 West Elm Street
with a yellow ukulele slung over my shoulder like some kind of
weapon. Tessa seems to like the music, even though it's nothing
special and has no lyrics. She lies on her bed and listens with her eyes
shut and plays with the lava of words inside her volcano. She says the
music helps her think.

So I play my yellow ukulele and I watch her think.

The best part is that she doesn't know I'm staring at her.

The worst part is that I really enjoy staring at her.

I feel like I'm losing balance, and the sensation is familiar. But
this time, it's completely different. My stomach hurts, my heart beats
faster, and I find it more and more difficult to talk.

It can only mean one thing.

I have a crush on Tessa Dickinson.

But I can't. I can't have a crush on her. I can't like her.

She doesn't like me back. And her sight is going to return soon.
And she isn't going to need me anymore.

She isn't going to see me.

Ever.

I won't allow myself to have a crush on her.

For the first few hours after my resolution, everything is fine. I go for a run at sunset—listening to loud rock music and looping around my neighborhood at least five times, until my quads are burning and I can't breathe. Then I busy myself with chores, helping Mom and Dad. For the first few hours, everything is fine.

But then I go on her blog and look at the picture on her "About" page. I look at her freckled face, at her smile—which is brighter than the yellow flowers in the background and way prettier.

That's when the feelings come back all over again, regardless of how tired I am.

Dizzying, falling, aching—

God, it hurts. Not like it hurts to blast the heavy bag or do a hundred push-ups.

This is a different kind of pain.

It's no use. I've passed the point of no return.

I have a crush on Tessa Dickinson.

I ditch the resolution to not think about her, since that is clearly not helping—instead, I go back to the homepage of her blog and scroll down, reading the words she's dictated to me over the past month. There's one poem that sounds like a song. I read it again and again, trying to hear the melody that belongs behind the words.

Sunlight is exuberant.
Thunderstorms are passionate.
Two extremes, and so much better
than nothing at all.

Cloudy skies are like nothing at all.
Apathetic.
Numb.
The feeling you feel when you have
no
idea
what
you
feel.

When everything has gone so wrong,
it no longer feels wrong.
There suddenly is no right or wrong.
There's just emptiness.

It would be better for the clouds to cry,
or better for the sun to shine.
But curse this bearing wall
where the sky is
nothing
at
all.

That's it.

I grab my ukulele from its usual spot by my desk, checking to make sure the strings are in tune. I start by playing a few chords: C, then C major 7. Then again. Then again. Then an F chord. It starts to sound like an actual song. I glance back at my phone screen to read the poem under my breath, putting the words to the music.

"Sunlight is exuberant… Thunderstorms are passionate… Two extremes, and so much better… than nothing at all."

Slowly, it all weaves together. And when morning comes, the song is complete. Well, kind of. It's a really short song because it's a really short poem. I can't improve upon Tessa's words or even add to them. All I can do is move them around until they work with the music.

And on Friday, when I show up at her house, I decide to sing it for her.

It's a stupid decision, really. I don't know why I go through with it. Maybe I just like to torture myself.

Or maybe I just like to see her smile.

I don't tell her what I'm going to play. She just sits on her bed and waits for the music. At least there's one consolation—she can't look at me as I sing. If she could, I'd never be able to do it.

I start strumming the ukulele, going through one set of chords. C, C major 7, F.

Then I add the lyrics.

"Sunlight is exuberant… Thunderstorms are passionate… Two extremes, and so much better… than nothing at all."

Tessa gets it. She recognizes it.

A smile blossoms over her face—just like in the picture on her blog. *Better* than the picture, because it's real life, and I'm the one who made her smile.

I think it's the most beautiful thing I've ever seen.

But I don't stop. I keep playing and singing.

"Cloudy skies are like… Nothing at all… Apathetic and numb… That feeling you have… When you have no idea… what you… feel. When everything has gone so wrong… it no longer feels wrong. There's suddenly no right or wrong. There's just emptiness."

I have to stop looking at her. If I keep looking at her, I'm going to mess up the song. It's surprisingly difficult to pull my gaze away.

"It'd be better for the clouds to cry… Or better for the sun to shine… But curse this bearing wall… where the sky… is nothing at all… At all… And I'm nothing at all."

That's all I have. And hell, singing is exhausting. My heart is beating harder than I'd like to admit, and my palms are damp with sweat.

I mute the strings with my right hand and finally look at Tessa again.

She's still smiling. "That's my poem."

I grin. "Yeah. I plagiarized you."

"It's beautiful."

It's really not. But I'm glad she thinks so. I'm glad she's smiling. There was a time, when I first met her, that I wondered if Tessa would ever smile. She seemed so angry and cynical. But now she's better. She's starting to heal.

"Weston?"

I refocus, but not on her—because I've already been staring at her this whole time.

I can't help myself.

"Yeah?" I say.

She's smiling again.

And it's definitely the most beautiful thing I've ever seen.

"Can you play it again?"

WESTON

JULY 30

TESSA IS LYING ON HER BED WITH HER ARMS FOLDED over her stomach, and she's wearing a pink dress, which somehow makes her even prettier. "I wish I could see everything we're doing."

Her voice is different than it usually is. Not miserable and longing, but looking for an idea. The way she sounds when she's in the middle of writing a poem and she doesn't have the whole thing yet.

I listen, because I know there's more.

"Like... I know I'm smelling things and tasting things and hearing things... but I also want to remember this. And you know how when you remember things, you remember how they *looked?*"

"Yeah," I say, thinking about it for the first time.

"Well, that's what I want." Tessa frowns at the ceiling. "Visual memories."

I force myself to take my eyes off her and actually think about what she's saying.

Visual memories.

Like pictures.

"I have an idea," I say, getting up from the desk. "I'm gonna take your hand. Is that okay?"

Tessa looks a little puzzled. "Yes…"

It's really just an excuse to touch her. She could get off the bed by herself. But it's more fun to grab her hand and pull her to her feet.

"Now we're gonna go to Target. Is that okay?"

Her eyebrows scrunch together. "Target?"

Mrs. Dickinson allows it only because the mall is within walking distance. It's not really a *mall*, just a Target and a Barnes & Noble and a few other stores squished into the same parking lot. And the walk isn't half as far as our little tour around town last week. And I get to hold Tessa's hand the whole time. So that's a plus.

"What are we doing here?" Tessa asks for the millionth time when we finally enter the store.

"You'll see," I tell her, grabbing a shopping cart despite the fact that I'm only looking for one item. "Get on."

"On what?"

I guide her to the end of the shopping cart and place her hands on the edge. She only laughs, as if it's a joke.

"That's not, like… legal."

"Aw, come on. You never have fun."

Tessa's eyebrows rise. "Excuse me? I do a lot of fun things… besides riding shopping carts like a reckless four-year-old."

"What could be more fun than riding a shopping cart like a reckless four-year-old?"

She sighs.

"Fighting?" I offer.

She wrinkles up her nose. "Fighting?"

"Yeah, you know. Punching people. And stuff."

"Is that what you do for fun?"

I shrug. "Sometimes."

She doesn't have a response for that one—she just has this look on her face, like, *Why am I hanging out with you?*

"Just get on the frickin' shopping cart," I say.

She sighs, but she's smiling, too. "Fine." And without further hesitation, she steps up on the end of the shopping cart and holds on tight.

I take the handle of the cart and start running through the aisles. Tessa laughs and I wonder if she's ever done this before—something tells me homeschoolers don't act like reckless four-year-olds, ever. Not even when they're four years old.

We're basically the only ones in the store, aside from a few employees—which means we can run through the aisles without getting yelled at. Or maybe we don't get yelled at because of other reasons.

I yank the cart to a stop when I pass an employee.

"Oh—excuse me?" I say.

The lady turns and looks at me, then does that classic double take. "Yes?" she says, in that *I shouldn't stare—it's rude* voice. "Can I help you find something?"

This is the moment where I'd typically crack a joke, like "Yeah, I seem to have lost my legs." But Tessa is here, so I decide to stay on topic.

"Can you tell me where to find Polaroid cameras?"

The employee glances between me and Tessa, who is frozen to the shopping cart, looking like a guilty four-year-old.

"Aisle ten."

I flash her a smile. "Thanks, ma'am."

And we're off again.

Tessa lets out a relieved sigh. "I'm surprised she didn't scold us for doing this."

"Yeah, well, there are some perks to being handicapped."

What the hell did you just say? What is wrong with you?

For a second, I'm paralyzed with anxiety.

But Tessa only blushes a little and says, "Is it really that obvious?"

She thinks I'm talking about her.

Haha.

Hallelujah.

"Uh, well…" I swing the cart into aisle ten and immediately spot the Polaroid cameras. "I have a solution for that, too."

Aviator shades. Super reflective ones so that nobody does a double take when they look into her slightly unfocused eyes. She might not be able to see them staring, but I know that I would give anything to look normal (except my right arm, since that would kind of defeat the purpose). For Tessa, reflective sunglasses disguise her blindness pretty well.

We buy the shades and one yellow Instax Mini. I use the money that her grandmother keeps giving me.

"This is a perfect idea," Tessa comments when we exit the store. "I can't believe I didn't think of pictures before. But you know, we could have just used my phone or something."

"Yeah, I know. But Polaroids are better."

She grins. "I didn't think uncultured teenage boys could appreciate Polaroids."

I laugh. "Here, put your sunglasses on."

Tessa slides the shades onto her perfect, freckled face. She looks like a movie star.

"Now stand right here," I say, guiding her hand to one of those barrier pillar things in front of the store's entrance. "Don't move."

She frowns. "Why?"

"Because I'm taking your picture, of course."

"Oh. Right."

She gives a little nervous laugh as I turn on the camera and step back.

"Strike a pose, Tessa Dickinson!"

She does, too. She puts one hand on her hip, one hand in the air, and turns her face to the sun—and she's smiling. I snap a picture of her, and the Polaroid immediately spits out a print. And now I'm smiling, too, as I give her my hand and walk her home.

Okay, fine.

Fine.

I'll admit it.

I'm in love with her.

TESSA

DAY 67

I WANT TO GO OUTSIDE AGAIN. AND AGAIN AND AGAIN and again. In fact, I want to go outside more now than I used to before the accident. Strangely enough, I feel safe with Weston. Almost as safe as I feel with my grandparents by my side. And now that he's revealed he knows how to punch people, I feel especially safe with him.

"Where will the wind take us today, Tessa Dickinson?" That's what he says when he shows up on Wednesday morning.

He doesn't mind chaperoning me anywhere, and I don't mind either—as long as it's within walking distance. Getting into the car is still an unsettling thought, one that will take more time to overcome.

But I plan on overcoming it.

I plan on overcoming anything that stands in my way.

Grandpa believes in me. Grandma believes in me.

Weston believes in me.

If he didn't, he would've given up long ago.

"I think I'd like to go to the bookstore," I say in reply to his initial question. "We could get coffee or something."

"Like a date?"

I feel a blush redden my cheeks. "What?"

Weston only laughs. "Kidding."

He moves across the room, closer to me. Against my will, I feel my heart rate quicken—just a little. I know he's going to offer me his arm. And I would be lying if I said that I don't get butterflies the moment we first touch. I would be lying if I said that I don't enjoy holding on to him, letting him guide me.

There was a time when I resented the idea of being dependent on someone else—whether that someone was my closest relation or a perfect stranger. But now, I feel different. About Weston, about my blindness, about everything.

He has helped me to see. (And *see* is a funny word to use when you're blind.) He has helped me to smell, taste, and hear.

Today, he takes me to Barnes & Noble. It's a bit of a walk from our house, but located in the same parking lot as Target, where we picked up the Polaroid. And speaking of the Polaroid, Weston takes it everywhere we go.

"You said you want visual memories, right?" he says, and I can hear a smile in his voice. "Your wish is my command."

I wear the sunglasses on the walk to the mall, but I take them off when we enter the bookstore. I read in an article once that it's considered rude to wear shades indoors—and I'd rather look blind than rude. So I perch them on the top of my head, next to my messy bun.

Weston guides me onward. My hand feels small in his—almost lost. His fingers are long, and his knuckles are rough. I wonder if that's from "punching people."

We slow to a stop, and the smell of coffee surrounds me.

We must be standing in line at Starbucks. I can hear steam hissing and people talking and blenders whirring. Weston asks me what I'd like to drink, and I tell him to order a grande iced caramel macchiato with coconut milk instead of real milk.

"Oh, god," he says. "You're one of *those* people?"

I feel a grin tug at the corners of my mouth. "Who are *those* people?"

"The people who make things more complicated than they need to be."

"Yes," I say, giggling. "I'm definitely one of those people."

It feels strangely perfect to be standing in line at Starbucks, holding a boy's hand and listening to him order coffee for me. I could almost get used to it.

Weston doesn't get anything for himself.

"I'm not allowed to drink caffeine," he says, but I can tell he's joking.

He didn't get anything so that he could hold my coffee *and* my hand while still giving me one free hand to feel with. I know because I've come to know *him*. And I'm amazed by how thoughtful he is.

Funny to think there was a time when I called him *thoughtless*.

We wander around the bookstore with no real purpose. I run my fingertips along the rows of books, thinking about all the millions of words I can't see.

"Hey, you ever tried reading braille?" Weston asks me at one point.

I shake my head. "I don't plan on being blind forever."

"True, but... you could still try it. For fun."

A little smile finds my face. "Fun? Like riding a shopping cart?"

"Not as good as riding a shopping cart, but... you know."

I laugh and sip my macchiato.

"Hey, uh... would you mind waiting here for a minute?"

My self-assurance falters. "What? Why?"

Weston laughs a little. "Um... I have to use the bathroom."

"Oh." I blush. "Sorry. Go ahead."

"You sure?"

"Yes," I say, nodding quickly. "Go ahead. I'll be fine."

"Okay." His hand slips out of mine. "Don't move."

I nod again, pushing a small insecure grin onto my face.

I don't notice the darkness until he's gone.

There is a bookshelf to my left and carpet under my feet. The store is doubtless crawling with employees and customers, but I suddenly feel all alone, as if I'm the only one here.

I feel vulnerable.

But I shouldn't. I should be stronger than this. I should be able to go at least five minutes without Weston by my side.

I lift my chin and take a measured breath, attempting to calm my uncalled-for nerves. Background noises have grown louder: distant voices, squeaking wheels, soft pop music on the radio. Then, nearby, I hear a book snap shut.

My heart jolts into my throat.

Footsteps approach.

Please be Weston.

Every part of me longs to hear his gentle, smooth, carefree voice—to feel his big warm hand slip back into mine.

But it's not Weston I hear in the aisle with me. It's another boy, old enough to be in high school. I can tell by the range of his voice.

"How's it going?" he says.

I have no idea if he's talking to me—there could be ten other people in the aisle with me, and I wouldn't know. Because I can't see. *I'm blind.*

"Hey," the voice comes again, closer this time. He's definitely talking to me.

I freeze up, unsure of what to say or do. Finally, I speak. And I sound small and timid.

"Hi…?"

The boy steps closer—I can tell by the vibration in the floor right in front of me. He smells faintly of cigarettes.

My heart beats faster, climbing into my throat.

"Are you blind?" the boy asks, his voice low.

I swallow, gripping the coffee cup in my hand. "Y-yes. I am."

"Are you here all by yourself?"

My senses begin to fire warning signals to my brain, telling me to get out of this aisle, telling me to get away from this kid. But I can't move. I don't know where to go.

I'm blind.

"Hey," the boy says again, and touches my arm.

I jerk away, bumping into the bookshelf behind me.

"It's okay," he coaxes, as if talking to a frightened animal. "I'm not gonna hurt you."

I feel his hand again—this time on my forehead, pushing a strand of hair away from my face.

My heart pounds. I can't breathe.

I don't know what to do.

I don't know what to do.

I don't know what to do.

Weston, please hurry.

"Leave me alone," I say. I mean for it to be firm, but my voice comes out in a whisper—broken, shaking.

Like me.

The boy only laughs under his breath. "You're really cute, you know." His hand latches onto my wrist and squeezes tight. "Why don't you come with me?"

WESTON

AUGUST 2

A BIG BAD CUSS WORD FLIES OUT OF MY MOUTH WHEN I find Tessa where I left her—when I catch that jerk harassing her. As I approach, I don't notice much about the guy—other than the fact that his pants are falling off his ass and he's got one hand wrapped around Tessa's beautiful little wrist.

The sight of it pisses me off more than words can describe. It's going to take a lot of self-control not to punch this guy in the face.

Instead, I try to play it cool.

"Yo," I say, walking right up to him. "Get your hands off my girl."

The punk glances up at the sound of my voice, but doesn't let go of Tessa. He does a double take. He looks at my prosthetic legs. And he laughs.

"What is this, the disability club?"

That's it.

I grab his wrist and twist his arm upside down, catching a couple of his fingers. Two—perfect. The fewer fingers, the more it hurts. I step into him, pulling his arm and pushing his fingers backwards. Tendons can only be stretched so far until they snap.

"Agh!" The guy flinches, going up on his toes.

It's a textbook lockout, and I can tell it hurts. I would smile if I wasn't so angry.

"Yeah, actually, it is," I spit back, giving him an equally sarcastic reply to his question. "Wanna join? Free membership with a broken finger."

He looks at me like I'm crazy, eyes flaring with pain. I want to snap his fingers off right now—but I also don't want to be arrested.

"Let me go, man!" the kid pleads, wincing even harder as I press him a little more.

I nail him with a long death stare, right in the eyes.

Then I release him, giving him a hard shove to send him staggering backwards.

He doesn't need to be told to get lost. He shoots me one last freaked-out stare, rubbing his poor disjointed fingers, before hurrying off in the other direction.

I turn back to Tessa. She's breathing hard, obviously shaken. Her body is stiff and her eyes dart back and forth, seeing nothing.

I feel like shit. How could I leave her like that?

I had one job.

"Are you okay?"

Tessa nods, and I know it's a lie. "Yeah, I'm fine… What did you do to him?"

"Nothing," I say, shaking my head. "Just tweaked his hand a little. I'm so sorry I left you."

"It's okay."

"No, it's not."

"Weston." Her voice is strong, despite the circumstances. "It's okay."

She reaches out for my hand, and I give it to her. But I feel even worse when her shivering fingers slip into the spaces between mine. There's a little red mark on her wrist where that guy grabbed her; I suddenly want to go hunt him down and smash his teeth through the back of his skull.

"It's not okay," I insist, forcing myself to stay grounded. Forcing myself to laugh warily and make a dumb joke. "Next time you'll just have to come to the bathroom with me and look the other... Oh, wait."

I get a tiny laugh out of her. And though I can tell she's still upset, I feel her hand relax into mine. I hear her let go of a shaky sigh. I sense her moving past it.

Please don't remember that stupid "disability club" comment, I think. *Please don't let this be the end.*

Tessa looks exhausted all of a sudden. Her voice is soft when she speaks up to say, "Would you take me home, Weston?"

I give her a sad smile she can't even see.

"Your wish is my command."

TESSA

DAY 68

HE CALLED ME HIS GIRL. HE LITERALLY SAID "GET YOUR hands off my girl."

I hear his voice in my head over and over again.

My girl.

Despite the gravity of the situation, I can't help but smile and get butterflies all over again. Really, it's the only thing he *could have* said. It might not mean anything. Weston is only trying to help me. And he only ever holds my hand because I'm blind and need a sighted guide.

I'm blind.

Weston's words aren't the only ones playing on repeat in my mind—the whole bookstore episode haunts me all night long. I don't mention it to my grandparents because I can't see what good it would do. Weston rescued me from that jerk in the end. I was unharmed.

But not unshaken.

I regret ever going outside. I was right before—I should have stuck with my resolution. People see me as blind and helpless and *pathetic.* Some people even take advantage of it.

I'm never going out again.

Not until my vision returns.

But Weston has no inkling of my resolve when he shows up on the morning of day sixty-eight. He just says, with his usual sunshiny optimism, "Where will the wind take us today, Tessa?"

I'm lying on my bed, still in pajamas, with a pillow hugged against my stomach. "Nowhere," I answer, feeling like a disappointment.

There's no need to explain. Weston knows where this change of heart came from.

His footsteps cross the room. I hear him sit down at my desk and sigh.

"You're going to let one asshole ruin your life?"

The words spark a fuse of anger in my chest. "One asshole already did," I spit back. "That drunk driver who hit us."

Weston is quiet for a long moment. I wonder if he's beginning to actually sympathize. But I'm wrong once again. If he pities me even the slightest bit, he doesn't let it show.

"You can decide how to respond to it, though," he says. "You're the only one to blame for your misery."

I exhale a hard, irritated sigh. "Why do you have to be so *righteous* all the time?"

"Me? *I'm* righteous?"

"Yes, you."

There is another pause, and this time I'm afraid that I'm being too harsh.

He's infuriating sometimes—but he also called me his girl.

Finally, he sighs again and says, "Listen, Tessa—"

"No, Weston," I interrupt. "At the end of the day, it's all the same. At the end of the day… I'm a handicap."

"You're not a handicap," Weston argues, his voice surprisingly curt. "You *have* a handicap."

I shut my eyes. "Oh, what's the difference?"

"There's a huge difference."

"And how are you such an expert?" The words shoot out of my mouth before I can think. "You don't know what it's like."

"To be a handicap?"

"Yeah."

Another silence.

For a split second, I wonder.

No.

There's no way he could possibly be—

"You're right," Weston says, immediately shooting down any suspicion that started to rise in my mind. "I don't know what it's like to be a handicap."

WESTON

3 YEARS BEFORE TESSA

SCHOOL WAS ALMOST OUT FOR THE SUMMER, BUT I could tell there was still a lot of confusion about me. I could tell lots of people were still wondering: how did I lose my legs in the first place? I felt the need to clear the air. And a small window of opportunity presented itself in the form of a speech assignment.

Mrs. Lloyd, our English teacher, announced in class that we were to write a persuasive speech on the topic of "change." It was like any other presentation—we were supposed to research a topic that we felt was important, write a speech about it, and then give the presentation to our class at the end of the following week.

But I just wasn't feeling it.

"What's your presentation going to be about?" Rudy asked me after class.

I shrugged. "Don't know. Maybe I'll just skip it and fail."

He looked at me like I was crazy. "Why?"

"Because..." I searched for a viable excuse. "My... voice sounds weird."

It was kind of viable and completely true. Though I had shown up late to the puberty party, it was worth the wait. My voice was finally beginning to deepen, which almost made up for the fact that

Rudy was still taller than me. I wondered if they could fix that by adding a couple of inches to my prosthetic legs.

"Well, I think you *should* give a presentation," Rudy said. "It's not a big deal. Just talk about something you're passionate about."

"Great idea. I'll talk about beating you up."

He just shook his head and smiled.

I decided to write something about social equality. About how students treat themselves and everyone else like shit, and why we need to stop. But it came out sounding angry. Or something.

Writing was never my strong suit.

I ripped up the first speech and tried writing a different one. The topic was similar, but focused more on the solution than the problem. Still, it felt fake. What did I know about any of this stuff? All I knew was what I'd experienced. And over the course of the past year, I had experienced a lot.

I wanted to talk about that.

I wanted to talk about me.

I wanted to talk about the two roads—the desert and the mountain range—and how everyone has a road to choose. And how most people choose the wrong road.

I wanted to talk about what I understood. It wasn't much, but it was better than parroting someone else's philosophy on social issues. If you ask me, I'd rather hear a speech from a kid who's been dragged through the mud than a kid who'd read about it online.

So that was exactly what I did.

The day came, Mrs. Lloyd called my name, and I walked to the front of the classroom. There was nothing to be nervous about, really. I'd gotten used to the feeling of all eyes watching me.

My notes were written on the five index cards I held in my hand. But they were notes for the speech that I wasn't going to give. I'd brought them with me just in case I changed my mind.

The class looked bigger from up front by Mrs. Lloyd's desk. She nodded for me to start whenever I was ready, and I nodded back in acknowledgment. Then I turned to face the class. Some of them looked interested; some looked bored; some looked apprehensive.

But they were all thinking the same thing.

And that was what I had to talk about.

I started by introducing myself.

"My name is Weston Ludovico… and I'm an amputee." I took a small bow and concluded, "Thank you. It's been great."

Everyone laughed—just a little. The heaviness in the air seemed to lift once that word was out there in the open.

Amputee.

I smiled at my captive audience and held up the index cards. "So I actually wrote a whole speech for today, but… I'm just not feeling it. So to hell with that." I paused to toss the cards in the wastebasket beside Mrs. Lloyd's desk. A murmur of laughs followed my sudden change of plans. "It was a boring speech, anyway. What I want to talk about today is something that I think needs to be said."

Not your typical opening hook, but it worked just as well. Everyone in the room was paying attention now. Especially Rudy. I caught his gaze, serious and grown-up. I decided to start by clearing the air—for his sake.

"So I'm sure all of you know that I was in an accident last year and lost my legs. It wasn't as exciting as a shark attack or something like that—and I won't go into the true story right now—but because of what happened… my whole life was turned upside down. And I felt that I didn't have any other choice but to try my best to turn it right side up again. That's why I'm here today. Not because I have to be, but because I want to be."

My classmates listened, silent and thoughtful and watching. But I felt like I was getting off topic, so I moved on.

"See, I have a problem—a handicap. But *I'm* not a handicap." I began to slowly pace the front of the room. "Sure, I may not *look* like everyone else. I mean, have you seen my ears? They're, like, way too big for my head."

Laughter from my audience again. It was a beautiful sound. Even Mrs. Lloyd chuckled despite the fact that I was totally hijacking my own presentation.

I grinned, turning to face the class. "I'm glad you're all laughing, because I want to be a stand-up comedian. And that's another reason why I had to recover… because whoever heard of a stand-up comedian who can't stand up? I mean, come on."

Okay, now we were just having too much fun. My classmates were laughing and so was I. For a second, it didn't even feel like school. For a second, I forgot that I was supposed to be giving a speech.

"So, yeah," I said, picking up where I'd left off. "I don't look like everyone else… but I *act* like everyone else. And that's the only way I can get through this."

I paused to look around at the eyes of my fellow students.

"Everyone's always treating me like I need help—and, sometimes, it's hard to resist giving in. It's hard to resist accepting what the world says about you… That you've got a disadvantage, a flaw, a problem. Because, these days, we're told that it's okay to let our problems control us. It's okay to be the victim. It's okay… because you have every right to be miserable." I shook my head slowly, sweeping the room with my gaze.

"But I want to tell you that it's not okay. It's not okay to let your problem stop you from doing anything you want to do. It's not okay to *be* your problem… because you're a *person*."

I smiled a little, the revelation hitting me as the words came. I wasn't even thinking about what I was saying. I was just thinking out loud, speaking from my heart. And everyone was listening.

"You're not your asthma," I continued, "or your diabetes or your depression or your anorexia or your social anxiety. You see, most people would look at me and say that I have every right to be miserable. But I don't. I have no right. I have *no right*. And neither do you." I paused to take a breath and to smile.

"You have a life, for crying out loud! You're sitting there and you're breathing in and out and you can probably see and you can probably hear and you can probably taste and you can probably smell and you can probably feel the sun on your face when you walk outside today. That's five really good reasons *not* to be miserable. And if you keep looking, you'll find new reasons all the time. But you've got to choose it. Over and over again. Every day, every hour, sometimes every *minute*. You've got to choose it. Just like I chose it."

You could have heard a pin drop in that room. Some kids were still watching me, and some were looking down at their desks with guilt in their eyes. But everyone was still listening.

"So maybe I should introduce myself again," I said, to wrap up the improv speech. "My name is Weston Ludovico… and I'm okay. I'm more than okay." I grinned. "I've never been better."

That was it. That was all I wanted to say.

Yeah, I was going to fail this presentation thing. But I didn't care.

I gave my classmates finger guns and said, "Thanks for listening." Then I walked back to my desk and sat down.

For a few seconds, there was silence—as if I'd just personally whacked every student upside the head, Mrs. Lloyd included.

Then one of the kids started clapping. Then another. Before I knew it, the whole classroom was loud with applause. My fellow students were smiling and clapping and turning around in their seats to look at me, as if unsure whether or not I was real.

I don't know what kind of response I was expecting, but I was pretty amazed.

Mrs. Lloyd gave me an A for that presentation.

TESSA

DAY 72

"I TOLD YOU I DON'T WANT TO GO OUTSIDE."

Weston laughs. "You also told me to get out of your house and never come back."

"And you directly disobeyed my wishes."

"And you've been enjoying it. Except for the thing in the bookstore."

"Yes," I say, crossing my arms over my chest. "The thing in the bookstore is the reason that I don't want to go outside anymore. I thought you of all people would understand that."

Weston is silent for a moment. We are sitting at the kitchen table this afternoon. Grandma has given us iced tea and left us to "talk." She thinks we're having a tiff, but we really aren't. I have no problem with Weston. I have a problem with going outside.

"What if there are no people around?" Weston offers at last.

I frown. "No people? There are people everywhere."

"Not everywhere. Not at the park."

"What park?"

"The one on Jefferson Street. You've never been there?"

I feel myself blush a little. "I... don't get out of the house much. Even before this happened."

"Why?"

I groan. "Why do you always have to ask *why*? You're no better than a two-year-old sometimes."

Weston laughs. "You just asked *me* a why question."

"But I don't ask questions twenty-four seven."

"Maybe you should. It's fun. Like riding shopping carts."

I roll my eyes, exhaling a tired sigh. He's trying to make me laugh, make me lighten up, make me chill. Unfortunately, I'm not very skilled in any of those areas.

"So why do you not get out of the house much?" Weston persists. "Is it because you're a typical writer?"

"What's that supposed to mean?"

"A recluse."

I lift my chin defiantly. "I am *not* a recluse."

"Oh yeah?" His voice shifts a little closer, and he's smiling; I can tell. "Prove it."

We go to the park, the one on Jefferson Street. I bring the Polaroid camera and Weston holds my hand—to guide me, not because he *wants* to hold my hand. I have to keep reminding myself of that.

The noises are mellow here. I hear no voices, just wind and birds and cicadas and the sound of cars driving by, obeying the slow speed limit. Pavement turns to grass under my feet. I feel sunlight on my skin, fractured by the cool shadows of trees overhead.

"What do you hear?" Weston asks me.

And at last, I smile. "Leaves dancing."

He guides me over to a park bench and I sit down. Then he steals the Polaroid camera and starts taking pictures of things. I hear the click of the shutter in different places around me. First in front, then behind, then farther away, then closer.

I close my eyes and fill my lungs with the fresh summer air.

"I hear a plane."

From somewhere behind me, Weston says, "Really? I don't."

I smile. "That's because you're not *listening*."

There is a moment of quiet. The muted drone of the plane gets louder.

"Oh, now I hear it." His voice moves closer. "Your hearing has probably really improved since you've been blind." I feel him sit beside me on the bench.

"Mm, yes," I agree. "That makes it all worthwhile."

"Hey," Weston says, "it could actually be cool if you let it be."

"Cool?"

"Yeah. You're like Daredevil."

I frown. "Daredevil?"

"Oh god," Weston says. "You don't know who Daredevil is?"

"I'm afraid not."

He sighs dramatically. "Typical uncultured teenage girl..."

I elbow him in the ribs, impressed that I can actually do it without seeing.

"Ow! Violent, too."

I roll my eyes. "Who's Daredevil?"

"A superhero. And he's blind."

"Really?"

"Yeah. He tries to save this guy from getting hit by a truck, and then he's blinded by this radioactive stuff that spills out of the truck—but that's also how he gets his superpowers. He can see with radar vision instead of his eyes. And then his father gets murdered, so he has to go avenge him. He's the 'Man Without Fear.'"

I smile, nodding contemplatively. "Sounds just like me."

Weston laughs a little. "Well, you can be the 'Girl Without Fear.' How about that?"

"Wishful thinking," I reply, "but okay."

I can't help but say things like that, to rain on his optimistic little parade—I know it drives him crazy, and that somehow makes me want to do it even more.

"What were you taking pictures of?" I ask after a moment's pause.

"Oh, just… stuff. The park. So that you can see it later. When you get your sight back."

I pull in a deep breath and then let it all out again. "I want to see *you* when I get my sight back."

Weston falls silent for a few seconds.

"In that case," he says, "we should take a selfie."

"A selfie?"

"Sure. Why not?"

I shrug. "Okay."

He inches a bit closer to me, so that our shoulders touch. I hear something clicking on the camera.

"I won't know where to look," I confess.

"That's all right," Weston says, "just close your eyes and smile."

So I do. And for one short moment, I feel the warmth of his body next to me. And I know that he's smiling, too—and it's one of the most perfect feelings in the whole world.

The shutter snaps.

WESTON

AUGUST 11

I TOOK A POLAROID OF HER WHEN SHE WASN'T LOOKING.
Which clearly wasn't as difficult as I just made it sound. I *was* taking
pictures of the park, but then I caught myself staring at her again.
She was sitting on the bench with her eyes shut and her head tilted
back, listening to that plane thirty thousand feet overhead. She
looked so beautiful, I couldn't help myself.

And now I have the satisfaction of owning a photo of Tessa
Dickinson that nobody else has ever seen.

"You like her, don't you?" Rudy says one day when we're grabbing lunch at a food truck after running at the track.

I decide to avoid the question and instead make pleasant conversation with the cashier girl on the other side of the window.

"Hot today," I comment, making Rudy sigh and look away.
"Especially for running."

"Running?" The girl's eyes widen. "You guys are running? That's
crazy."

"Yeah, well, my friend here is training for the Olympics—"

"No, I'm not," Rudy mutters.

The cashier girl doesn't acknowledge this. She just giggles and
says, "Running is *awful.* I sprained my foot last summer, and now I

still get these nasty foot cramps when I run."

"Mm." I nod sympathetically. "That's tough."

It takes all my self-control not to grin knowingly at Rudy. He casts me a sidelong glance and I know we're thinking the same thing.

She has no idea.

That is, not until we pay for our food and walk away from the window to the picnic benches that are scattered across the patch of grass out front. Then she sees my running blades and her jaw drops a little. I just grin and give her finger guns.

"You shouldn't do that to people, you know," Rudy says, taking a seat at one of the tables.

I sigh. "Why not? I've got to have *some* fun with it."

He gives me a serious look. "Sounds like you've been having enough fun lately. With Tessa."

"Yeah, well." I sit down across from him and don't say anything else.

He raises an eyebrow. "Well?"

"Well what?"

"You're avoiding the question."

"Now you sound like Henry."

Rudy sighs. "*Wes…*"

"Fine." I groan, resting my head on my fist. "I like her. A lot."

"Is she cute?"

Instead of replying with my biased opinion, I reach into the pocket of my shorts and take out the Polaroid—the one sacred picture of her that no one else has except for me.

Rudy grins as I hand it to him. "Conveniently, he has a photo of the girl *in his pocket.*"

"Shut up."

He laughs, then looks from me to the photo, then back to me, then back to the photo.

I narrow my eyes. "What?"

"You're in love."

I can't deny it. All I can do is smile like an idiot and say, "She makes me feel like a whole person again."

That's because she's blind, my brain tries to reason. *That's because she can't see what you look like.*

Rudy gives me back the Polaroid and says, "Have you told her yet?"

I shake my head no.

"Are you going to?"

"There's no rush," I say, glancing down at the photo of Tessa.

"Something tells me you're not planning on telling her at all."

I shrug. "Maybe I won't."

"What are you gonna do, then?"

"I don't know! I don't think that far ahead. I guess I'll just... get over her. And move on."

"Assuming she *wants* you out of her life when she can see again."

"She won't need me to run her blog for her anymore."

Rudy rolls his eyes. "And what if *she* has a crush on *you*? What then?"

To be honest, I hadn't thought about the possibility. I *still* don't think about it. What a stupid idea.

I shake my head. "She doesn't. She can't."

"Why not?"

"I don't know. Because... I just... I can't imagine anyone having a crush on me."

Rudy laughs. "Are you kidding, Wes? *I* have a crush on you. And I'm as straight as it gets."

I shoot him a teasing smirk. "Clearly, if the way you were making out with Clara today is any indication…"

"We were *not* making out," Rudy says defensively, turning red.

"It looked pretty slobbery to me."

"Says the guy who's never even *kissed* a girl before."

I'm about to come back with some kind of defense—even though I can't deny it—but that's when the cashier girl calls Rudy's name. I give him a smack on the arm as he leaves to pick up our food.

Yeah, it's true, and I'm not ashamed to admit it: I've never kissed a girl before. I only went out with Clara for two seconds, and since the amputation, I guess I've just resigned myself to the idea that nobody would ever want to go out with me. I guess I've just accepted the role of class clown who makes stupid jokes about himself and picks on his best friend.

Until Tessa came along. (Or until I intruded on Tessa's life, however it happened.)

I don't know what I'm going to do. I don't know if I'm going to tell her about my disability. I don't know if she has any feelings for me, or if she'd even miss me if I vanished from her life. I don't know much at all.

But I know one thing.

I want Tessa Dickinson to be my first kiss.

TESSA

DAY 84

I MISS GOING TO CHURCH. IT'S BEEN ELEVEN WEEKS since I last sat in the congregation and listened to my grandfather preach. Eleven weeks since I curled my hair and put on my Sunday best and smiled at all the church ladies, who usually give us enough baked goods to feed an army.

I feel a hollow spot in my chest when I think about it. And even though car rides still give me anxiety, things are better this week. I've gone outside so much lately—with Weston by my side. There's no real reason why I should avoid going to church anymore. Except for the fact that all my friends there will see me as I am. Blind.

But I think I can face it.

If Weston is by my side.

So I decide to invite him, last minute, on Saturday night. It's eight thirty-five, and when he picks up the phone, I hear a cacophony of voices on the other end—little boys all shouting over each other.

Weston's voice interrupts the chaos, sounding a distance away from the phone. "Guys! Just… listen for a second, okay?"

There is a moment of silence.

"Henry's in charge. Don't light the house on fire."

The shouting immediately resumes, but then I hear a door shut, cutting in with silence.

"Tessa? Hi. Sorry about that."

I giggle. "It's okay. Are those your brothers?"

"Mmm." He doesn't sound too pleased with them. He sighs into the phone and says, "Anyway, what's up? Need me to write something down for you?"

"No, actually…" I press my lips together, searching for the best choice of words. "I was calling to ask you if you'd like to, um…"

My heart starts beating faster. Why is this making me so nervous? I shake my head and refocus.

"I'm thinking of going back to church," I say. "Tomorrow. And I was wondering if you'd like to come with me. I don't know if you're a Christian, but…"

Now I'm just babbling. I decide to shut up and let him answer the question.

"I don't know if I'm a Christian, either," Weston says, and I can hear him smiling. "But I'd love to come."

"Really?"

"Hell yeah. Oh—sorry. I won't say that tomorrow, I promise."

I can't help but laugh. For a moment, I feel so happy I could burst.

"What time should I come over?" Weston asks.

"Oh, um. Nine thirty should be good."

"Cool," he says, still smiling. "See you then, Daredevil."

My instinctual response is, "See you."

Only after I hang up with him do I realize that I *won't* actually see him. I blush at my mistake, but I'm too giddy to care.

I might not see Weston, but Weston will see *me.*

And I want to look my best.

WESTON

AUGUST 20

WHEN I SHOW UP AT 52 WEST ELM STREET ON SUNDAY morning at nine thirty, Tessa answers the door. I'm shocked—for a couple of reasons.

First, because she answered the door all by herself.

Second, because she is the most beautiful girl in the whole world.

Her hair is curly today; some of it is pulled back and some of it is falling around her shoulders. She's wearing a blue dress and it makes her eyes look even brighter. Something is different about her face, though. Her eyelashes are darker, and—

"Weston?" Tessa says somewhat nervously when I am speechless for too long.

"Oh. Sorry. Hi."

She lets out a little relieved laugh. "Gosh... you scared me for a second."

I rub the back of my neck, feeling my face turn red. "Did you think I was a kidnapper?"

"No." Tessa rolls her eyes in that righteous way of hers. "I know what your knock sounds like."

"You do?"

Now *she's* the one blushing—as if she's spoken without thinking.

"Come on in," she says, leaving the door open and stepping back inside. "Grandma's almost ready."

I figure Mr. Dickinson must already be at church.

The living room is quiet and clean and washed in sunlight. I wonder if Tessa can feel its warmth as it pours through the eastern windows. She makes her way over to the couch and sits down.

I have to stop staring at her. Not because anybody is going to catch me doing it, but because it's driving me crazy.

She's driving me crazy.

For once in my life, I have no idea what to say. The wall clock ticks, ticks, ticks.

Five seconds pass.

I sit beside her on the couch, leaving two feet of space between us.

Five more seconds pass.

I can't do it. My gaze lifts back up to her face.

Her eyelashes are *definitely* darker.

"Are you wearing makeup?" I ask, without thinking.

Tessa smiles just a little. "Yeah," she says. "Grandma helped me with it. This feels like… a special occasion."

"You don't need it, you know. You look beautiful without it. But you look beautiful with it, too. You always look beautiful. Even when you're crying."

There you go again, Weston. Not thinking.

Tessa's eyes have widened a little, and her face is brighter pink. She whispers, "Weston!" As if I've just said something totally out of line.

"Sorry," I murmur, but I can't help smiling. "I don't mean to embarrass you."

She shakes her head slowly. "I'm not embarrassed…"

There seems to be more to that sentence, but she doesn't say anything else. She just sits there with her curly golden hair and her unrealistically blue eyes, and more than anything in the world, I want to hold her hand.

Not for the sake of guiding her somewhere—just for the sake of touching her.

In fact, I'm close enough that I could do it right now.

Both her hands rest in her lap, on the lacy fabric of her dress. It would be so easy to just reach out and take her hand. I can almost feel it—the sensation of her skin against mine, our fingers woven together. She has small, pale, delicate hands: made for writing poetry.

Before I know it, my right hand is disobeying me, moving silently toward hers—then I freeze. I hesitate. I second-guess myself. What will she think if I hold her hand for no reason? She'll know that I have a crush on her. But do I care if she knows?

Tessa sits there in the sunlight and has no clue that my hand is awkwardly hovering six inches away from hers. She has no clue about my inner struggle.

I'm about to do it—I'm about to *actually* do it—when Mrs. Dickinson enters the room. My hand immediately zips back to my side.

"Hello, Weston. Right on time. Is everyone ready to go?"

Tessa nods and takes a deep breath. "Ready."

I'll wait until we're in church. Then I'll hold her hand.

Hopefully that's not considered a sin.

TESSA

DAY 85

I DON'T SIT IN THE PASSENGER SEAT—IT STILL GIVES ME bad memories. The PTSD, the *again and again and again,* triggers more easily when I sit in the passenger seat. So instead I sit in the back, and Weston does, too. Grandma drives us to church, where Grandpa has already been preparing for service, hours in advance.

When we get out of the car, Grandma offers me her arm. I know that Weston is with us, but I can't feel him. I almost want to ask Grandma if he can guide me instead. But how would that sound? It would sound as if I *like* him. And the last thing I want the church ladies to think is that I have a boyfriend.

But I suppose I should have considered that before inviting him in the first place.

I am greeted with unparalleled enthusiasm by the regular church members. They all seem so pleased to see me, and I'm surprised by how happy I am to be here. The sounds and scents of church welcome me with more potency than they ever have in the past. I hear voices echo up in the tall ceilings of the chapel, words like sparrows in flight. I smell elegant perfumes and colognes, scattered with hints of pepperminty breath. I smell lilies, too. There must be fresh bouquets of them at the ends of the aisles.

A few questions come up about Weston, but he answers them all for himself, luckily saving me the burden of blushing and pretending he's "only a friend." The church ladies seem rather taken with him, so much so that I'm convinced he won't leave today without being forced to accept some kind of baked goods.

Grandma guides me to our usual pew and I sit down. Weston takes a seat beside me, and at last I feel like I can relax.

While everyone is still milling about, Weston says to me in a low voice, "There are flowers in here."

"Mm, yes, there are," I reply, relishing the way his warm, soft breath touches my ear when he speaks.

"What kind?"

"Lilies," I say.

"Good answer."

I smile.

After praise and worship—which I manage to get through very easily, knowing all the lyrics to all the songs—the sermon begins.

I love to listen to my grandfather preach. Not so much for what he's saying as the way he says it. He has a natural gift with words, making them flow like gentle, artful rivulets. I'm convinced that my poetry skills are inherited and probably skipped a generation. Grandpa can make a sermon sound like a sonnet.

I can hear the joy in my grandfather's voice. It's done him a world of good to see me in the congregation today. I know it. I know it because of all those nights he spends at my bedside, praying. I know it because he's smiling. I know it because he reads from the gospel:

"'And in that same hour, he cured many of their infirmities and plagues, and of evil spirits; and to many that were blind... he gave sight.'"

I try to focus on the words, but I can't seem to pay much attention to anything when Weston is sitting beside me. During the pauses between Grandpa's words, I can even hear Weston breathing—quiet inhales and exhales. For some reason, this observation makes my heart speed up.

Of course he breathes, Tessa. He's alive.

Slowly and discreetly, as if doing something unlawful, I slide my right hand out of my lap and let it rest against the seat—the small space between me and him. I know that his hand is there, too. I can feel the faintest warmth radiating off it.

And I want to hold it. I want to hold his hand.

But I'm too nervous to move a muscle.

Grandpa continues reading, "'Then Jesus answered and said to the messengers, Go your way, and tell John what things you have seen and heard: the blind see, the lame walk...'"

At that moment, we make contact. We touch. Our hands breathe against each other on the seat of the pew. I feel his sandpapery knuckles against my unblemished ones. Then he rubs his thumb against my hand in a small circular motion.

My heart does ridiculous things—fluttering and pounding in my chest. There's an ocean in my stomach, swelling and crashing and aching. My face is warm with a rush of blood.

We're not even holding hands.

Just touching.

Just a little.

That's when I begin to realize—there is one more sense besides sight. One that Weston hasn't shown me yet. One that I've been using all this time, without even noticing how beautiful it is.

Touch

WESTON

AUGUST 25

IS IT WRONG OF ME TO WISH THAT TESSA'S SIGHT would never return?

That's the question I ask myself as I sit on the floor of the shower with hot water running over my head and down my back. I usually take a bath—because it helps my phantom pain—but tonight I just want to close my eyes and feel the water pound me, burn me.

Is this what Tessa feels like all the time?

In the darkness, drowning?

How stupid and selfish I am.

Just because I'm stuck with my problems for the rest of my life doesn't mean Tessa should be. She's going to get better. And I'm going to stay the same. I'm going to stay the broken boy who sits on the shower floor and lets the water run over him—because he can't even stand up without prostheses. I'm going to make myself smile even when I feel like crying. I'm going to stick to the mountain trail even when I feel like giving up. I'm going to reply to "How are you?" with "Never been better," even when it isn't true.

I'm going to be the same. But I'm never going to get better.

And Tessa is.

How will I deal with it? When she calls me and tells me that her sight is starting to return? Will it happen all at once or a little bit at a time? Will she be able to see everything right away or just shadows and vague shapes?

Will this be our last week together?

How will I answer her when she's freaking out about her vision returning? How will I fake my own excitement for her when all I feel is dread gnawing at the pit of my stomach?

How will I let her go? Will I just stop showing up at her hyper-organized house, with the yellow walls and the polite grandparents and the sunlight pouring through the windows? Will I not pick up the phone when she calls? Or will I talk to her and tell her that I can't see her anymore?

Will I tell her *why*?

Will I give her a piece of the truth, but not the whole truth?

I think up a few possible replies.

Tessa, you don't understand. I'm not what you think I am.

I have a problem. I have a handicap.

You don't want to be with me.

You don't want to see me.

Please don't see me.

Please don't look at me.

Please let me be a ghost, let me be gone.

Just let me vanish.

It starts out as an explanation to Tessa, but it turns into a plea, a prayer, a cry to a God that I'm not sure even exists.

Just let me vanish.

My throat aches and I feel like I'm suffocating on the steam locked in the shower with me. I bury my dripping face in my hands and I clench my teeth together.

Just let me vanish.

TESSA

DAY 91

WHAT IF I NEVER GET MY SIGHT BACK?

That's the question I ask myself on the morning of day ninety-one. I'm still in bed, covered in twisted sheets, with my face tilted up toward the ceiling. My cheeks are stiff with lines of dried tears.

What if the doctors are wrong, as they so often are? What if this isn't transient cortical blindness? What if it's just cortical blindness? What if nothing can cure me?

What if I never get my sight back?

It's been twelve weeks—the minimum amount of time Dr. Carle believed it would take for my vision to return. But I shouldn't be looking on the bright side. I shouldn't be *realistically optimistic.*

There's no such thing.

I know that Weston will be here soon, so I force myself to get out of bed and navigate my room. I go through the motions of dressing, washing my face, and braiding my hair. It no longer feels dangerous to be alone in my room.

It just feels… numb.

I

  feel

    numb.

Weston knocks on the door and Grandma answers it. I listen to their voices murmuring under the thin floors. Then I hear his footsteps on the stairs. I'm sitting on my bed, which isn't made. Normally, I would bristle at the thought of leaving my bed a mess—but this morning I feel no motivation to do it.

No motivation to do anything.

Except sit here.

And look at the darkness.

"Good morning, Tessa."

His voice is as constant as his visits—smooth, bright, optimistic.

A tired thought returns to me, something I pondered a few weeks ago.

I wonder if he's ever unhappy.

"Hello," I say, in a voice as tired as my soul.

Weston moves to my desk. I hear the chair slide out of its usual place.

A few seconds of quiet elapses.

He doesn't ask me how I am.

Instead he says, "Is something wrong?"

Instinctually, I shake my head. Because he doesn't want me to tell the truth. He doesn't want something to *actually* be wrong. He just wants me to be a little ray of sunshine all the time.

Like him.

But I can't.

I'm not.

I'm falling apart at the seams.

I'm *blind.*

For a tense moment, I am unable to speak. Then words come out on their own. No longer numb, but steeped in misery.

"I'm just so sick of not being able to see."

Weston has no reply for me. Not for a few long moments, anyway.

After the hesitation, his voice comes. "Well, there's still one more sense you've forgotten."

I haven't forgotten. I know what it is. I began to recognize it that day Weston sat beside me in church.

But instead, I act none the wiser and say, "Which one is that?"

"Touch."

I hear my desk chair being dragged across the floor, then set in front of me. I am sitting on the edge of the bed with my legs crossed. Weston sits in the desk chair right in front of me. He's close; I can tell. But I don't reach out to find him.

"To feel," he says, voice softer. "To touch."

This time, he doesn't even have to ask if he can take my hands—I'm expecting him to. After a moment, his gentle fingers lift my wrists out of my lap. Then he whispers the words I've been dying to hear, but afraid he would say.

"Touch me."

I am a mess of nerves, but I follow his command without a word of objection. He leaves his arms suspended in the space between us, and I touch him.

My fingers traverse the ravines between his—smooth palms on one side, rough knuckles on the other. His skin is warm with life, and I imagine it to be suntanned, like Grandma described.

I move up to his wrists, feeling the orchestra of muscles and bones there.

His hands are strong enough to punch people, but delicate enough to type poetry and pick flowers and make waffles for me. There are veins in his wrists, too—ribboning around his forearms like Michelangelo's sculpture of David. I know that he's blond, and the hair on his arms must be golden.

For a moment, I let my hands explore the landscape of his skin. I listen to my unsteady breath—my shivering inhales and exhales.

Then, suddenly, I pull myself away, as if I just realized that I'm doing something wrong. My inappropriate feelings in church were nothing compared to what I'm feeling right now. My heart is pounding everywhere all at once—and the ocean in my stomach is beginning to ache.

This is more than just skin on skin.

I don't know how to explain myself. I don't know what to say to Weston.

But apparently words no longer need my consent to leave my mouth.

I hear myself whisper: "I wish… I wish I could see your face."

He says nothing in reply. Instead, he takes my hands again and places them on his face.

My heart stops altogether.

For a moment, I don't know what to do. But there's no need to think.

I feel.

I feel his face. I feel the smooth skin of his forehead, the shape of his eyebrows. My fingertips barely even make contact—but still, I can almost see him in my mind's eye. I can feel him. I can feel his eyelashes and his nose and his ears—the place where his soft hair begins. My fingers trace the line of his jaw, then end their journey at his lips.

That's where I freeze, unable to move. I'm touching his lips.

He smiles, and I feel it happen under my fingertips. I feel the corners of his mouth lift into that signature grin Grandma tells me he is never without. One of my hands drifts away, but one remains on his face—and the pad of my thumb finds a tiny dimple on his cheek.

My heart hasn't stopped pounding—if anything, it's only grown more chaotic. My pulse whooshes through my ears, and it's dizzying and painful and wonderful, all at the same time.

Weston finally speaks, his voice just as quiet as before. "What do you feel?"

And this time, I can't reply.

I feel…

I feel…

I feel.

WESTON

AUGUST 27

IT WAS SCARY, LETTING TESSA TOUCH ME. BUT IT WAS also the most amazing feeling I've ever experienced.

I'll never forget the way her fingers traced my arms and my face—warm, shivering, scented like some kind of hand cream. I wish I could go back and live that moment over and over. Because I have no idea if anything like that will ever happen again.

But there I go, being selfish again.

This is about Tessa now.

And we're exploring what it means to *feel*.

Touch isn't the only way to feel. Sometimes you can feel without touching anything at all. There's this feeling called *adrenaline*—and I'm pretty sure Tessa doesn't experience it very much.

For me, adrenaline is fistfights and one-hundred-meter sprints and skateboarding tricks that might kill you. But I'm trying to accommodate Tessa, so I decide to take her to the amusement park. Or I guess I should say, I bribe Mrs. Dickinson into dropping us off at the amusement park one afternoon.

I tell Tessa where we're going, only to be sure she's okay with it before I spend all my money on tickets. And for the first time since the day at the bookstore, she seems genuinely excited to get out of the house. Even when we went to church, she had this apprehensive look on her face—but today, she's all smiles. (And she's beautiful, but that's beside the point.)

On the drive there, she still insists on sitting in the backseat—and I insist on sitting back there with her. I wonder if Mrs. Dickinson still has PTSD from the accident, since she was in it, too. I almost ask her about it, but then I stop myself, figuring that would be rude—especially if the answer is yes. So I just keep my mouth shut on the painfully quiet car ride and practice self-control to not hold Tessa's hand until we get out of the car.

In the parking lot, Mrs. Dickinson goes through the rudimentary mom-talk: *Are you going to be okay? Do you have enough money? Do you have my cell phone number? I'll pick you up in two hours. Be safe.*

Finally, she drives off and I have Tessa all to myself. It feels like an important job to be her chaperone.

The best part is that I get to hold her hand.

The worst part is that this may be the last time.

It's already been twelve weeks. But I push those thoughts to the back of my mind and instead focus on what's happening right now.

The sun is shining and the sky is scattered with white clouds; I'm holding onto Tessa Dickinson with one hand and our little yellow Polaroid with the other; everything is okay.

More than okay.

Never been better.

I buy the tickets to the park with the money that Mrs. Dickinson insists I take every week. I don't actually spend that many hours working on Tessa's blog, but the few hours do add up. And now, it's paying off.

Once we're inside the gates, time seems to pass at warp speed. Tessa holds on tight to my hand and asks me to describe things. I do a terrible job, having no talent with the lava of words—not like she does. Everything is colorful and bleached in sunlight. It's easy to describe things like that to her, because she could see before and she knows what colors and sunlight look like. I can't imagine explaining those things to someone who has never seen anything their whole lives.

Just thinking about it makes me feel lucky.

Legs aren't half as great as colors are.

The first ride I convince her to go on is the swinging chairs. I can tell she's still apprehensive about anything new, but she seems willing to be reckless for today.

"You'll do it with me, right?" she asks.

"No. I want to capture this historic moment on film."

"But—"

"Come on, please? I'll buy you caramel macchiatos with coconut milk instead of real milk for the rest of your life."

Tessa laughs. "You really want me to do this, don't you?"

"Mm-hmm. And if you could see my face right now, you wouldn't be able to say no."

Finally, she relents. I stand to the side and take pictures with the yellow Polaroid, and I watch Tessa experience adrenaline for possibly the first time. She screams and laughs and everything is a blur of color. It sounds like music, her happy scream. I've never heard it before, but now I want to hear it for the rest of my life.

"What did you think?" I ask her when she gets off the ride. Her hair is a mess.

Tessa smiles and catches her breath. "That was amazing."

"Good. Should we try a roller coaster next?"

She looks a little freaked, but laughs anyway. "Why not?"

I like this spontaneous version of Tessa Dickinson.

There's still lots of Polaroid film left, so I take pictures of everything as we head over—the bright, loud, sunlit colors. And of course, Tessa. But I only keep two photos of her for myself. Or maybe I keep three. I don't know. Who cares, right?

She's wearing that yellow dress again, and now she's eating cotton candy and she looks like something from a magazine. Pop music is playing from everywhere, and this park is bigger than I remember it being when I was a kid. They have a new roller coaster that would terrify Tessa if she could see it. But she can't, so I underestimate its height and manage to drag her on it with me.

"Something tells me this isn't a good idea," she says after we are strapped into our seats.

"I thought you were Daredevil."

"No!" She laughs, shaking her head. "I'm not."

I take her hand for the eight hundredth time and say, "Well, if you get scared, just… close your eyes."

She smacks me in the arm. And now I'm laughing. And now we're rolling forward, up the chain lift. When we reach the top, I shout, "You're missing out on quite a view, Tessa! I can see Lake Placid from here."

Tessa gasps. "No, you can't. Oh my god, this is the top, isn't it? We're gonna fall, aren't we?"

I smile and nudge her shoulder. "No, we're not gonna fall. We're gonna fly."

And we do. I get another dose of Tessa's happy screams right in my ear. The adrenaline makes her squeeze my hand until I feel pins and needles. But it's worth it just to hear that beautiful sound, mixed with the rush of wind in my ears.

When the ride is over, Tessa grins and says, "Let's do it again!"

I raise my eyebrows. "Seriously?"

She giggles. "Maybe I'm more of a Daredevil than I thought."

"Called it."

Those two hours fly faster than the roller coaster. Tessa pays closer attention to the time than I do, and we're only five minutes late to the parking lot, where we meet Mrs. Dickinson. She smiles when she sees Tessa so happy.

"Have fun?"

"We sure did!" Tessa replies.

I guide her over to the passenger seat and open the door. For a moment, a puzzled frown crosses her wind-blushed face. She knows this is the passenger seat.

But instead of explaining, I just lean closer and whisper, "Girl Without Fear."

For a split second, she hesitates. Then she smiles. Then she gets in the passenger seat and buckles up.

I've never felt more accomplished in my life.

On the drive home, the windows are down. It's almost sunset, and golden sunlight is reaching through the windshield to illuminate Tessa's hair. She rests one hand on the window's edge, weaving the air with her fingertips. Her grandmother plays some kind of happy folk music, and I watch Tessa from the backseat and I think about how different she is compared to the day I first met her.

Mrs. Dickinson notices it, too. She pulls me aside when we get back to her house. Tessa goes up to her bedroom and Mrs. Dickinson stops me in the kitchen and says, "I want to thank you, Weston."

"For what?"

Mrs. Dickinson gives me that modest smile of hers. "For everything. You've helped Tessa in ways that… I don't think anyone else could have."

"She's helped me, too," I say, hoping Mrs. Dickinson won't ask me to elaborate on how exactly.

"Well, I hope you know how appreciative we all are. Tessa, especially. She might not tell you this, but… she's very fond of you."

Fond. The word does something to me, however old-school it might be. I try not to read into it, even though it doesn't take much reading-into to convince me that Rudy might actually be right—Tessa Dickinson might have a crush on *me.*

"I hope," her grandmother continues, "that you two will still be friends even after her sight returns."

I nod slowly, though it's difficult when my heart is sinking. "Yeah, I hope so, too."

It's a lie. I want to be so much *more* than friends with Tessa. But, at the same time, I don't want anything to change. I don't want her to see me.

With one last reassuring smile and a pat on my shoulder, Mrs. Dickinson leaves the room. I go upstairs and knock on Tessa's ajar bedroom door.

"Come in," she murmurs from inside.

When I open the door, I find her standing at the window. It's a lot like the first day—her back to me, and her hair a mess.

But it's nothing like the first day.

And the window is wide open.

"Is it a pretty sunset?" Tessa asks in a soft voice.

"Yeah," I say. "It is pretty."

Not as pretty as you.

I have the Polaroids in my pocket—all of them. Every single picture I've taken (besides the four of Tessa I decided to keep) since the day we bought the camera at Target. Moving as silently as possible, I take a sticky note, a pen, and a rubber band from Tessa's desk.

She stands at the window and looks at nothing while I write a short message on the note, stick it to the top of the stack of Polaroids, and wrap the rubber band around it twice. There's a little box of printed photos sitting on the lower shelf of her nightstand. I noticed it before and decided it would be the dead drop location for these new photos. Tessa will find them eventually.

I place the stack of Polaroids in the box on her nightstand.

Just in case this is the last time.

TESSA

DAY 92

TONIGHT, THE BUTTERFLIES OF SLEEP DON'T EVEN come to my room. I'm still wide awake—flooded with energy. For the first time in ninety-two days, I feel like I'm finally, finally, *finally* not afraid anymore. I feel strong, brave, capable of anything.

Just like Grandpa said on that night so long ago. Really, it was only a few weeks ago. But it feels like so much more time has passed. What was my life even like before Weston? Safer, quieter, but... less.

My life was less.

How foolish and prideful I was to try to push him away. I wish I could tell him how glad I am that he stayed—perhaps, still, I'm a little too prideful to come right out and say it.

The truth of the matter is, I can't sleep.

I roll onto my side and speak into my phone. "Siri, what time is it?"

"It is eleven forty-three p.m. Good evening, Tessa."

I sigh, pressing my eyes shut and wondering whether or not it would be rude to call him at this hour. He might be asleep.

Evidently, I don't care. I push the button again, and before I know it, I'm telling Siri, "Call Weston." I hold the phone to my ear and wait for him to pick up.

After four and a half rings, he does.

"Tessa?" His voice is low and groggy, but my name sounds like magic on his lips.

I grin. "Hi. What's up?"

He laughs softly. "Sleeping. How about you."

"I'm sorry," I whisper. "I just… I couldn't sleep. I'm still thinking about today."

"Mmm."

I hear the faint rustling of bedsheets, which makes me realize that we are both in bed at the same moment, though a couple of miles apart. For some reason, that thought warms me from the inside out.

"When I was a little kid," I say, "my grandma would tell me stories if I couldn't sleep."

"Like, make up a story on her own?"

I nod. "Yeah. Some of them were stories that her mother told her, growing up."

Weston is quiet for a moment. I close my eyes and listen to him breathing. I remember the way his face felt under my fingertips.

"Do you want me to tell you a story?" he asks at length.

My eyes ease open and I feel myself smile. "Would you?"

"Yeah. But I'm not sure how good I am at telling stories. That's more your kind of thing."

I shake my head, settling back against my pillow. "You'll do fine. Just… take your time. Words will come when they want to."

"When they want to?" Weston echoes. "So words have a mind of their own, huh?"

"Absolutely."

He doesn't seem convinced, but that's okay—he doesn't have to be. I'm the writer, and I know more about these things.

"Okay," he says, taking a measured breath and letting it all out again. "So once upon a time… there was this bird."

"A bird?"

"A bird."

"Got it."

I close my eyes and wait for the rest of the story. Listening to his gentle voice in the darkness like this, I can almost imagine he is lying beside me. Not in an inappropriate way, but an innocent way. I can almost imagine holding his hand and feeling the warmth of his body in my sheets.

But as it is, I have only his voice on the other end of the phone. The other side of town.

It is enough.

"So this bird was kind of… well, he was kind of a jerk," Weston says, continuing the story. "Nobody else thought so. In fact, they all thought he was pretty cool. But he was a show-off, you know? Always trying to prove something."

I frown, finding the opening of this story a bit strange—but at the same time, I'm curious to know where it's headed. I close my eyes and listen.

"Anyway, one day this bird was out flying with his friends and he decided to show off by flying higher than anyone else could. His friends tried to tell him not to, but… he wouldn't listen. So he flew up, up, up—above the clouds, where the wind was stronger. And it knocked him out of the sky.

"The wind spun around him and crushed his wings and the next thing he knew, he was lying on the ground, looking up at the sky. His wings were broken—both of them. Not the kind of broken that gets better over time, though. The kind of broken that never gets better. This bird knew that he would never be able to fly again. But he knew *how* to fly. So not long after that, he met this other bird—

and she was blind."

My eyes open at that word, *blind*. I suddenly realize that this is more than just a story. It's not so much fiction as it is metaphor.

I thought I was listening before, but I'm all ears now.

"The blind bird felt like she had nothing left, and so did the show-off bird. They were actually really similar, even though the blind bird didn't realize it—because she couldn't see his broken wings.

"Still, he taught her how to fly. He pushed her out of the tree and she fell a few times, but she always got back up and tried again." Weston pauses for a moment, laughing softly. "She was stubborn as all hell, this blind bird."

I feel myself smile.

"And she learned how to fly, just like any bird with vision. And, even better than that, her vision was coming back to her. Pretty soon, she would be just like everyone else. But the show-off bird wouldn't be. He'd never be able to fly again, and he knew it. And he wouldn't let her stay on the ground with him—not when she was capable of so much more."

My eyebrows pull together in a puzzled frown. I say nothing, listening carefully. I don't understand this story. But at the same time, I understand it perfectly.

"He knew," Weston continues, "that they could never fly together. They could never be together."

I wait for more, but that's it. That's the end of the story.

It's unfinished.

It's happening still.

It's happening now.

It's about us.

After a long moment of silence, I hear Weston take a breath and whisper, "Tessa? Are you awake?"

I'm about to reply, but I decide not to say a word. I don't know *what* to say. The story haunts me and confuses me. It makes no sense to me.

So I decide not to speak—to let him think that I'm sleeping.

Another silence slips by, and I can still hear him breathing on the other end of the phone. Soft and steady, inhales and exhales.

Finally, he says, "Goodnight, Tessa..." and his voice is barely audible as he adds, "I love you."

The phone disconnects.

And here I am, in the darkness, awake.

Here I am, alone in my bed, with my heart aching, pounding, pushing against my rib cage.

Here I am, with tears in my eyes and one hand pressed against my lips and a smile forming underneath my fingertips.

He loves me.

Oh, Weston.

I don't think I've ever been happier in my entire life.

Despite everything, *he loves me.*

Oh, Weston.

I love you, too.

I love you and your broken wings.

WESTON

AUGUST 28

"YOU'RE QUIET TONIGHT," TESSA SAYS, FOR THE FIRST time ever.

She's right; I am quiet.

I have been quiet, ever since last night, when she called me on the phone—when I told her that stupid story about the birds. I don't really know what to say anymore. I've said everything I want to say.

I told her that I love her.

Even if she *was* asleep, I still said it. Because I couldn't help myself.

Now we are walking home from the park, the one on Jefferson Street. She's holding my hand and keeping the weary conversation alive. And the sun is painting the sky as it rolls toward the horizon.

"I really enjoyed our time yesterday," Tessa says as we turn down West Elm Street.

"Yeah?" I grin, looking over at her. "What was your favorite thing?"

"The roller coaster. Definitely."

"Me too."

For some reason, tonight feels like the last night. And I don't know why. I just get the feeling that Tessa's sight will return any time now. And then I'll be gone.

I'll vanish.

When we reach her house, the windows are dark. Tessa's grandparents are out at a Bible study or something like that, but they told me where to find the spare key—at the top of the doorframe. I reach up and find it easily, then unlock the door and let us both inside.

I've never been in her house this late, so it takes a minute to find the light switch that turns on the two lamps in the living room. Tessa's hand slips out of mine and she wanders over to the big picture window, which faces the west. Right now, it frames the sunset.

Tessa stands there for a moment, looking at the world she can't see. The house is quiet and warm and softly lit. It still smells of lavender and laundry detergent, and in some ways, I wish the grandparents weren't gone.

The best part is being alone with her.

The worst part is being alone with her.

I pull in a deep breath, moving over to the window and standing beside her.

"Is it a pretty sunset?" she asks.

I smile. "Yeah. It is pretty."

Not as pretty as you.

"Describe it," she says. "What does it look like?"

I take another breath, glancing out the window—but only for a second. It's an ordinary sunset, and I'm not poetic like Tessa. I can't make something out of nothing.

"Well," I start off, "it's… mostly pink. But there's orange, too. The clouds are thin and streaky near the horizon… but then they spread out more, higher up. Like sponge paint, you know? It's like a perfect fade of color, from blue to pink…"

But I'm not looking at the sunset.

I'm looking at her.

I'm *staring* at her.

And she has no idea.

My heart starts beating faster and harder, and my stomach is doing somersaults inside of me.

More than anything in the world, I want to kiss her.

And she has no idea.

She's looking out the window, but not actually *looking*. Her eyes are even more unrealistically blue in the soft light of the sunset.

"Weston?" she whispers, breaking my trance.

I've gone silent for too long, I guess.

She reaches out with both hands and finds me. They are perfect hands—resting against my sides. I feel their warmth through my T-shirt and I wonder if she can feel my heartbeat bursting out of my skin.

For once, I'm the one without words.

Tessa's breath is unsteady and shivering as she says my name again. "Weston?"

"Yes," I manage to whisper.

She's whispering, too. As if we're not alone in this deafeningly quiet house.

"Are you the bird with the broken wings?"

I don't know why the question surprises me—of course Tessa would think there was more to that story than meets the eye.

"Yeah," I say, unable to take my gaze off her face. "Yeah, I'm the bird with the broken wings."

Tessa is silent for a moment, but I know that another question is coming. And I don't want her to ask it. I don't want to answer. I don't want her to know.

Because right here, right now, everything is perfect.

The last drops of sunlight ease through the picture window, and Tessa's hands are warm against my sides, and I feel like my heart is going to explode as I take one tiny step toward her.

I don't think.

I just lean in closer until I am two inches away from her mouth.

Then I whisper, "I'm gonna kiss you. Is that okay?"

It's not fair, because I don't give her any time to reply. Instead, I press my lips against hers. Without permission.

So this is what kissing is like.

Wow.

Even if I could describe it, I don't think I would. It's not something that's meant to be described—not something even Tessa Dickinson could put into words.

Her soft lips move against mine and it's the most incredible feeling in the whole world. For a few seconds, the stars align. Everything is okay.

More than okay.

For probably the first time, I've *really* never been better.

Then, suddenly, I realize what I'm doing—I'm kissing Tessa Dickinson.

The revelation hits me like waking up from a dream.

My heart stops pounding.

I pull away from her lips.

Somehow, my hands have drifted to Tessa's lower back—and her hands are resting against my chest. Her breath shivers in and out of her lungs, warm against my skin.

How could I?

What was I thinking?

I wasn't.

"Oh, god," I whisper, letting go of her and stepping away. "I'm so sorry."

I feel like that broken bird, falling out of the sky all over again. One minute I was flying higher than everyone else—above the clouds, above the world. Lost in the blue.

But now,

I hit the ground.

And hell, it hurts.

"I'm so sorry," I say one last time before turning away from her and heading for the front door.

"Weston," Tessa calls after me, and it burns to hear my name on her lips.

To know that I kissed those lips.

How could I?

What was I thinking?

I wasn't.

"Weston!"

I don't stop. I open the front door and I step outside. I shut it behind me.

I run home, in the dark, with my heart cracking and aching and bleeding in my chest.

I vanish.

TESSA

DAY 94

HE KISSED ME.

He literally *kissed* me.

I'll never forget the way that felt. Soft, sweet, dizzying. He asked my permission, but didn't wait for a reply—and even if he had, I don't think I would have been able to reply. How do you reply when a boy asks if he can kiss you? Especially when you've never even *seen* the boy? Especially when you want to kiss him back?

For once in my life, I didn't overthink it. I just let it happen. I let myself fall. I let myself fly.

And what magic it was. I thought his lips felt good under my fingertips—they felt even better pressed against *my lips*.

But in a split second, the moment of perfection ended. He pulled away from me and said, "Oh, god, I'm so sorry," and just like that—

He was gone.

I tried to make him stop, but he wouldn't.

The front door opened and shut.

And I was alone in the house.

I went to bed early. Even when Grandma and Grandpa returned from Bible study, I didn't go downstairs. I pretended to be asleep. I heard Grandma come in to check on me and leave a kiss in my hair.

I didn't stir, despite how shaken I felt inside.

Every atom in my body was buzzing with life, energy, curiosity, joy, fear... I don't know how to describe the way I felt. Words refused to avail me in places where they used to be so steadfast and ready.

Now it's morning, and I'm still thinking about the kiss—still reliving it over and over again in my mind.

I may be a chaos of emotions, but I know one thing for sure: I've fallen for Weston Ludovico. I've fallen head over heels in love with that stubborn, infuriating, obnoxiously optimistic boy... and I can't imagine life without him.

Why did he leave so suddenly? Was it me or him? What happened? How could everything be so golden one minute and turn to confusion the next?

He said he's the bird with the broken wings... but what does that even mean? What could possibly be broken about him? Was he being literal or metaphorical?

It doesn't matter—whatever reason he apologized for, it's not important. No matter what, I love him.

I love Weston Ludovico.

The very thought puts a stupid, awestruck smile on my face.

Maybe he thought he was rushing into it—kissing me out of nowhere like that. And, yes, it was sudden—I sure wasn't expecting it. But I wanted it to happen, even if I hadn't contemplated it before. I'm *glad* it happened. And I don't want him to think he should be sorry for it.

So I find my phone in my bedsheets and tell Siri, "Call Weston."

He has to pick up. He *always* picks up.

And when he does, I'll tell him.

I'll tell him that I love him.

He'll have nothing to be sorry about.

But as I lie in bed and press the phone to my ear and listen to it ring and ring and ring and ring and ring and ring—

I realize that I'm wrong.

He's not going to pick up.

My heart sinks down to my stomach as the call cuts to his voicemail.

"Hi, Weston," I begin, my voice soft and cracking. "I just wanted to tell you…"

Not like this.

I shake my head, refocusing.

"I'd like to talk to you," I say. "Please just… call me back."

I wait for the time to run out on the message so it will hang up the call. Then I drop my phone in my bedsheets and I wait.

And I wait.

And I wait.

And I wait.

For five days, I wait.

And he doesn't call me back.

Sight

TESSA

DAY 100

I SEE A SMALL POINT OF LIGHT IN THE CENTER OF MY field of vision. I blink, then squint, then try to understand what I'm looking at.

Then it hits me—

I can see.

I can *see.*

"I can see!" The words burst out of me as I bolt upright in bed.

Whoa. Not a good idea.

A wave of dizziness crashes over me, making the point of light blur and swirl. I press my eyes shut, and total darkness greets me.

So it's not just a dream.

It's real.

I can *see.*

"Tessa?" I hear Grandma's voice in the hallway, panicky. "Are you all right?"

"Yes!" I laugh like a lunatic despite the wave of disorientation clouding around my head. I hear my bedroom door open and Grandma rush inside. "I can see something! A little point of light. It's not much, but it's... it's something."

"Oh, Tessa!" Grandma wraps her arms around me and holds me

close. She's laughing, too. And I'm hugging her back, and pretty soon Grandpa comes in and joins the party. We are a mess of tears and joy.

They ask me all kinds of questions, but I have only one response for them: I see a tiny speck of white light in the center of my field of vision. And I'm dizzy again.

Grandma hurries downstairs to call Dr. Carle and schedules an appointment for later today.

By the time they can examine me at the clinic, the point of light has grown into a bigger circle. I can see the blur of shadows moving in front of me. The dizziness remains—as intense as when I first came home from the hospital. But now, I welcome even the unpleasant side effects. It means something is changing—changing for the better.

"You'll still need to get plenty of rest," Dr. Carle tells me after the examination. "And try to be patient; it could take a week or more for your vision to return to normal. I want to see you back here in a week."

As soon as I return home, I give Weston a call. He hasn't made any attempt to contact me since the night he kissed me, and silence from him is so unexpected and feels so cold, I hardly know what to make of it. In fact, I have *no idea* what to make of it. I'm confused. I'm *so* confused.

But I call him anyway. Because my sight is returning. And that's exactly what we've been waiting for this whole time. Weston has helped me through the bleakest days of my life. He's been as much a part of my struggles as Grandma or Grandpa.

So I tell Siri, "Call Weston," and I listen to the phone ring.

And ring.

And ring.

And ring.

He doesn't pick up. His voicemail comes on.

I know it's because of the kiss.

But why is he being so apprehensive about it? Weston is never shy about anything. If he wants to know whether or not I like him back, he's going to have to talk to me.

So why is he refusing to answer my calls?

I let out a long sigh, but I'm too excited about my vision to hang onto the sadness about my relationship with Weston. Instead of hanging up, I leave him a voicemail.

WESTON

SEPTEMBER 4

"HI, WESTON. IT'S TESSA. I JUST WANTED TO LET YOU know that… my sight is coming back! When I woke up this morning, I could see these little points of light. Anyway, I've been to the doctor and she thinks my vision will go back to normal within a week. Isn't that amazing? And it's been exactly one hundred days, just like Dr. Carle said it would be."

Her voice falls to a lower tone. "I know you're… avoiding me. Because of the kiss. But I just want you to know that you have nothing to be sorry about. I was actually…" She pauses; she laughs a little. "I was actually waiting for it to happen. And it was wonderful. Beautiful. Indescribable. I want to see you, Weston. When my sight has returned completely. I want to *see* you. So please call me back. Please."

Click.

"End of messages," the electronic lady tells me. "To erase this message—"

I hang up my phone and drop it on my chest. I'm lying on my bed, looking up at the ceiling.

I just couldn't answer her call.

I couldn't talk to her.

I couldn't explain.

Not without *telling*.

And I couldn't tell her.

I can't.

Still, her voicemail is a sledgehammer to my heart. Just like I thought it would be.

I press my eyes shut and ignore the sting of tears. I wish this could somehow be easier.

Stupid, selfish Weston. There you go again.

It's true—I wasn't thinking about Tessa. I wasn't thinking about what would happen when her sight returned. I wasn't thinking about how she would feel if I vanished.

I was thinking about myself. How she made me feel. How she made me forget that I'm different.

Wonderful, beautiful, indescribable.

That's how her kiss felt to me, too.

Did she really say that she was *waiting* for it to happen?

Did she really say that she *wants* to see me?

Apparently, Rudy was right. Tessa Dickinson does have a crush on me.

The revelation would be mind-blowing if I didn't know the reason why.

She likes me because she has no idea.

And once she finds out...

I don't know what will happen.

I don't *want* to know what will happen.

But how am I going to stop it?

Tessa is stubborn—if I've learned nothing else about her, I've learned that. She doesn't give up when it comes to something she cares about. She stands her ground and fights. She screams and cries, and she says whatever she thinks. The volcano erupts.

How can I stop a volcano?

I can't.

The only thing I can do is answer the phone the next time she calls—and try to convince her to forget about me.

Not like it will work.

Not like I *want* it to work.

Oh god, I don't even know what I want anymore.

I want to be normal.

TESSA

SEPTEMBER 7

OVER THE COURSE OF THE NEXT FEW DAYS, MY SIGHT returns completely. The point of light I originally saw is like the glow at the end of a tunnel; it slowly opens up, giving me back a full field of vision. For a while, everything is so blurry I can't recognize a thing—and I'm bedridden with a splitting headache. But by the time Thursday comes, I can see clearly enough to use my phone.

Who would have thought I'd ever be so overjoyed to simply text my friends? Or choose an outfit to wear? Or watch the sunlight pour through my bedroom window and paint yellow patterns on the floor?

It's similar to the feeling of coming home after a long time away—everything is familiar, but different. Nothing has changed, yet everything seems new. My room is bright and white and beautiful, and everything is in its proper place except for a few things on the desk that are only slightly out of symmetrical alignment.

I don't have my old sight *back*; instead, it's as if I have brand-new eyes—eyes that see things I've never noticed before. It takes one hundred days of darkness to appreciate what a miracle it is to see. Shadows and light and texture and colors…

All of it is glorious, but bittersweet.

Because Weston still hasn't called me back.

I find the notebook that he gave me so long ago, and look at my big, messy, chicken-scratch letters. I read the line I wrote on the first page, and I can still hear Weston's voice speaking those words to me.

There's nothing you can't do.

Why hasn't he called me? It doesn't make sense.

Grandma and Grandpa have been wondering about Weston, too—they keep asking why he hasn't come by to see me. I say that he's been busy with school. It seems plausible enough, but I can tell they don't quite believe me. The truth is, I don't want to burden my grandparents with the situation—partly because I'd hate to seem unhappy or ungrateful, and partly because I would have to tell them the whole story (including the fateful kiss).

For some reason, I find it much easier to talk to my blogging squad about my problems.

LIV: TESSA HOW ARE YOU FEELING

ME: a lot better actually

ME: my headache FINALLY went away

MARIA: yayy!!

ALLISON: PRAISE THE LORD

ME: yeah fr

KATE: So glad to hear you're doing better, Tessa! It must be quite a transition omg...

GRACIE: I can't even imagine

ME: it's been pretty crazy

ME: but good

ME: I guess

ME: ugh idk mixed emotions

LIV: ????

LIV: TELL US EVERYTHING

LIV: if u want to lol

ME: ahhh well

ME: Weston is kind of not talking to me anymore

GRACIE: WHAT?????

GRACIE: WHY

MARIA: When did this happen?

ME: right after he kissed me

GRACIE: UH

GRACIE: WHAT

GRACIE: AFLKJSDLSAKFADLKAJS

LIV: HE KISSED YOU???

ALLISON: WHAT HAPPENED

ALLISON: PLEASE SPILL

ME: lololol I kind of knew he liked me

ME: and so one night we were coming back home from a walk and my grandparents were out so we were alone in the house and I was asking him to describe the sunset to me and then he got really quiet and he just kind of

ME: kissed me

LIV: ASDFGHJKASLDKJAL

ALLISON: sldklkhsljDLFJLKASJAlkj

GRACIE: I'M SCREAMING

MARIA: what!!!!

RAQUEL: WESTESS WESTESS WESTESS

ME: lol I knew you were going to say that Raquel

GRACIE: WHAT DID YOU DO??

ME: nothing! After he kissed me he said he was sorry and he left! I tried to stop him but he didn't listen and I've been calling him almost every day and he doesn't pick up.

LIV: ughhhhh

LIV: boys

ALLISON: ^^^

RAQUEL: tbh that's pretty weird. He hasn't talked to you at all?

ME: no!

ME: I have no idea what to do.

ME: I thought we understood each other?? Like I thought I knew him. But apparently not. This is just so unlike him.

GRACIE: yeah I agree with Raquel that seems really out of line. Especially after everything you've been through.

ALLISON: BUT THE QUESTION IS

ALLISON: DO YOU LIKE HIM????

ME: yeah

ME: I do like him

ME: a lot

LIV: asdfghjklslakj

LIV: tell him!!!

LIV: maybe he's just afraid he made the wrong move and thinks you're offended or something idk

ME: well I kind of did tell him in one of my messages

ME: but he still hasn't called me back

ME: WHAT SHOULD I DO GIVE ME SOME ADVICE

KATE: Well didn't you say that he kept coming to your house even though you told him not to? Like he was really stubborn about it?

ME: yeah

KATE: so you should do the same thing to him.

GRACIE: ^^^^ WHAT SHE SAID

MARIA: exactly. give as good as you get.

ALLISON: yeah just keep calling him I'm sure he'll be annoyed enough to give in eventually lol

ME: mm you're probably right.

LIV: AGREED. Don't stop bothering him until he talks to you!

ME: okay okay lol

ME: I'll try him again.

I close out of the Instagram chat and, out of habit, press the home button to tell Siri, "Call Weston."

Though the conversation with my friends has reignited my determination, I don't feel very hopeful that Weston will actually pick up the call.

But maybe Kate and the other girls are right—if I don't give up, eventually *he* will.

So I wait and I listen to my phone ring.

And ring.

And ring.

And—

"Hello?"

WESTON

SEPTEMBER 7

"WESTON!" TESSA'S VOICE SIGHS THROUGH THE OTHER end of the phone, sounding relieved and thrilled and frustrated all at once. "Why haven't you called me?"

I should have known that would be the first thing out of her mouth. I should have prepared myself for it. But I didn't, just like I don't prepare myself for anything.

And I have no answer.

"What's going on?"

"Nothing, I just…" I pace my room, shoving my fingers through my hair. Afternoon sunlight pours through the windows and it reminds me of her.

Sunlight is everything,
And all at once.

I press my eyes shut and say, "I just didn't want to hurt you."

"Hurt me?" Tessa repeats. "You're hurting me by not talking to me."

I sigh. "Look, I'm sorry. I got your voicemail, and I'm glad your sight is returning… That's awesome. But that means you don't need me anymore, so—"

"What?" Tessa sounds appalled. "I don't *need* you anymore? Weston, you *kissed* me."

I swallow, feeling my face redden. "I'm sorry."

"Why? Don't you like me anymore?"

"Tessa—"

"I wasn't asleep, you know."

My mouth opens and shuts again as her words hit me.

I wasn't asleep.

"W-what, you mean when—"

"When you told me the story about the birds," Tessa says, her voice soft and shaky. "When you told me that you loved me."

It's a relief and a punch in the gut all at once. I shut my eyes, leaning back against the wall.

After a long moment of silence, Tessa speaks again. "Do you take it back, Weston?"

"No. Of course not."

"Then there's no need to be sorry. Because I want you to know that... I love you, too." She pauses, laughing a little. "I *love* you, Weston. I never thought I would say that, but it's true. And I need you now more than ever."

If only she knew how much her words break my heart.

My grip tightens on the phone in my hand and I press my eyes shut. I shake my head even though she can't see me. I shake my head to tell myself, *No, you can't have her.*

"Weston," Tessa says, "I want to see you."

"No."

"Why not?" Her voice is beginning to harden with frustration. "Weston—"

"Look, Tessa, whatever you imagined me to be like, stick with that. Pretend I don't exist anymore. You don't need me, not really. You'll forget about me eventually."

"Are you insane? I can't *believe* what you're saying!"

"Well, you have to believe it. Because it's true."

"It is *not* true." Tessa's voice cracks, and I can tell she's starting to cry. "I know you, Weston—"

"No, you don't!" Now I'm losing it, too. My throat is tight as I force the painful words out. "You don't know me, Tessa. And you don't want to."

I hang up on her.

The silence slaps me in the face, cold and cruel. It *is* me. Silence.

Stupid, selfish silence.

I look at the sunlight coming through the window, and all I can think about is Tessa Dickinson, with her unrealistically blue eyes full of tears.

Stupid, selfish Weston.

What have I done?

TESSA

SEPTEMBER 7

MY HEART BREAKS WHEN HE HANGS UP ON ME. FOR A moment, I can't believe it.

Patient, kind Weston.

I pull the phone away from my ear and I stare at it.

Tears have already started overflowing my eyes and streaming down my face. I feel just the same as I did one hundred days ago. Wretched, crushed, broken into pieces.

I feel like I've lost everything all over again.

And I can't do anything about it.

And I feel like it's all my fault.

But what could I have done to prevent this?

Nothing.

Nothing.

Nothing.

This isn't me; this is him.

Just like that, my pain gives way to anger. My fingers clench around my phone and my broken heart hardens in my chest.

What is *wrong* with him?

I know there's something. I know there's a reason why he doesn't want me to see him. But it can't be any big deal—Grandma would have told me.

How can he treat me like this?

How can he act like my feelings don't even matter?

How can he say that I'll forget him?

Clearly, he's the one who doesn't know *me*.

Ignited with a burst of hot anger, I throw my phone to the floor. But it doesn't hit the floor. It hits my photo box on the lower shelf of my nightstand, knocking it over and sending the contents spilling out.

I groan, looking at the mess of photos on the floor. Then I notice something new: a stack of photos I've never seen before, held together with a rubber band and labeled with a sticky note.

Frowning in confusion, I climb off my bed and sit cross-legged on the floor. I pick up the stack of photos, turning it over in my hands and reading the sticky note.

Here are all the things you didn't get to see.

-W

"Weston," I whisper, touching my fingertips to the handwriting.

These aren't just any photos.

They're the Polaroids.

The ones he took for me.

My heart softens when I see his words. My anger falls away, like a cocoon. And the butterflies return to my stomach, fluttering and warming me from the inside out.

With shivering hands, I pull the rubber band off the stack of Polaroids and start looking through them one at a time.

The first photo is of me standing outside the front entrance of Target, wearing that pink dress and those reflective sunglasses. I smile, remembering that day so well. How he forced me to ride the shopping cart like a reckless four-year-old.

I lay the Polaroids out on the floor as I go through them one at a time.

There are photos of everything—sunlight coming through trees, the jars of flowers I smelled but never saw, me again sitting on my bed and holding Weston's yellow ukulele, more flowers, the river, the center of town, the inside of the bookstore, the brightly colored rides at the amusement park, the blur of swinging chairs, the crazy roller coaster (which looks much more frightening than I imagined), a squirrel climbing a tree, me sitting on a bench at the park on Jefferson Street—

And us.

There's a photo of us.

Weston and me, side by side, sitting on the park bench, taking a selfie.

My heart stops the moment I see it.

Weston.

I set the other photos on the floor and stare at the one in my hand.

His face.

I *see* him.

Even if the photo is slightly out of focus and a bit over-exposed, I can *see* him.

And Grandma was right.

He is quite a good-looking boy.

Blond hair, gray-blue eyes, suntanned, smiling—he matches her description to a T. But I notice other things about him, too. Like his perfect teeth and his beautiful eyelashes and how he does, in fact, have a scattering of freckles—just like me.

If optimism had a face, it would look like his.

Though I still have tears on my cheeks, I feel myself smile. I leave the rest of the photos scattered on the floor as I lie back down on my bed. I can't stop staring at the Polaroid in my hands.

I can *see* him.

I hold the photo against my heart and I press my eyes shut and I whisper, "I don't care what you say, Weston. You never gave up on me—and I'm not going to give up on you."

I won't give up. I won't give in.

I'm going to do just the opposite.

I'm going to outsmart him.

WESTON

SEPTEMBER 8

"WHAT ARE YOU GOING TO DO?" RUDY ASKS ME AT THE track on Friday.

It's a crappy day—rainy and overcast, kind of like a projection of how I feel. School is out for the day, but I've convinced Rudy to stay behind and run with me. Really, I just want to run by myself. I want to run until I can't breathe, until my muscles are burning, until I can't feel the aching pain in my heart. I don't want to talk about anything—especially not Tessa.

But, of course, Tessa is the first subject Rudy brings up.

"I'm not going to do anything," I tell him, fitting my running blades on and tossing my backpack into the grass.

"Did you talk to her?"

I sigh. "Yeah. I told her to forget about me. That she didn't need me anymore. That she doesn't want to know me."

Rudy crosses his arms over his chest, giving me that judging frown. "And what did she say then?"

"I don't know."

"How do you *not know*?"

"I hung up, okay?"

"What?"

"Look, just *drop it*." I stand up and begin pacing the starting line of the track. "Whatever was going on between us… it's done. I'll get over it, and Tessa will too. It's just a matter of time."

Rudy stares at me like he doesn't even know me. Like I'm a stranger. Like I've changed or something.

But I haven't changed.

I *don't* change.

For a long moment, there is silence—hanging in the air like the heavy gray clouds overhead. I stop pacing the line and shut my eyes, letting go of a sigh.

Rudy doesn't speak—he just stands there and looks at me.

Finally I mutter, "What."

"Nothing," he says. "I just… I guess I thought you were braver than that."

My eyes open, but I don't look at him. I look at the grass under his feet. A flash of anger sparks somewhere inside me, and a fire ignites in my fists. For a second, I feel attacked. Like I want to fight back, I want to punch someone. But not Rudy.

I want to punch *myself.*

"Look." I sigh, still unable to bring my gaze to his. "I wasn't… expecting it to happen like this."

"Well, it has happened," Rudy says, taking a few steps forward. "And you can't undo what you've done. She loves you, Weston—do you really want to throw all that away?"

Finally, I look up and meet his eyes. "Of course not. But she only loves me because… she doesn't know."

Rudy squints at me, disgusted. "Are you kidding me? Do you really have such a low opinion of her?"

"Hey, I don't have a low opinion of her. I love her too, for crying out loud—"

"Then why not tell her?"

Why not.

If only it was that simple.

I can't reply—I don't know how. All I can do is stare at him and feel the anger pumping through my veins.

Stupid, selfish.

"Oh, I get it," Rudy says at last, nodding but still looking at me with that judgmental frown. "This isn't even about Tessa—"

"Of course it's about Tessa—"

"It's about you."

Another silence cuts in, and I don't do anything to stop it. Words abandon me. I can't reply; I can't even defend myself.

Rudy takes another step closer, looking me right in the eyes. "You once told me that Tessa made you feel like a whole person again. Well, news flash, Weston: you *are* a whole person. I see that, Tessa sees that, and her grandparents do, too. So do your parents and your brothers and all our friends at school. No, Weston—" he shakes his head slowly, lowering his voice "—the only one who doesn't see you as a whole person... is you."

Again, I can't reply. All I can do is stare at him.

"You talk the talk," Rudy continues, "You act all cool and confident, like none of this bothers you; but I know that it *does* bother you. I've seen it in your eyes, man. And it'll probably bother you for the rest of your life, but that doesn't mean you should punish yourself for it. And you shouldn't punish Tessa, either. Because even though it'll hurt you to let her go, it'll hurt *her* even more."

For a full minute, I'm speechless. I don't think I've ever heard Rudy say that much all at once. And I've certainly never heard him give *me* advice. Suddenly, our roles are reversed—he's the one telling me to toughen up.

And he's right.

"You've gotta face her, Weston," he says. "You've gotta tell her the truth. You'll regret it if you don't."

I'll regret it.

Of course I will.

And, hell—I've got plenty to regret already.

For a few seconds, all I can do is stare at him, feeling like I've just been beaten. Feeling like I'm on the ground looking up at the sky with blood in my mouth, thinking, *What just happened?*

"You're right." The words come out on their own, and my voice sounds defeated. "I've been…" I stop to let out a miserable, sarcastic laugh. "I've been a coward."

Rudy shakes his head. "I don't think you could ever be a coward, Wes."

I give him a wry smile. "Well, you're right. I do put on a show. I *try*. Really hard. I try to pretend that none of it bothers me." I pull in a deep breath, taking my eyes off him and scanning the track around us. "But it does bother me. And I'm just… I'm scared. Tessa thinks I'm someone that I'm not."

"That's not true," Rudy says. "Come on, man—have you forgotten about that speech you gave us? When you said, 'you're not a disability; it doesn't define you'? It makes you different and more badass, but it's not *who you are*. Tessa knows who you are. She's always known who you are."

For a moment, I don't say anything. I just think about his words. I let them hit me, one by one—I let them leave bruises.

Tessa knows who you are.

Finally, Rudy breaks the silence and says, "So *now* what are you going to do?"

I take my gaze off the ground and look up at him. "I'm… going to see Tessa?"

"Say it with conviction!"

"I'm going to see Tessa."

"Confidence!"

"I'M GOING TO SEE TESSA!"

Again, we must look like quite a pair—two boys at the track on a rainy day, not actually running, but having a very unlikely argument over a girl. An argument that, surprisingly, Rudy wins. Ten to zero.

I start laughing, unable to stop myself.

Rudy grins and says, "You have to promise you'll talk to her."

"Promise."

He sticks his hand out. "Shake on it."

"Fine."

But I don't shake his hand. I grab hold of it and pull him into a hug. He's not expecting it, and that's why I do it. For the rest of my life, I will do whatever it takes to throw him off guard.

I slap him on the back and say, "Where would I be without you, Rudy?"

He just laughs and hugs me. "You'd be dead, pansyass."

TESSA

"GOOD MORNING, TESSA," GRANDMA SAYS WHEN I ENTER the kitchen. She's smiling, and I can see it. I've missed the way she smiles—warm and constant, like the sun.

I smile in return and take a seat at the table. Grandpa pours three cups of coffee—one for each of us. At last, things are back to normal.

Almost.

Grandpa greets me with a cheery good morning, too. "How are you feeling this morning, Tessa?"

The question no longer seems like a threat. Without thinking, I steal Weston's favorite line.

"Never been better."

Grandma squeezes my hand.

I know that it's time to apologize—in fact, I should have apologized a long time ago. But before I even begin my speech, I know that my grandparents forgive me.

When Grandpa takes his seat with us at the table, I speak up.

"I wanted to tell you both how sorry I am for the way I acted," I say. "I handled everything so badly… and I treated you both like dirt. It was wrong of me."

Grandma gives me a sympathetic look. "Oh, sweetheart, there's no need to apologize."

"You were going through a lot," Grandpa adds.

"But that's no excuse for the way I behaved. Especially with the whole business about the ad in the newspaper, and Weston, and… I should have trusted that you both knew what was best for me. But instead I was… angry."

Grandma puts a hand on my shoulder and says, "You were *afraid.*"

The word comes to me like a missing puzzle piece. *Afraid.* It's a gloriously frustrating thing when someone else finds the perfect word to describe something that you had no idea how to explain until this very moment.

"That's right," I murmur. "I was afraid."

And Weston helped me to not be afraid.

Weston took me outside and showed me the world.

He taught me how to smell and taste and hear and touch.

He taught me how to let go.

To fall.

To fly.

"Well," Grandpa says, pulling me out of my thoughts, "we're just glad you're all right. Our prayers were answered."

I smile. "Yes, Grandpa. They *were* answered." I can't help but stand up and come around the table to wrap my arms around him. He hugs me back, and Grandma joins in after a moment, too. We are a warm, tangled mess of love, patience, and forgiveness.

I can't imagine having a family better than this.

When Grandpa leaves for prayer meeting at the church, I decide to bring up the topic of Weston. Actually, Grandma is the first to bring it up.

She clears the breakfast dishes and says, "I know I've asked you this already, but... Do you know why Weston hasn't come around in a while? Is everything okay between you two?"

I blow out a long sigh, unsure how to explain it all. Finally, the word *no* comes out of me.

Grandma frowns, looking puzzled. "Have you called him?"

"Multiple times. For a while, he wouldn't answer. Then I finally got him to pick up the other day, and he was so..." I shake my head, searching for the right word. *Impatient. Unkind.* "Different."

Grandma says nothing. She just watches me and listens. I can tell, by the expression on her face, that she knows something I don't know.

And I can't stop myself from asking about it.

"Weston is keeping something from me," I begin slowly, tracing my finger over the wood grain of the tabletop. "Isn't he?"

Grandma doesn't reply with words—but the look in her eyes is confirmation enough.

"Grandma, *please.*" I lean forward, lowering my voice. "Please tell me what it is."

She shakes her head resolutely. "No. I promised him I wouldn't. He's just going to have to tell you about it himself."

I pull in a deep breath and let it all out again, slumping back in my chair.

Grandma folds her hands on the table and says, "Why don't you tell me what happened between you two."

I launch into a detailed explanation, leaving out a few of the specifics—like the kiss, and the way I felt when I touched him, and the way he confessed that he loved me over the phone that night.

"I just don't know what to do," I admit, leaning against the table. "Weston doesn't want me to see him. But I can't just let him walk out of my life like that. We've become... really close."

"You're right," Grandma says, "You can't let him walk out. You have to talk to him. *Truly* talk to him."

"But I've tried! And he refuses to listen. He's so stubborn."

Grandma gives me a playful smirk. "Like someone else I know."

I sigh through a little smile. "True. But he didn't give up on me when I was a brute. So I don't want to give up on *him*."

"Then don't," Grandma says, as if it's that simple.

"He doesn't answer my calls," I explain. "How am I supposed to have a conversation with him when he doesn't even give me the time of day?"

Grandma thinks for a moment, frowning thoughtfully. At last, she says, "What number do you call him on?"

"His cell phone."

"Did you try his home phone?"

I shake my head. "I don't have his home number."

That's when Grandma smiles, a tad mischievous. "I do."

"Really?"

She gets her phone book, which is impressively organized, and I find two numbers under "Ludovico." I decide to use the landline in case my name shows up on their caller ID. Grandma leaves the room to give me some privacy, and I dial the Ludovicos' home number.

And wait.

And wait.

And wait.

Finally, someone picks up.

"Hello?"

It's not Weston.

This boy's voice sounds younger than Weston, but not much younger. I try to recall the names and ages of his brothers. It must be the thirteen-year-old one.

"Is this Henry?" I ask, wondering for a moment if I've dialed the wrong number altogether.

"Yep!" the boy replies, putting my anxiety to rest. "Who are you?"

"I'm Tessa."

"Holy crap, really? Like *the* Tessa?"

I smile, feeling a blush wrap my face. Apparently I'm famous in the Ludovico household.

"Hey, Weston!" Henry yells, a short distance away from the phone. "Tessa's on the phone!"

I wait for a response, wondering if Weston will actually agree to speak with me.

"You're what?" Henry says, presumably to his brother. "...Oh. Uh, Tessa?"

"Yes?"

"He's not home."

I sigh, but can't help grinning at their failed attempt to deceive me. "I know that he *is* home, Henry. So I would appreciate it if you told your brother to get on the phone right now, or else I'll show up at your house and talk to him in person."

There is a long pause. When Henry's voice returns, he sounds a bit intimidated. "Uh... okay. Hang on a sec."

I hear the telltale clatter of a phone being set down. Then a few moments of quiet while Henry goes to deliver my message to Weston. I listen to the white noise and the soft murmur of a television in the background and I wait.

And wait.

And wait.

Finally, the phone picks up again, and Weston's smooth, gentle, sunshiny voice says, "So you're threatening me now, huh?"

Relief melts over me and I smile. "Weston."

I hardly know how to begin, what to say first—what to say at all. I know that our last conversation ended in tears, but in some strange sense, I feel as though it never even happened. I feel like, even when we argue, we know each other's hearts. Even through the confusion and the secrets and the lies—I know him. I know that he loves me.

And I love him.

"Weston, I found the pictures."

"Yeah?" He's smiling, too. I can hear it. "Do you like them?"

"I love them." My eyes have already begun to sting with tears. I am filled with happiness and heartache—too much of it for one person to contain. I feel like I'm going to burst. "You know which picture is my favorite?"

Weston laughs softly. "Hmmm… The squirrel?"

"No." I roll my eyes. "The one of you and me."

He goes quiet for a minute.

And I can't talk because my throat is closing up with uncried tears.

Finally, Weston whispers, "That's my favorite, too."

"It's kind of funny, actually." I laugh and sniff, drying my tears with my fingertip. "Because I already knew what you looked like."

"Really? How?"

"I asked my grandmother to describe you, a while ago. And you look just like I imagined. Better, actually."

He doesn't respond at first. There is a splintering silence, one that I can feel.

Finally, Weston asks in a weak voice, "Your grandma described me?"

I swallow, nodding slowly. "Yes. But… she left out something. Something important."

Weston exhales, and I hear it crackle through the phone's speaker. "I made her promise to."

For the first time ever, he confirms that it's true. I feel a lead weight sink into my heart.

"Weston," I begin, taking a deep breath, "I know you're keeping a secret from me."

WESTON

SEPTEMBER 9

"I KNOW YOU'RE KEEPING A SECRET FROM ME."

My heart stops beating when she says it.

Then she adds, "Whatever it is…I don't care."

I close my eyes and lean back against the wall. Noah and Aidan are in the living room watching TV, and I keep my hand cupped over the speaker of the phone in an attempt to block out some of the noise. Henry is trying to listen in, but failing miserably. My replies to Tessa are short and confusing, out of context.

"Weston, I want to see you," Tessa continues, repeating the words that punched me in the stomach the last time she said them. "I refuse to give up on you. And you might think that just because I'm no longer blind, I don't need you anymore—but you couldn't be more wrong. I *still* need you, Weston. I thought my life was so… perfect before all this happened. But now I realize that nothing can be perfect without you—"

"But I'm not perfect," I interrupt, trying to stay grounded in the reality of the situation—despite the way her love confession makes me feel weak in my nonexistent legs.

"I know you're not perfect," Tessa says, with a little sad laugh. "But neither am I."

I'm not sure if I'm supposed to agree with her, or say something like "You're perfect to me."

"Weston," Tessa says again, with more determination in her voice, "I want to see you. And I mean it about showing up at your house. I'll find your address and I'll come knocking on your front door."

I groan, reaching up to rub my forehead. I'm definitely not going to win this battle.

"Or," Tessa adds, "if *you* want to pick the place where we meet, I'll give you sixty seconds to do so."

For at least twenty of those sixty seconds, I think about it carefully. A place to meet her. A place where she'll *see me* for the first time ever. I don't want people around. Not even my family. Not even her grandparents.

"The park," I decide at last. "The one on Jefferson Street."

"Okay then." Tessa sounds satisfied, finally. "What time? Three o'clock tomorrow sound good?"

I nod, already feeling my heart rate quicken. "Yeah, sure. Three o'clock. Tomorrow."

"I'll call your cell when I get there," Tessa says. "Just in case I can't find you."

A wry smile finds my face. "Good idea."

"So I guess I'll… see you then."

See me.

Oh god.

"Yeah, I guess so."

"Okay," she murmurs, and I can hear her smile. "I love you."

The words make my stomach do somersaults all over again. It feels just like the moment before I kissed her. I suddenly remember how much I want to do that again. It was amazing.

I'm just about to reply with, "I love you, too," when I catch Henry still staring at me from the doorway with a teasing smirk on his face.

So instead I just clear my throat awkwardly and say, "Ditto." Then I hang up the phone and push past Henry, intentionally nudging his shoulder.

"Ditto what?" he nags.

I blush. "Shut up."

I run upstairs and shut myself in my room. For a few seconds, I brace myself against the door and look around and take measured breaths. My room is so much the opposite of Tessa's. There is no feng shui here: my clothes are scattered across the furniture and floor (despite thousands of attempts to keep them inside drawers), my ukulele is sleeping in my unmade bed next to a pair of boxing gloves and a pile of homework, and I still have that messy collage on the wall above my bed—pictures of mountains and Paralympic runners and motivational quotes and cut-up pages from the comic about the Six Million Dollar Man.

I am a mess. I am loud and unfiltered and I laugh and cry at all the wrong times.

I am nothing like Tessa Dickinson.

Yet, still—by some miracle—Tessa Dickinson likes me.

Loves me.

Despite the irony of the whole thing, I smile. I walk across the room to my empty sock drawer (which is now a drawer for things that are more special than socks), and I take out the four Polaroids of Tessa.

In one, she's sitting on the park bench.

In one, she's eating cotton candy.

In one, she's laughing in front of the swinging chairs.

In one, she's smelling a bunch of flowers with her golden hair framing her face.

Just looking at the photos, I can't imagine what I was thinking before Rudy smacked some sense into me. Was I really going to let her go? Pretend she didn't exist? Break her heart?

Still, the fact remains: I have a handicap and Tessa doesn't. How will she look at me when she first sees me at the park tomorrow? How will she react? How will I react?

I thought this part was over—the reactions. Everyone I know has already "reacted" a long time ago. Even people I don't know, like the homeowners in my neighborhood that I run past during my laps around the block. It's been a long time since I had to face someone I know—someone I love—and let them *look* at me.

With Tessa, it will be even harder.

But to see her again, to touch her again, to kiss her again…

I would give both my arms for that.

TESSA

SEPTEMBER 10

I FIDGET ANXIOUSLY IN THE PEW DURING CHURCH service. All I can seem to think about is *seeing Weston.* I imagine his face from the Polaroid. I anticipate seeing his smile, his dimple, his freckles, his beautiful eyelashes. I wish he were here, right now, in church, sitting beside me. I wish he were holding my hand.

On the ride back home, I sit in the passenger seat beside Grandma. The windows are down and the warm summer breeze flows through the car, pulling at my already-messy bun. I can't seem to keep the smile off my face, which of course raises all kinds of suspicions on Grandma's part.

"Looks like you and Weston made up."

I turn to face her, still grinning. "Yeah. We agreed to meet today. At the park."

Grandma looks surprised. "My, my."

I know what she's thinking—because she knows Weston's secret. And I'll know, too. In less than three hours. The radio clock reads sometime after twelve.

"I'm so nervous," I admit, pressing a hand to my heart. "I can't believe he actually said yes."

"Well," Grandma says, "from what I overheard, it sounded like you threatened him."

My face warms with a blush, but my smile doesn't fade. "Maybe."

Then I realize what Grandma just implied.

"Wait, you were listening in? What else did you overhear?"

For a torturously long moment, she says nothing. She just smiles and turns on the directional, pulling into our driveway. Then, after we park, she finally replies, "I heard you say that you love him."

I let go of an exhale, but it's not a relieved sigh. In all honesty, I don't know what I feel. I'm still smiling, still blushing, still nervous.

But I've never been better.

When I don't say anything, Grandma puts one hand on my arm. "He's a good person, Tessa."

I look up at her and let the words melt into me. They are true and warm and kind and everything all at once.

Oh, Weston.

I nod slowly, feeling the sting of tears already—long before I lay eyes on him. "I know he is."

These are the longest three hours I've ever experienced.

When I was a little girl, I would wake up at five a.m. on Christmas Day, alert with anticipation and joy. Those felt like long hours back then—I could have sworn that years passed while waiting for Grandma and Grandpa to wake up. But now, I don't think time has ever moved more slowly.

I sit on my bed and I stare at the clock on my phone, draining the battery by keeping the screen alight and watching the minutes tick by. I could write poetry or answer blog comments, but I fear the words will come out as gibberish. My nerves spark and dance and refuse to calm down. My heart is a reckless beast, my stomach a cage of butterflies.

When I have only thirty minutes left, I decide to start getting ready. I put on the yellow sundress and fix my messy bun. Then I stand in front of the mirror and stare at my reflection. I could put on makeup, but something inside me doesn't want to.

I remember the words Weston spoke that morning before we left for church.

You don't need it, you know. You look beautiful without it. But you look beautiful with it, too. You always look beautiful. Even when you're crying.

Oh, Weston. Always saying whatever you think.

I decide to leave my face alone. Instead, I take the notebook out of my desk drawer—the notebook he gave me to write down the things I didn't want to tell him.

Sitting on the floor in a patch of afternoon sunlight, I start thumbing through the notebook.

On the first page, in horribly messy handwriting, it says:

There's nothing you can't do.

I exhale a shaky sigh, letting my fingertips graze the letters.

There is more in this notebook—poems and fragments of poems and words worth thinking about. I penned them in my blind chicken-scratch handwriting and it felt good. It felt needed.

But then, Weston was always giving me what I needed—even when I despised him for it. Even when I dug my feet into the ground and refused to budge, he somehow convinced me to keep going.

Patient, kind.

No matter what.

At last, it's two forty-five. Time to leave.

I take my phone and I walk to the park, the one on Jefferson Street. Afternoon sunlight pours down on our lovely little patch of the world—shimmering on the trees and sparkling in the shower of lawn sprinklers. I try to focus on my surroundings—enjoying the sights and smells and sounds of everything—but I find it impossible to focus with my heartbeat raging in my chest.

When I reach Jefferson Street, I pull out my phone and dial Weston. The park is exactly how I imagined it to be—peppered with shade trees and benches, crisscrossed with gravel paths that converge at a fountain in the middle. I follow one of the trails, walking slowly and aimlessly.

The phone rings twice before Weston answers.

"Hello?"

"Hey. It's Tessa. I'm at the park."

"Me too."

My heart rate spikes. "Really?" I turn around in a circle, scanning the park—the trees and the benches and the random old couple walking their dog. "Where are you? I don't see you."

Weston laughs, soft and warm—the way he does when I don't get a joke. But I also detect a hint of nervousness in his voice.

"Well," he says, "I can see you. Standing by the bench."

I sigh, spinning around again—my gaze darting and searching. "Weston, where are you—"

There. I see him.

I see him walking down the path toward me.

Oh my god.

Oh my god.

Oh

my

god.

The air rushes out of my lungs.

My phone slips out of my hand and drops into the grass.

My heart stops beating.

I can barely breathe.

I feel everything, and all at once.

My eyes sting with tears and my vision blurs.

My hands drift up to my face and cover my mouth.

My head moves slowly back and forth.

No. Yes. Oh my god.

Weston says nothing. He just walks up to me and wraps his arms around me. I can't help but notice that his hands are trembling a little.

It's almost like being in a dream—I can't control myself. My body shivers as I collapse against him and hug him tight, and the tears spill out of me along with the words: "Oh my god... oh my god..."

I hold onto him and he holds onto me and I press my forehead against his shoulder and I cry. My heart is still pounding, but slow and heavy—it feels broken. Broken because of Life.

Because of what Life has done to Weston.

Broken because I love him so much more than words can say.

I remember what he told me on the phone: *You don't want to know me.*

Oh, Weston.

I never want to let go of you.

But, after a moment, I do.

I pull back a few inches to look up into his face—into the face of optimism, which looks much less optimistic at the moment.

"Don't cry, Tessa," he says, barely above a whisper.

"Well, you're crying, too."

He laughs a little, broken and sad. "I liked you better blind, Captain Obvious."

I pull him against me once more, unable to stop myself. I wrap my arms around him and I don't let go. I cry into his T-shirt. And I can hear his heartbeat under my ear.

At last, I speak, my words rushing out in a choked whisper. "Oh, Weston, I'm so ashamed."

"Don't be."

"But I treated you so badly." I pull back to look him in the eyes. "How could you not hate me? You... you've lost so much. And I've lost nothing. Who was I to complain about my stupid temporary blindness?"

"No," Weston interrupts, placing his hands on my shoulders. "I needed you to be that way. I *needed* it. Because for once, I was judged as a *person*—not as a sob story." He smiles a little. "That's why I made your grandparents promise not to tell you."

For a moment, I am shocked into silence. I can do nothing but look into his eyes. He brings his hand to my face and gently dries my tears with the pad of his thumb.

"I couldn't hate you," he continues, in that same soft voice, "because I knew what you were feeling. I was there too, once. I was scared. And helpless. And I felt like my whole world was falling apart." He pauses to smile a little, looking down. "I know I don't have the best bedside manner... but I could understand things that your grandparents couldn't. I could show you how to suck it up and get on with your life. As hard as that is."

Again, I am speechless. Words have deserted me. All I can do is stand here in the speckled sunlight and stare at him. Stare at this boy who can't possibly be real—stare at this stubborn, patient, kind, obnoxiously optimistic boy. Stare at this boy I can't imagine life without.

Weston slowly averts his gaze to the ground. He lets go of me and murmurs, "You can see, now, Tessa. What do you see?" He shakes his head, exhaling a small depressed laugh. "Do you see why we can't be together—"

"No, Weston," I interrupt, taking hold of his arms and looking up into his face. "You know what I see?"

His gaze drifts back up to mine, and I notice the tears in his beautiful gray-blue eyes. "What?"

I take one step closer to him, feeling myself smile. "I see the bravest person I have ever met."

His smile returns just a little. "No, that's you," he whispers, gently pressing his forehead against mine. "Girl Without Fear."

I laugh, but it comes out sounding more like a broken sob. My hands drift up to his face, and his to mine. I close my eyes and feel.

I feel my heart exploding.

I feel the space between our faces disappear.

We kiss.

And it tastes like sunlight.

ACKNOWLEDGEMENTS

Wow. How do I even begin to thank all the amazing people who made this book possible? My heart is spilling over with gratitude. Most especially for you, who has arrived at the last page of this book — the fact that you are reading these words makes me dizzy with gratitude and joy. I always love reading the acknowledgements page in a book because it's where a little-known truth is revealed: although writing is a lonely art, you can't do it alone.

First, Katie. Thank you for being my writing buddy since before I can remember. Thank you for always believing in me. You inspire me beyond words and if it weren't for you, I never would have discovered how much I love writing. (Which means I owe you pretty much everything.)

Mom, thank you for reading those hundreds of books to me and Katie growing up. You made me fall in love with stories.

Dad, thank you for dreaming big with me — when I aim for stars, you lift my bow and arrow and help me shoot for the galaxies instead.

I want to give a huge thank you to my editor Jen, who is an absolute genius and believed in this book before the rest of the world got to see it. Thank you for your emails that made me cry happy-tears (in public!)

I also want to give a big thank you and a virtual hug to my real-life Instagram squad — you know who you are. Thank you for inspiring and uplifting me, and for boosting my confidence when I needed it most. You girls are awesome. (#TeamWaffle)

And finally, thank you to my entire blogging community and the WritersLife Wednesday community. You guys inspire me every second of every day and I wish I could personally hug each and every one of you and tell you how much your support means to me.

And last but definitely not least, thank *you*.

For reading this book.

For making my dreams come true.

Rock on,
Abbie

(NOT) THE END

FOR YOU!

You know how some books have that unfortunate sticker (totally ruining the front cover) that tells you there's Bonus Content™ in the back of the book? And did you notice how I *don't* have one of those stickers on the front cover of this book?

That's because I have something so much better for you:

www.100daysofsunlight.com
(A whole website of bonus goodness!)

On this site you'll find
- Exclusive Q&As with the author (me!)
- *100 Days of Sunlight* merch
- The book's official playlist
- Aesthetics + pretty things
- Giveaways (!!!)

And the giveaways are *especially awesome* because all you have to do is sign up and you're automatically entered for a chance to win an AUTOGRAPHED + PERSONALIZED paperback of *100 Days of Sunlight!*

And if you want to do something *super* nice for me, go leave a review for *100 Days of Sunlight* on its Amazon or GoodReads page. I'm an indie author so I love and appreciate every reader who takes the time to give my book a good rating. ;)

Don't want to miss when I release new books? Join my email circle and receive personal updates from yours truly – sign up at: www.abbieemmonsauthor.com

Also follow me on:
- youtube.com/abbieemmons
- facebook.com/abbieeofficial
- instagram.com/abbieeofficial

You're the best!!

- Abbie

ABOUT THE AUTHOR

ABBIE EMMONS has been writing stories ever since she could hold a pencil. What started out as an intrinsic love for story-telling has turned into her life-long passion. There's nothing Abbie likes better than writing (and reading) stories that are both heartrending and humorous, with a touch of cute romance and a poignant streak of truth running through them.

Abbie is also a YouTuber, singer/songwriter, blogger, traveler, film-maker, big dreamer, and professional waffle-eater. When she's not writing or dreaming up new stories, you can find her road-tripping to national parks or binge-watching BBC Masterpiece dramas in her cozy Vermont home with a cup of tea and her fluffy white lap dog, Pearl. If you want to see Abbie in her element (ranting about stories) just type her name into YouTube and search.